Dorothy

I've made you a
special shelf at last!
I hope you enjoy the book.
All the best!

John McIvanc

ANSYLIKE

ANSYLIKE

J. D. McGrane

The Pentland Press Limited
Edinburgh • Cambridge • Durham

First published in 1994 by
The Pentland Press Ltd.
1 Hutton Close
South Church
Bishop Auckland
Durham

ISBN 1 85821 174 3

Typeset by CBS, Felixstowe, Suffolk
Printed and bound by Antony Rowe Ltd., Chippenham

This book is for Belinda Brennan who shared in the writing of Ansylike's tale and without whose help this would never have been finished.

My thanks also to:
 Brendan 'Boss' Loftus; a rare example of wisely-used power.
 Frank Lean for his bemused encouragement.
 Angharad Lloyd who gave me more ideas than I could fit into a trilogy.
 Ged Challis for technical expertise.
 Phillip and Sarah for their patience and company.

CONTENTS

Chapter One

THE LAST INN

Wearily, and with much grumbling, a small band of dwarves approached the tavern. There was a faded, creaking sign above the door. It boasted that this was the last chance for those in need of food and drink to satisfy their appetites before entering the Lands of Desolation.

Groblic was a veteran of many a poor lodging. He was a dwarf who knew a poxy inn without having to sample the watery flies' pee that passed as ale. He heaved his backpack off his shoulders and concealed his disappointment under a curse at the fleas that were having their dinner from his legs.

"Well, here we are at last!" proclaimed Haldriel, who was leading the adventurers, and who was renowned for looking on the 'bright side'. Pushing open the oak door, he entered and peered through the steam and smoke. It was certainly as grim, as Groblic had foreseen, and the smell was stronger than an ogre's armpit.

Following Haldriel, the rest of the dwarves trooped in and made their way to the corner where the ale was being tapped from a huge barrel.

The beer-man was a giant of a man with a head of hair that a bear would've been proud of. He greeted his customers with a grin and four beerpots in each hand. "Ale for the gentlemen? It'll quench a dragon's thirst! Perhaps you'd like to try our wines?"

Haldriel took the first pot of ale. After a long gulp, which obviously was to his satisfaction, he ordered that a dozen flagons should be brought to a table in a back room. He also ordered six flagons of wine and four bottles of mead.

Groblic tasted the ale, which was unexpectedly good, and looked around for a table waiter from whom he could order some food. The ox, roasting on a huge iron spit over the central fire, was nicely brown and the juices were collecting an a flat pan which lay underneath, suspended by chains. A lean-limbed, skinny maid wielded a slicing knife and deftly carved three plate-sized portions of meat. Groblic drooled!

Following Groblic's gaze, Haldriel noted the source of his pleasure and ordered that meat and seasonal vegetables should be brought with the drinks to their room. Before they attracted any more attention, he turned and led the weary party off, to the secluded chamber. There they would be able to eat and drink in privacy.

Knowing that his comrades would not want to mix the serious business of eating with thoughts of their Quest, he resolved to say nothing of it until the morning. After a sound sleep in a snug bed, a bath, breakfast and a pipeful of the excellent smoking weed that grew in these parts, they would all have more stomach for danger. Around the table the dwarves sat, recounting tales, singing songs, and eating until they were ready to burst. Ale was brought in at regular and increasingly frequent intervals, accompanied by side dishes of meat, toasted bread rolls, spiced vegetables, and fruit which had been preserved in honey.

After many hours had passed, Groblic moved to a comfortable armchair at the fireside, rooted out his clay pipe and began to fill its intricately carved bowl with strongly-scented weed. It was a weakness that he was trying to resist, with little success. He found himself unable to fully relax without the succour of the fumes and the reassuring feel of the clay stem between his teeth.

He noted that the young girl who had been carving the meat in the communal room was now stacking logs by the side of the fire. Her movements were deft and assured as she shifted each piece of firewood. The muscles that flexed beneath her tanned skin showed that she would make a formidable opponent in a street fight.

At the top of each boot she wore a sheathed knife. With growing interest, Groblic noted that she had a slightly lighter coloration around each wrist. It was the unmistakable mark of an archer. Only the customary wearing of archer's greaves could leave such a pattern.

"Curious," thought the dwarf as he puffed a smoke ring in the direction of the hearth. "Perhaps she hunts for game in the woods. Probably she..." Pretending to choke on his pipe smoke, Groblic concealed a gasp. Shifting his feet from the stool on which they had been resting, he peered more closely at the maiden's hair. He had seen pictures of 'elf-locks' in tomes that he had studied before he left home. "She's an elf!" he shouted, unable to contain his excitement. "An elf! Here, of all places. We've found one at last."

The maid, startled and unprepared for this sudden attention, attempted to retreat. Dropping the log which she was holding, she backed away, but only into the arms of Haldriel.

"Are you certain?" queried Cledrin, a dwarf to whom little was ever certain, except that when you thought that things couldn't get worse, they always did!

There was anger and anxiety in his voice. Molesting the staff, in an inn where you intended to spend the night, seemed like a bad idea. So, rising to his feet, he started to come to the maid's defence. He saw to his relief that there was no need.

Haldriel had already released his grip and was staring fixedly down his long nose at a dagger which tickled the hairs in his left nostril. Groblic had a similar problem. His head was raised as high as his short neck would allow and the dagger under his chin had already drawn a trickle of blood.

Cledrin couldn't resist a grin and he looked at the rest of his companions who were standing or sitting as still as they could manage. He noted that Obolin had his legs crossed and was swaying alarmingly from side to side. The mixture of mead, wine and ale that he'd drunk would ensure that he would sleep soundly! It was obvious that for once he had the initiative. He dared not move but determined to make peace before any more blood was spilt.

"Put down your knives, girl," he insisted. "We do not mean to harm you. Forgive the rudeness of my friends. Their manners are rough. We are simple folk. We seek information and we think that only the elves can help us. Our forest is dying and our efforts to replant it have failed."

Groblic and Haldriel collapsed into each other's arms. So swiftly had the maid moved that their balance had been lost and, as one, they fell to their knees. The maid sheathed her knives and made herself comfortable in the chair which Groblic had vacated. She rested one booted foot on a stool, pointed a long, slender finger at Cledrin and spoke.

"Are you the leader? Shall I talk with you?"

Cledrin had heard the many stories of elven enchantments, but her voice was as gentle as a raindrop on a saddle. Suddenly he regretted not bathing when they came across a stream some eight days ago. He was aware of the tangles in his beard and the pipeweed stains on his uneven teeth. He sighed.

"I am called Ansylike. I am, indeed, elven, though only on my father's side. Why have you come here? What do you want of me?" She addressed Cledrin who had begun waving his hands in agitation as if to quieten his friends, although there was no need. They were all silent. She watched as Cledrin's hands met each other and knitted, which stopped his fingers wriggling somewhat. He was unable to speak and gazed sidelong into the fire which was burning merrily. Suddenly he was aware that he hadn't changed his underclothes in a very long time.

"I bought a new set of linen in Trelisa, that town on the other side of the mountains," he proclaimed. "It was only seven moons ago! I...." Then he clasped his hands to his blushing cheeks as if to hide his embarrassment. The room was suddenly filled with an hysteria of dwarven laughter and Ansylike joined in with a shriek of glee.

"Maybe I have a spell that works on dwarves,'" she chortled. This caused a further outbreak of mirth and many of the company renewed their interest in the ale pots, the bad feelings easily forgotten. The tension was gone. Groblic, although he had received a small injury, was joining in the fun at Cledrin's expense. The blood on his neck merged into the general layers of grime and if there was a scar, well, it would be another battle wound to tell tales about!

Putting his empty ale pot on the table, Groblic noted that the supplies of drink in the room were getting low and hoped that more would be delivered before he got back from emptying his bladder outside. He headed for the door. The inn was certainly a dirty and grimy place, as he had expected. He ran a finger along the wall and it was soon covered in grease and soot. Whoever was in charge of the cleaning, didn't take their work very seriously.

"Perhaps I'd better talk to you all later when you've had time to rest further and gather your wits." Ansylike poked Cledrin with the toe of one boot and got to her feet. "I might be missed if I stop here long. I'll be back before the moon sets. Have you decided where you are to sleep tonight? The rooms upstairs are the safest. I'll make sure that the beds are made up." She waved once, turned swiftly and was through the door before any of the dwarves had time to question the arrangements she was making on their behalf.

Obolin remembered that he too needed to go, urgently, to the latrine and followed Ansylike. In the communal room the waiters were moving swiftly between the tables carrying trays stacked with meat and steaming vegetables, pies, pastries, bread loaves and honeyed fruit. Others bore foaming beer pots, bottles of mead and flagons of wine and weaved their way around the room, uncannily avoiding the flailing arms of the patrons. It certainly appeared that a good time was being had by all. At some of the tables sat gamblers. Various games of dice, cards and chance would determine who would be leaving with empty purses at the end of the night. The stakes, however, didn't seem to be very high and dwarves found it easy to resist that particular temptation.

In one alcove Obolin noted a man sitting alone. He was drinking from an ornate metal beer pot and reading a leather bound book. On the table in front of him rested a long wooden flute. It seemed strange to Obolin that a minstrel should not be playing when there was money to be earned. By his clothes, which were travel-stained and frayed,

Obolin judged that he was unlikely to be a rich man. Perhaps he was learning the words to a new song to entertain the guests later. Passing quickly by, Obolin lifted the latch on the stout door and went out into the cool, night air.

Silver stars glittered and twinkled and Groblic wished, as he studied the intricate patterns, that he had the knack of remembering them. It was said that some people could tell where they were by the stars. They could tell directions and which way to go. Groblic was ready to believe that this was true but reluctantly accepted that it would always be beyond him. Perhaps he was too old to learn, but at only 134 he had really not reached maturity. He considered the possibility that wisdom might come to him with age, but dismissed this swiftly. No dwarf had ever claimed that knowledge was anything other than experience! They didn't think much of books and passed knowledge on by word of mouth.

With a last glance at the sky, he shrugged and turned to go and bumped into Obolin, who had sneaked up on him. As it was their bellies that collided, neither dwarf was damaged, but it rather shook them both. Obolin recovered first and decided that he had better apologise in case the ale had put Groblic into a mood for a fight. He had seen this companion of his put a bare fist through a stout oak door and had a fair idea of how it might, just as easily, put a lasting dint in his jaw.

"Alert as ever!" he declared. "No-one can catch you by surprise. Are you coming back to the feast? I think I owe you a draught of ale, or two, for interrupting your thoughts." Saying this he offered a short arm in a gesture of friendship as he swayed gently from side to side.

"In a moment," replied Groblic. "I was just looking at the stars."

"'The silver that we cannot reach?'" quoted Obolin. It was a line from an ancient dwarven ode, but there was some truth in it. Poems often said what was obvious but unrealised until it was actually written down. Only the most fanciful, however, really thought that the stars were silver or holes in the sky!

"A map in the sky. That's what I was pondering. If we could work out where we were by a better method than our maps, then we could work out where to find silver that we could mine...and gold too."

"It is said that the elves know of such things and never lose their way," mused Obolin. "Perhaps that girl, Ansylike, could tell you how it's done. You'll have to ask her. Of course she's only a half-elf but she seems friendly enough. Now let's return."

"Did you notice anything odd about the latrine?" asked Groblic, changing the subject abruptly.

"Indeed I did," laughed Obolin as he followed his companion. "Too clean to be natural! Why, there was hardly any smell at all and no flies buzzing around. At that last inn, the stink was enough to make a dung beetle puke! I can't understand why all that glazed pottery and enamelled metal should be wasted in such a place! Still, it's a pleasant change."

"There was the sound of running water. I think they've diverted a stream to flow through the latrine, but why would anyone go to so much trouble to keep the air fresh?"

There was no time for further speculation as the two dwarves had reached the back door of the inn. It was too noisy for them to converse without shouting. Obolin noted that the minstrel was no longer reading and he was no longer alone. Seated next to him in the alcove was none other than Ansylike. The pair of them were engaged in earnest conversation, but Obolin was too far away to catch any of their words. He made his way to the serving table where the same hairy bear of a man was still filling pots with ale. He had to wait for a short while to catch his attention, so he stood patiently and took the chance of another glance in the direction of the alcove. The beer-man caught sight of Ansylike and his voice roared above the general hubbub.

"Get your skinny tail over here, Spud, and see what your customers want! Do I have to do everything myself?" There was no real anger in his voice but Ansylike sprang to her feet and came straight over. Her face was clouded. Seeing Obolin, she relaxed somewhat, but still seemed a bit disgruntled. It appeared that she was not fond of being ordered around, which was a bit odd for a serving maid! "See to this gentleman, will you. I've a dozen tables waiting and there are two-score thirsts to be quenched."

His manner was rough and it was obvious that he would stand for no arguments. Obolin did not have the chance to say anything before Ansylike had grabbed a tray and begun to fill it with pots of ale.

"You just go back to your room and I'll be there with ale for you all before you've had time to sit down. Shall I bring more food? No, you don't need to answer that."

Before she had finished talking, the tray was full and she was striding purposefully towards the back room. Obolin followed, although he had been instructed to go on ahead. He shrugged and swerved to avoid a table waiter who was carrying a tray of steaming pies. There was no sign of any lessening in the activities in the inn. Business seemed uncommonly good! A small argument had broken out over one of the tables of gamblers, but none of them were reaching for their weapons yet. No doubt it was only a matter of time before they'd come to blows.

Time passed and eventually Ansylike joined the dwarves. They were considerably mellowed and several were asleep. The table was awash with spilt ale and wine. Several puddles had formed on the floor and were gradually drying. No doubt the cleaners would be claiming extra pay in the morning!

Chapter Two

BANDITS

Haldriel waved Ansylike over to a vacant seat by the side of the fire and drew up one for himself. Most of the other dwarves had fallen into snoring slumber and were curled up on chairs, benches and, in two cases, on the floor. Deftly avoiding them, Ansylike dropped herself into the wide, wooden armchair. At once she seemed relaxed. Her long legs easily reached the stool which Haldriel pushed towards her, and she put her booted feet on it.

"Our problem is simple," he said, and was interrupted by an insistent knock on the door. The tall minstrel flung the door open, waved a steel broadsword through the smoky air and said: "We're under attack! All of you who can stand are called to arms. Quickly as you can!"

There was no doubting the urgency in his voice. A sudden thud in the woodwork and the emergence of a spearpoint through the window frame convinced all of the need for action.

Obolin was at the door with a battle-axe in his hands before Groblic had time to pull his war-hammer from his sack. The other dwarves prepared themselves for the fray.

All were confident. Twelve, fully-armed dwarves should be able to see off any measly human opponents. Haldriel was tightening the string of his crossbow. He had already loaded a quiver of bolts across his back and slipped a pair of bracers over his wrists. When he saw that all were ready, Groblic started to turn down the lanterns. One of the dwarves' main advantages was their ability to see very well in the darkness.

Ansylike seemed to have no difficulties either. She quickly stripped off her skirt, revealing thin-bladed throwing knives which she had strapped to each lean thigh.

"Do you need a sword?" asked Cledrin. "I have an elven leaf-blade that you might find useful." So saying he unsheathed a cruelly sharp weapon and offered it to Ansylike. She accepted it. In the light of the fire it gleamed with streaks of scarlet. It seemed to anticipate the blood which it would soon spill. Ansylike felt a surge of power as she wielded it and knew that it was no ordinary blade.

Out in the grounds a battle was raging. It was difficult to make out who was attacking and who was defending. The dwarves were, however, well used to such confusion and knew exactly what to do. Obolin recognized the minstrel who was in the thick of the action, parrying a grim-looking rogue and slashing with his broadsword at a man who fought with a scimitar. In a few strides Obolin was there and, with one blow of his battle-axe, he sent an arm, still gripping a scimitar, through the air. He didn't bother to finish him off, but turned his attention to the minstrel's other adversary.

Groblic's war-hammer flashed, spun and thudded. No ordinary shield could withstand its force. Wood splintered, metal buckled and bones shattered under its weight. A particularly gruesome-looking man bore down on him only to fall at his feet, a crossbow bolt protruding from his chest. Haldriel never missed! A severed head bounced by and came to rest a pace or two to his right. Casting a glance in the direction from which it had come, Groblic saw the man who had been serving the ale. In each hand he wielded an axe with deadly efficiency. The force of the blow carried an arm, shoulder and still screaming head into the darkness beyond.

Cledrin, however, was having problems. His axe had splintered on a tough suit of mail and his shield was dented and ready to give way. He parried a blow from a scimitar with a deft thrust of his axe handle and whipped its jagged point across the eyes of his foe. It was not enough. The curved blade caught him across the chest and ripped through his leather armour. He fell back, bleeding and unable to block the fatal blow that, he thought, must follow.

It didn't. One of Ansylike's knives appeared in the chest of his foe. She was on him in a moment and had cut his throat before he hit the ground. She bounced away leaving him to clutch wildly at his wounds. Cledrin knew better than to sit and stare. As he rose, he grabbed for the scimitar and wielded it with both hands to slice at an unfortunate opponent's hamstring. The blood-loss and shock of his wound was too much. His vision blurred. Suddenly he felt himself being dragged backwards. His weapon slipped from his grip and he was unable to resist.

Ansylike threw the last of her daggers and shifted the leaf-sword into her right hand. It was not her favourite weapon, but she considered herself to be reasonably proficient. The sword, however, seemed to have a will of its own.

Its balance was perfect. It was made for no other purpose than to bring death and this it did with startling efficiency. She moved like a cat. No man felt the lick of her cold steel and lived! Blood trickled down the shaft, over the hilt and coloured her wristguards. Springing from her haunches into a battle stance, she let fly with the blade and neatly lopped a head from its shoulders. Blood smeared her face and hair, but none of it was her own. Seeing that Obolin was besieged by three men, she raced to his rescue. Seconds later Obolin stood alone. Around him were the scattered remains of his opponents. He stood in awe. Well used to battle though he was, he had rarely seen anything as lethal as Ansylike. She paused momentarily and Haldriel fired a bolt at the inn sign above her head. It gave way and fell, catching her a glancing blow. Unbalanced, she stumbled and the sword flew from her grip. Haldriel checked that they were in no danger. He put down his crossbow, picked up her sword and hurled it into the darkness.

Before much longer the battle was over. The bandits were defeated and had fled, leaving many of their number dead. In the communal room the injured were having their wounds tended. The minstrel was supervising and he seemed to be proficient in the use of healing herbs.

There were a few serious injuries but no-one was in danger of dying or losing a limb. The beer-man was once again pouring ale and several of the waiters were loading trays with food. The smell of roasting meat and pastries mingled with the aroma of herbs.

In the back room the dwarves had gathered again. In the chair by the fire was Ansylike and she did not look very healthy. Cledrin sat opposite her. His wound was deep but the blood had stopped flowing. There seemed to be no infection and he would be fine after he'd rested. Dwarves were renowned for their toughness and Cledrin had recovered from far more serious injuries in the past. In fact, his appetite was just beginning to return. His armour had saved him from a fatal injury.

Of more concern to him was the state of Ansylike. Her face, he noted, was pale and drawn. He'd looked briefly at the wound on her head and judged it to be of no significance. It didn't account for her present illness. He suspected that she had been struck by a poisoned weapon, but it was difficult to tell. She was covered in so much blood, but none of it seemed to be hers.

Haldriel had taken charge and ordered several of the dwarves to go outside and keep guard. He didn't seem to be concerned about Ansylike, although he couldn't be unaware of her condition. It was he who had carried her in and borne her to the fireside. He rested a hand gently on Cledrin's shoulder.

"It wasn't your fault. You were not to know. Elven blades do not work any magic for us. It was a gift given in friendship. She will understand." As he said these words, Haldriel squeezed Cledrin's shoulder a little too hard for comfort and Cledrin couldn't stifle a gasp of pain. To his relief, however, he saw Ansylike open her eyes. They stared blankly for a moment before focusing. Then she grinned.

"What hit me? I was just enjoying a decent fight when the lights went out!" She rubbed her head and removed her feet from the stool. In what must have been a reflex action she ran her hands over her boot-tops and over her thighs. The daggers were not in their sheaths. "All four! I hope they found their marks."

"Indeed they did!" Haldriel assured her. "We are grateful to you. Cledrin owes you his life."

As if this was a signal, understood by all, the dwarves tapped their tankards with their fingers. It was a polite form of applause. Haldriel held up his hands after a few moments to shush them. "Obolin too has cause to thank you. I, however, must offer my apologies. I knocked you senseless with the inn sign!"

"A mistake?" queried Groblic. "A bad shot?" As he said it his voice tailed off. Haldriel did not make 'bad shots'. The other dwarves looked uncomfortable and waited for Haldriel to explain himself.

"I have seen battle-lust before, never in an elf, of course. If you had continued to fight you would have fallen, or killed us all. It was that sword of Cledrin's. It was a trophy that should have stayed on a wall and not have been brought into action again. Such things belong to the darker ages. We should not have any dealings with them."

"In the 'darker ages'," replied Ansylike, "elves fought with dwarves. That's why my kindred are only to be found in The Desolation. Was the sword forged to kill dwarves? Is that why it frightened you?"

There was sorrow in her voice but Haldriel noted that her left hand stroked the top of her boot where a dagger had been, until recently, stowed. He would have to be very careful.

Cledrin was a little less subtle. "You have already proved yourself to be a friend," he declared. "Why not hear our story and help us? We cannot pay you well, but we offer a chance for you to meet your own folks. Come with us into The Desolation beyond the mountains. You will be more than welcome!"

Ansylike was lost for a suitable reply to such a ridiculous proposal. It was, however, too wild an idea to be ignored. "Tell me then," she said, "why you have come so far? The Desolation is no friend to dwarves and you are unlikely to find any elves. They will not welcome you if you do chance to come across any. Their memories are long and they are hardly likely to have forgotten how your folk betrayed them." She stood, swaying a little and clutched her forehead as if to shield her eyes from the light of the fire. Instantly Cledrin was at her side. He supported her elbow and helped her back to her seat. Obolin looked in and was puzzled by what he saw. It seemed that Cledrin was taking an unhealthy interest in the welfare of an elf.

Half-elf, he corrected himself, but still a sworn enemy. He made his excuses and left the room.

"We have a good vein of silver," began Haldriel. "It's been mined by our people for an age and it has kept us in good stead. The mountains have been kind to us. We work the metal and sell our goods. We buy food and anything that we can't make ourselves. Now, however, we have a problem. We've cut down too many trees."

Ansylike pursed her lips. She could see where the conversation was leading. Dwarves destroying forests was nothing new. She maintained a grim silence.

"We plant new ones, of course," continued Haldriel, "but to no effect. They just won't grow. The soil washes away in the spring rains and the hills are bare. We have ore to last for a generation but no wood for the furnaces. That's why we need the help of the elves." He waved his arms expansively. "Unless we have help our people are doomed. We cannot survive without the trees to smelt our ores. We can't plant the trees ourselves. Only elves know the secrets of the seeds. Please help us!" There was a silence, broken only by the gurgling of wind in over-full guts.

Ansylike looked at the faces of the dwarves she knew by name and couldn't resist a smile. They seemed so serious. Their faces were streaked with grime, smoke and blood. She was reminded that she too would be looking no better. A bath and a long rest would be needed before she was presentable. The silence, however, was too much for her to bear. The dwarves were waiting for her answer so she wasted no more time and gave it.

"Of course I'll come with you, although I don't see how I can be of much help. Your cause is indeed a worthy one and I have no wish to stay here any longer. I would like to travel again. I had intended to cross the mountains when I'd found suitable companions. Now seems like as good a time as any other." She noted the relief on their faces and began to regret her hasty decision.

The door opened and Obolin strolled in. He placed four knives on the table. "None dented!" he said. "I think these belong to you. I had to search for your sword, though. It was stuck in a tree." Before the sword had time to rest on the table, Haldriel had seized it, beating Cledrin by an instant. He was through the door before Obolin had time to say another word.

Cledrin stood in front of the door, wide-eyed.

"It's a magic sword!" he gasped. "I had no idea when I gave it to her. It's a weapon from the dark days." He relaxed a little as he saw that Ansylike had made no move. She cradled a cup of mead in her hands and was looking at him archly. She averted her gaze and looked into the fire which was beginning to die down. Cledrin continued, "She fought as if she was possessed. Haldriel saw the danger to us all and knocked her unconscious. He shot the inn sign from its hinges while she was under it and threw the sword away." Almost breathless, he paused. Obolin didn't look convinced and sought confirmation from Ansylike. She, however, continued to study the dying embers in the hearth and said nothing. It was time for bed and such matters could be sorted out in the light of the morning. To be invited into The Desolation beyond the mountains was all she wanted, although she didn't know why. Fate seemed to call her. So far, her life had been a series of escapes. With something to aim for, she felt that she was taking a positive grip on her destiny. Although the company was a bit strange, they were likeable enough and dwarves made solid allies once their trust had been gained. Cledrin seemed to have taken a liking to her already and would probably protect her in a tricky spot.

After tonight's attack, Ansylike was fairly sure that there would be no further trouble from the bandits. Still, there was no sense in taking risks. She decided to sleep in her clothes. Not, however, the ones she was now wearing. They were streaked with blood. Quickly she shed her garments and washed in a basin of cold water that had been left by her bedside. From a wooden trunk she withdrew a clean set of clothes and put them on. She judged that it would not be necessary to wear her leg knives or boots. That would be carrying wariness a little too far! She lay on her bed and pulled the rough blankets over her, hoping that sleep would come quickly.

Meanwhile, the dwarves were making their preparations for the night. Haldriel and two others would stay on guard in the backroom. Three, including Obolin, would join the sentries outside. The rest of them would retire to the sleeping-quarters that Ansylike had booked for them. They carted their possessions, including weapons, upstairs. Cledrin noticed that the communal room was by no means empty. He caught sight of the minstrel who was standing by a heavily shuttered window, apparently inspecting the lock. He was still wearing his broadsword. Cledrin decided that now would be a good time for a chat.

The minstrel could hardly fail to notice his approach as he clinked and clattered in his metal-link shirt. He turned to face the dwarf and grinned broadly.

"You must be Cledrin!" he declared offering a hand in greeting. "Spud told me about you. I gather you've persuaded her to join your company. Did she tell you that I'd be with you for at least part of the way?"

"Spud?" queried Cledrin. "I prefer to call her by her proper name. She introduced herself to us as Ansylike. That's what you should call her if you have any manners!" Cledrin bristled indignantly. His armour jingled as he puffed out his chest.

"I stand corrected, Cledrin," replied the minstrel. "Only her closest friends are permitted to call her Spud. You haven't known her long enough for that. Now won't you have a seat by the fire while we talk? I must get some sleep soon, if I'm to see anything of the morning with a clear head."

Cledrin took the seat which was offered and made himself comfortable. He was somewhat annoyed that the minstrel was on familiar terms with Ansylike and that he was not.

"You have the advantage of me," he began with exceeding formality. "You know my name but I do not know yours."

"Andric," replied the minstrel, "and in case you haven't already guessed I am Ansylike's brother and a half-elf."

Cledrin had not guessed and the relief that he felt made him want to rise from his chair and shout with joy. Instead he composed himself. Dwarves were not given to such displays of emotion.

"Ansylike's brother?" he stuttered. "'This inn is overrun with elves! We've travelled the length of the land in search of elves and now we find two in the same tavern. I just can't believe it." His ill humour evaporated and in its place was a feeling of happiness that he had not felt since the journey had begun. "And you are to accompany us? Well, this is a good start. How can we fail?" He laughed and Andric joined in. Dwarves seemed remarkably easy to get on with, despite their reputation to the contrary. He hoped that Cledrin was typical of his race but suspected otherwise.

Both were inclined to talk long into the night but they were weary from the exertions of battle. After Andric had yawned for the second time he decided to leave for his room before he started to fall asleep in the chair.

Cledrin also decided to get some sleep but not in the room with the rest of the dwarves. He took his chair and carried it up the stairs to the first landing. It seemed a good place for an extra guard. He placed a battle-axe across his knees and crossed his arms.

It seemed to Ansylike that she had hardly closed her eyes before she was woken by a crash outside her room. She flung the blankets aside, grabbed a pair of knives from under her pillow and stood at the door. There was definitely some commotion on the landing so she shifted one knife to her belt and went out. At the end of the corridor she could make out the figure of Cledrin. He was rolling on the floor, apparently engaged in combat with a chair. His battle-axe had slipped to one side and Ansylike saw that he was lucky not to have rolled over it. A door opened behind him and a dwarf that Ansylike didn't know by name walked out in a nightshirt. He kicked the axe to one side and poked Cledrin with a hairy foot.

"Some guard you make, Cledrin. When will you ever manage to stay awake for a whole night? Shake yourself down and go to bed. The whole inn will be in an uproar."

He waited until he was sure that Cledrin was at least partially alert and in no danger of doing himself any further mischief. Then he sighed, went back into his room, and closed the door firmly behind him.

Cledrin gathered himself unsteadily to his feet and saw Ansylike at the end of the landing. She was smiling at his obvious embarrassment. Once again he felt rather foolish!

As Cledrin got to his feet he couldn't help noticing that Ansylike looked even better now she was clean. Her clothes were different too. She wore closely-fitting, green pants that were held under her bare feet by wide straps. Her shirt was loose but gathered in at the wrists and waist and was of a fine weave that almost made it look like spider-silk. It was of a dazzling, pure white. Her raven-black hair was cut short and didn't reach her collar. Around her slender waist she wore a leather belt with a dagger stuck casually through it. Cledrin resolved to buy a new set of clothes for himself in the morning and have a bath!

"So you are the cause of all this noise. It would be a brave bandit who would try to sneak past you!"

There was a hint of laughter in her voice, but Cledrin accepted her comment as a compliment. He retrieved his axe and walked towards Ansylike. He couldn't help wishing that dwarven maidens were as fair.

"I must have fallen asleep," he said.

"Fallen indeed!" She couldn't resist this little dig at poor Cledrin's expense. He looked a bit uneasy so she continued. "After you had fought so hard this evening, I'd have thought you'd earned your rest. If you must keep guard, why don't you sit outside my door? I'll certainly be able to sleep a little sounder knowing that you're there."

"Then I shall!" replied Cledrin, glowing with pleasure. "You won't be disturbed again before breakfast." This time he was even more determined to stay awake. He had a lady to protect!

Ansylike thanked him and returned to her room. It would no longer be necessary for her to sleep in her clothes. Even a dozing dwarf would be enough to ensure her safety. She checked, once again, that the shutters over the windows were secure and got ready for bed.

Chapter Three

OUT OF THE INN

In the morning Ansylike was woken by a sound like rocks being rolled around in a tin pail. It took her a moment or two to identify the noise. It was dwarven snoring outside her door. Cledrin had obviously fallen asleep despite his efforts. Sunlight was streaming through the cracks in the shutters as she decided to leave her bed. The basin was still full of dirty water so she decided to leave washing for later. She was never at her best in the mornings and always felt a little irritable until after breakfast.

She had finished dressing and was pulling on her boots when there was a gentle knock on the door.

"Come in," she called as she slotted two daggers into their scabbards. There was another knock on the door. Somewhat wearily she crossed the room and opened it. To her surprise Cledrin stood there with a bowl of hot water in his hands and a drying cloth over one arm.

"I thought you might need these," he said, "and breakfast will be served soon."

She took the offered basin and went back in. Cledrin closed the door gently behind her and resumed his guard duty. If he had noticed that she had not thanked him, he said nothing of it.

Before long the dwarves, Ansylike and Andric, the minstrel, were seated round the table enjoying a hearty breakfast. Instead of ale there were flagons of unfermented fruit juice. The bread was still hot and the butter was fresh enough to have been churned that very morning. There was a whole side of roasted bacon being sliced by the beer-man at one end of the table. Between each place was a platter of tomatoes and fried eggs. There were steamed mushrooms and boiled potatoes. Pancakes were piled high, with honey dripping over them. Haldriel grunted with satisfaction as he cut himself a third slice of bread. He noted that Obolin had egg and grease from the meat trickling down his beard. He would have to remind him of his manners before they dined again in refined company.

The rest of the morning passed in preparation for their journey. The sun was high in the sky before they were finally ready to leave. Cledrin had insisted that they buy a donkey to carry some of their possessions and had busied himself loading it up. The party was far smaller than Andric had expected. To his surprise, he found that only five of the dwarves intended to make the trip. Haldriel was their leader so, naturally, he would go. Obolin, Cledrin, Groblic and one other who introduced himself as Tharl Wolf-slayer would make up the rest.

Ansylike noted that he was the one who had scolded Cledrin the night before. She hoped that there was no bad feeling between them.

The first part of the journey was over well-kept roads. On either side of them were fields where a variety of plants grew in lush profusion. Haldriel wished that the lands around his home were so fertile.

Even the rows of hedges bore flowers that would, no doubt, turn to tasty berries later in the year. They would make good wine. The farm buildings were arranged into small squares for easy defence and seemed to have few windows on their ground floors.

There were animals grazing contentedly and some raised their heads to stare at the passers-by.

"They certainly know how to manage the land around here!" he declared to Andric. He had a garden back home, which was rare for a dwarf.

"Good soil, I expect, and not much to do except grow things and eat," retorted Obolin grumpily. He preferred to be working at the forge or in the silver-mine. Air didn't seem healthy to him without some smoke or dust in it. He was missing his home and the sort of work he was used to. He had begun to wonder if he would ever see it again.

"When will we reach those mountains?" sighed Groblic. "They seem no closer and we must have been walking at a fair pace. Just how far away are they?"

"We should reach the foothills before tonight," replied Andric, "then we can make camp. We'll have to choose our route through the pass very carefully. Even at this time of the year there's snow on the peaks. It sometimes melts and brings showers of stone down. I don't want to be under a rockfall!"

"Wise words, Andric. We'll take your advice and make camp before it gets dark," agreed Haldriel. "I hope we can find a safe place for a good rest." His feet were aching and his shoulders were sore where the straps of his pack dug into them. He would have to lighten the load before long.

Cledrin was having no such problems as his donkey was carrying nearly all of his baggage. He whistled a cheery tune as he strolled along, ignoring the occasional glare from Haldriel and Obolin. Ansylike too seemed to be making good progress. Despite her slight build she was carrying a large framed pack without trouble.

The foothills marked a sudden change in the scenery. The path they'd all been following had narrowed to little more than an animal track and that, too, petered out. Andric called them to a halt.

"I'll go on ahead a little way first," he said. "There are too many good sites for an ambush in these hills and I want to examine the ground carefully before we go any further." He unslung his pack and lowered it to the grass. "Keep watch. I'll be back before long."

Haldriel nodded in agreement and unslung his own pack. Cledrin led his donkey over to a tasty-looking patch of grass and let him graze. He had a sudden thought and turned to Ansylike.

"Why do they call you 'Spud'?" he asked. "It doesn't seem like a term of affection to me."

"I'll tell you one day," she replied and, seeing the disappointment on his face, added, "but as we have become friends you can call me Spud too. I'm sure it will be easier for you to pronounce."

Cledrin was gleeful and went off to boast to the other dwarves. Soon they would all be calling her Spud, with his permission!

Andric returned and said that the way ahead seemed safe, but they'd better camp where they were for the night. There was plenty of grass for the donkey to fill up with. He might not be so fortunate the next day. It was obvious that they would need to post a guard and the freshest of them would have to take the first shift. Cledrin immediately volunteered.

This was generally agreed to be a good idea. As there were only seven of them all would have to take a turn. Cledrin would be least likely to nod off if he were given first duty.

A fire was lit and a stew was soon bubbling over it. The fresh meat would have to be eaten first. They also had a supply of dried food which would last a few days. After that they would have to hunt in the wild and survive on what they could catch. It was not a cheering prospect. Ale and wine were also in short supply. Secretly, Haldriel had stashed two bottles of fiery drinking spirit in his pack for medicinal purposes and celebrations.

Cledrin's sentry duty passed without incident. He woke Obolin whose turn it was next. All of the others seemed to be fast asleep on the grass. Each was wrapped in an oiled blanket to keep out the damp. Ansylike had taken off her boots to use as a pillow and so that her daggers were close to hand. The fire had burned low but was in no danger of going out yet. Just to make sure, Cledrin carefully placed a few more logs on it. The smell of the wood-smoke would help to keep animals away. He noted that the donkey was close by, tethered to a stake in the ground, then prepared for a peaceful night's sleep.

Clouds had gathered overhead, but there was no rain. The moon was hidden and Obolin was thankful that he could see so well in the darkness. He was not prone to falling asleep and there was no chance of anyone sneaking up on him. So it was to his amazement that he saw the wolf gazing at him from less than a dozen paces away! He hefted his sturdy war-hammer with both hands and cast an eye around in case there were any more of the beasts.

The wolf gazed at Obolin and made no move. It was near enough to reach him in one bound but it simply laid its head on its paws and waited. Obolin decided that it was time to summon some help and edged his way towards his sleeping companions until he was close enough to reach one with his boot. He kicked at the prone figure carefully, but hard. He didn't want to be unbalanced in case the wolf chose that moment to attack.

Andric woke and saw the danger at once. He was on his feet in an instant, and seized a brand from the fire. He shouted to wake the rest of his companions and waved the burning stick in the air. With a snarl of anger the wolf rose to its feet and sprang at him. This creature didn't seem to be worried by fire!

At once there was confusion in the camp. From out of the darkness the wolves descended. Their claws were as deadly as their fangs and they ripped and tore at their prey. Cledrin was borne down but the wolf was dead before it reached the ground with one of Ansylike's daggers through its neck. Soaked in blood, Cledrin rose to his feet and aimed a blow at the back of another who was defying Groblic's attempts to batter it with his war-hammer. He caught it a crippling swipe across its haunches and hefted his axe for the next one.

Haldriel stood with his crossbow loaded, ready to fire. Andric had gathered his sword and neatly whipped it across a wolf as it tried to grip his leg.

Tharl Wolf-slayer was deadly efficient in his approach. He wielded an axe as though it was a part of him. On his left arm he wore a small shield of iron with a curved, cruel spike in its boss. In his right hand was the weapon that had earned him his name. 'Wolfsbane' gleamed as if it were silver under a full moon, catching the reflected glow. It scythed through fur and flesh. It knew no mercy and neither did Tharl. He had his reputation to consider as well as his own skin. Before him, however, was the biggest wolf he had ever seen in his long life.

It was as tall as Cledrin's donkey! Its bared, yellow teeth were the size of fingers and it looked hungry. Very hungry! He didn't have time to adjust his stance and trusted to luck. He raised his shield, braced his arm and struck upwards with his axe. He caught the wolf across its ribs and his axe buried itself up to the hilt, then was wrenched from his grasp. He fell back under the weight of its attack, impaling it on the spike of his shield. Still it wouldn't die! It moved back, shook the axe free and prepared to spring again. Then it dropped lifeless with one of Haldriel's crossbow bolts through its skull!

Tharl retrieved his axe. Luckily it was not damaged. He moved back into battle.

Ansylike threw her last dagger and grabbed two burning logs from the fire. They were her only defence and not very effective. She had to leap from side to side, duck and parry as wolves sprang at her from all directions. Above the sound of snarling and growls, she heard Haldriel call.

"Catch, Spud!" and she saw him throw Cledrin's elven leaf-blade in her direction. It was in her right hand before she had time to consider. Once again she set about delivering bloody death.

Groblic, she saw was in no immediate danger. His war-hammer crunched bones and splintered teeth. Haldriel was reloading his bow faster than she thought was possible and his missiles found their targets with unerring accuracy. Tharl had lost his shield, but used his axe for parrying and attack. Cledrin had found an unusual ally. He stood in front of his donkey and guarded its head. She watched as it kicked with precision at a wolf which tried to spring on its back. It seemed to be as deadly as Cledrin! The wolf retreated into the darkness to lick its wounds. Her blade flashed again and caught another one a slicing blow across its eyes. Almost blind it stumbled away.

Andric shouted, "They're falling back. Don't follow them. Stand around the fire. There could be more of them out there." All heeded his advice except Cledrin who stood guard over his donkey and wouldn't leave it. Both stood and waited for a moment, but there was no sign of a renewed onslaught. The donkey's ears twitched and Cledrin peered into the night, but the wolves seemed to be gone. The danger was past.

Ansylike collected her knives and wiped each one carefully. When she'd found all four she walked towards Haldriel and offered him the leaf-sword. He raised his hands in refusal.

"No, I trust you now. Keep the sword. We're not in any danger from you. The sword doesn't seem to have any control over you. Accept it in the spirit in which Cledrin gave it. I have the scabbard. It will fit well on your belt."

Obolin and Tharl exchanged dubious looks. Cledrin was pleased and rubbed his hands together, urging her to accept it. Andric said nothing and merely scanned the rocks for any sign of danger. If he had any thoughts on the wisdom of this act he was unwilling to share them.

Ansylike was happy to keep the sword and nodded agreement. It was finely balanced and suited her well. It was not too heavy, like Andric's steel blade, and its curious lettering fascinated her. When she had the chance she would study it carefully. The writing looked like elven runes and could hold many secret powers.

Wounds had to be tended before the party could rest again and Cledrin put more wood on the fire to heat water. Few of them had escaped without injury, but all considered themselves fortunate to be alive. At least none of them would spend the next day being digested in a wolf's gut.

The rest of the night passed without any event and the dwarves were much refreshed when they woke at dawn. It had been a cool night, but not unpleasant. At least there'd been no rain and the dew was light. Andric and Ansylike were on guard and had nothing to report. The carcasses of the slain wolves were scattered around the campsite. Some of them were huge! Haldriel, however, was only interested in recovering the bolts he'd fired at them. All could be used again. He didn't have the skill to make new ones. Obolin, however, had an interesting discovery to report. He bent carefully over one of the dead wolves as he spoke.

"This animal has a chain around its neck! This was no ordinary hunting pack!" He was examining the body of the one which had destroyed his shield and nearly taken his life. "This was no chance encounter. These creatures must have disposed of many who tried to take this route into the mountains. They must be guarding this path. I wonder why!" As he reached for the chain Andric shouted a warning.

"Don't touch it!"

He was too late. Obolin hurtled backwards through the air and came to rest against a boulder. He raised a smoking finger to his eyes as if in amusement, then passed out.

"What was that?" cried Cledrin as he went to help his friend.

"Draw your sword, Spud," said Andric, "and cut its head off."

Haldriel and Tharl went to their fallen comrade. Cledrin acted to protect his fair friend and hastened to the wolf, standing between it and Ansylike. His expression was grim and lines of worry creased his face.

"No!" he shouted at her as he held his arms out. "Give me the sword. I will not allow you to put yourself in danger. Obolin could have been killed. If we have to cut the head from this creature, then I will do it!"

There was no doubting his determination. Ansylike paused and stood still. Andric said nothing so she drew her sword and offered it, hilt first, to Cledrin. He took it and swept the head off the wolf before she had time to step back. Both of them were splattered with blood. In the light of the day they saw that it was a sickly, unnatural purple.

"Ugh! You could've waited a moment," complained Ansylike, wrinkling her nose.

The wolf's severed head bounced a few paces and disappeared. The body before Cledrin vanished. Where it had lain on the grass was nothing but a dark stain. That too changed until there was no sign that blood had been spilt. Cledrin stood with the leaf-sword in both hands. Its point was embedded in the turf. He looked over his shoulder at Ansylike, who could only shrug. She'd seen little of enchanted animals and magic swords and could offer no help. Cledrin left the sword in the ground. On the grass was the chain that had been around the wolf's neck. He gazed at it and saw that it was silver. He was not tempted to pick it up. He did not want his fingers burned!

"Is it safe to pick that up?" asked Ansylike.

Andric regarded it thoughtfully and shook his head. "I doubt it," he replied. "It gave that dwarf a nasty shock! You'd better see if he's still in one piece."

Ansylike didn't move. She suspected that she was being hoodwinked into getting out of the way while Andric tried to pick up the chain. He cared too little for his own safety. She was used to that but it was unreasonable and it annoyed her. A wrinkle of anger appeared on her forehead.

Groblic noted it and backed off to a safer distance. He knew very well what dwarven women were like when they were angered and suspected that elves were no better. He had more scars from his wife than from his opponents in combat! Dwarves have a reputation for never running from a battle, but they generally know better than to poke their noses into a wasps' nest!

The frown suddenly vanished from Ansylike's face and she put a hand on Andric's shoulder.

"Let me," she said. "I have an idea. Roll a rock over it and see what happens." The tone of her voice was calm and betrayed none of the annoyance that she'd briefly felt.

This seemed a sensible suggestion to Groblic and he took a few more paces backwards and started to look for a suitable stone. There were many close to hand but he saw no reason to find one quickly. He was not keen on flying backwards through the air and having his fingers set on fire! There was a sudden pop behind him and he turned to see what had happened. It took him a moment to realise that there was no longer any need to find a stone.

Andric and Ansylike looked at each other. Neither of them had touched the silver chain, but it had vanished in a small cloud of acrid smoke. All that was left to show where it had been was a charred patch of grass. There was no point in them standing and watching any longer. Whoever had sent the wolves would know that they'd been slain and might be sending another batch! They had little time to lose. Obolin would also need attention before they could continue on their journey. Discussion would be better held while they travelled. They left the mystery to be solved at another time and both of them scanned the hills as if they could anticipate what dangers lay ahead.

Obolin was not showing any signs of waking up. Haldriel had looked carefully at his hand and arm and found only slight damage. He seemed to have no more than a little soot on one finger and this had been easily wiped away. Andric looked on with growing anxiety. Haldriel stood up. There was nothing that he could do.

"We can't stay here and I don't see how we can go on unless Obolin recovers soon. The mountains will be difficult to cross and we cannot carry him. One of us will have to return with him to the inn. Perhaps they could catch up with us later."

This was a sensible idea and typical of Haldriel's optimism. Who would volunteer to return?

"I'd better take him back," said Cledrin. "I can tie him to the donkey. I can catch you up in a day or two. You will remember to mark the trail for me to follow?"

"I'd better come with you. I did not intend to leave this party of adventurers so soon but we have a better chance if I accompany you to the inn. We also should be safer when we set out to follow you." Andric's words were a heavy blow to all of them, except Haldriel.

"You should be able to catch up with us. I'm sure that Obolin and Cledrin will be well protected by you. We will not be too far away. Let me tell you of a few things that we should have bought at the inn." Haldriel had thought of more than just a few things, but he was in earnest. He passed Andric a small pouch of silver pieces to pay for his provisions and made him repeat the shopping list.

Groblic had heard enough. He knew well that Cledrin was reluctant to part from his elven friend and ushered him to one side while the others kept watch.

"Let's get Obolin onto the saddle. The sooner a journey is started, the sooner it is finished."

It was a saying that Obolin was fond of repeating and Cledrin appreciated the sentiment. Groblic had a kind heart. He needed one. How else could he put up with a wife who had the temper of a troll!

The decision had been made and Andric scouted ahead as Cledrin led his donkey and its sleeping burden back on the trail to the inn. He turned and waved to his sister who was leading the small band of dwarves back into the peril of The Desolation. He hoped that he would see her again. He did not have the confidence of Haldriel.

The sun was high in the sky before Ansylike called them to a halt.

Andric, Cledrin and the donkey, carrying Obolin, had long since passed out of view. Ahead of them was the pass through the mountains and it was empty. Ansylike looked carefully, but could see no creatures moving. There were birds wheeling around in the sky, probably carrion crows or hawks, and signs of nests up an the rock walls. She really had no idea how to tell the difference between one bird and another.

There were no trees in the valley itself. On one side though, starting a hundred paces up, were small, scrubby bushes. They were stunted. Their branches all seemed to be dragged in the same direction as if by a strong wind, although the air was now still. Haldriel had noticed the bushes too. He pointed them out to Groblic who nodded. They both knew what was growing up in the rocks.

"We can't miss a chance like this," explained Haldriel. "The roots of those plants have the power to heal certain types of injuries and they are often collected by our people. We call them 'urixcroc', or 'rix' for short. I think we should climb up there and harvest some."

Groblic nodded again in agreement, but looked to Ansylike for her decision. Tharl was already unpacking his rope. It seemed like a good idea to Ansylike, as any healing herbs would come in handy. They had already seen enough injuries and no-one knew what perils they would meet on their journey.

"Let's make sure that nothing is waiting to ambush us first," she said looking keenly around. "We'd better keep a careful watch while we climb. Shall I go first?"

Tharl laughed at the idea. He was not too bothered about giving offence. Dwarves were better than anyone at rock-climbing. It was ridiculous for anyone to think otherwise. He cared little if Spud thought she was in charge. He didn't really like anyone he had met since he had left the mountains and cared nothing about hurting their feelings. He only respected warriors. All others were farmers or traders. Farmers were peasants and traders were robbers who didn't use violence. He despised them all. Groblic was anxious to cover for his friend's lack of manners. He tried to smooth things over by chuckling as if it were something of a jest.

"Come now," he said to Ansylike. "You don't think that we would ask a fair maiden to do such dirty work? They can grub around for the roots. You can stand guard with me. Let Haldriel and Tharl collect the rix." He smiled and saw that Ansylike did not seem ruffled. He considered them all to be fortunate. He knew that there was no point in upsetting anyone. They would have to get on and work together or perish.

"I'll stand guard with you," she agreed cheerfully.

Ansylike unloaded her backpack when she reached the base of the rock wall and looked carefully around. There was no sign of danger so she unstrapped her weapon belt and took it off. Without all that weight she felt much more at ease. She sat on a soft, sandy patch of ground and relaxed while Groblic kept guard. After a moment's thought she pulled off her boots, wriggled her toes and soon dozed off. The sun kept her warm enough, but Groblic put his cloak over her when he saw that she was sound asleep. Groblic felt protective. She looked like a child and he wondered what it was that had led her from home at such an early age. He resolved to ask her when he got the chance. Now, however, was not the time. Haldriel and Tharl should have reached the urixcroc patch and should have started to dig them out. There was no sign of them! He couldn't hear them and he couldn't see them! Where could they have gone? The rope dangled limply against the face of the cliff but there were no dwarves at the top of it. He peered up and saw that the bushes were exactly as before. They had not started work. He was just beginning to enjoy himself again too! Regretting their decision to harvest the herbs, he looked around, but there was still no sign of danger. Not that it was much comfort. The reputation of The Desolation was well deserved. Wild magic ran free here and danger was everywhere!

Groblic thought for more than a moment. Should he wait? He had heard no calls for help and he did not want to wake Spud. He could climb the rope. He could climb another piece of rock to get a better view of where his friends ought to be, but he couldn't do much if he were to be attacked on the face of the rock. It was sheer and he would need both hands to hang on. He'd better wake Spud, he decided, and warn her that things were not going according to plan.

He checked that her daggers and her sword were well out of her reach before he tried to wake her. He shook her gently by the shoulders. There was no response. He lifted her head in one hand, tapped her chin and called for her to wake. Still she didn't move. He shook her shoulder again and she curled up tighter and shuddered deeper into sleep. He called for her to wake. As he did so, a shadow passed over, then another. With dismay he realised that the carrion birds were circling lower. They were expecting dead meat to feed on. They would not take him nor his elven friend! He heaved his weapon onto his back, dropped his shield and scooped Ansylike into his arms. There was an overhanging rock some 300 paces away and there he would make his stand!

His legs were short but he covered the distance quickly. Running on stone was natural to a dwarf. Under the outcrop he paused and lowered Ansylike gently to the ground. She was still wrapped in his cloak. Groblic hefted his war-hammer into both hands and prepared for battle. He was confident. Carrion birds were always cowardly and would not persist once one or two of their number had been killed. So intent was he on watching the birds that he didn't immediately notice that Ansylike was stirring. She rolled out of the cloak and lay, spread out, on the ground. She was face down in the sand and her back heaved as she drew in deep gasps of air. She drew herself up to her knees and shook her head as if to clear the sleepiness away. Unsteadily she rose to her feet and staggered a little before steadying herself against the rock wall.

"What happened?" she asked. "Where are the others?"

Groblic explained briefly, not taking his eyes off the birds who had now shifted their attention back to where Ansylike had been sleeping earlier. Occasionally one of the braver ones swooped low, but there was no prey for them yet and the rest hung back.

"We'd better get back to where we left Haldriel and Tharl. They must be in trouble. Those birds know when there is likely to be a meal and I think they're expecting to be eating dwarf before long!" Ansylike's words were slurred as if she had been drinking wine all morning. She still leant heavily against the rock and looked as if she was ready to collapse. She was not wearing her boots nor her belt, so she had no weapons to fight with and she could not climb very far in bare feet. Groblic thought she was unlikely to be much help!

"You stay here. You still look half-asleep and..." Groblic's words trailed off as he had a sudden inspiration. "It's those plants! They must be far stronger than the ones we have at home. We normally collect the roots and boil them to make a healing brew, but anyone who drinks it falls into a deep sleep. These ones must be powerful enough to put anyone to sleep just by smelling the scent. Not that I noticed any scent in the air, but it certainly would explain why you are so drowsy. Haldriel and Tharl must have been overcome by it!"

"Then why didn't they fall to the ground? That doesn't explain how they disappeared."

"Perhaps there's a cave in the rock that we couldn't see. Perhaps they are there, fast asleep. Those birds will attack them and they'll be unable to move. Come on! You can help after all!" Groblic was insistent. He held his war-hammer in his left hand and took Ansylike by the waist and hurried her along. Despite his support she stumbled frequently, but it didn't take long to get back to the rope which was ominously still. Ansylike pulled her boots on and rolled over in the process. Her head was obviously not too clear. She spat sand out of her mouth and shook her head again. Already she was feeling sleepy.

"Put this over your mouth. It will keep you awake." Groblic held out a cloth which he had soaked in liquor. He had remembered that people at home were warned not to drink any alcohol when they were given 'rix' to heal their wounds. He hoped that the same effect would work here in The Desolation. If it didn't, they might all be food for the birds! He took a long swig of mead and offered the flask to Ansylike. She found that it tasted sweet and delicious and she was reluctant to hand it back. She looked on sadly as the dwarf put the stopper firmly back in. Then he started to climb, keeping roughly parallel to the rope.

The rock was solid enough and his fingers found easy holds. Despite the war-hammer across his back he moved swiftly up and reached the ledge where the lowest bush grew. From here he could see that there was indeed a cave, in fact several, set well back. He decided to report on his progress and called down to Ansylike.

"There's a cave not too far above me. I think that's where I'll look first. What are the birds doing?"

"Go on. The birds are keeping their distance and there is no sign of anyone else around. I feel much better and I'll climb up if you need any help." Ansylike hoped her voice sounded more confident than she felt. Without waiting for a reply she grabbed the rope and gave it a tug to make sure that it was secure, then began to climb after Groblic. Her boots gave a good hold on the rock but they were not designed for such work and she was glad of the line to hang on to.

She reached the ledge where the rope was anchored and looked up at the sheer slab of rock above her. It made her feel giddy. It was as if she was going to tumble backwards at any moment. She was aware of the enormous weight that towered above.

Suddenly Groblic's head appeared in view. He leaned over and dangled another rope.

"Grab this and tie it around you. I'll haul you up and you can see what we've found."

She did as she was told and was glad of the comfort of the rope round her waist. She took a moment to brace herself before she shouted back to Groblic that she was ready. Then she began to climb. When she reached the next ledge she saw that Groblic had tied himself firmly to the boulder behind him. He had been paying out the rope to her from around another rock so there was even less chance of him losing his grip. She had been in safe hands. The carrion birds had not moved any closer so there was no threat from them at the moment. She had time to steady herself and edge carefully along the ledge towards the cave.

The sight inside was grisly, but it was better to be in a cave than out on the rock. At least there was no chance of falling to a sudden death! Amongst the scattered bones of animals were some that were definitely human. All were picked clean, probably by the birds.

The sleeping dwarves were nestled in this dreadful place of death as if they were in their own beds at home. Ansylike cast a wary eye around the cave to make sure that there was no other danger. Satisfied, she called back to Groblic who was watching her carefully.

"How are we going to get them out of here? Can we lower them on your rope? I don't think that they're dead, just sleeping." Ansylike was careful to breathe through the cloth and wished that she had a bottle of wine with her in the cave. Her head was not very clear and she was aware that she was staggering, even as she spoke. Groblic quickly attached a rope to Haldriel wrapping it twice around his waist. Between the two of them they had soon got their friends to the ground. They were fast asleep and Tharl was snoring, peacefully unaware of the danger he had been in.

Chapter Four

DREAMS AND SCREAMS

Groblic and Ansylike carried the sleeping dwarves, one at a time, to the shelter of the rocky outcrop and waited for them to recover their senses. While Groblic kept watch, Ansylike went to collect some wood for a fire. She was careful to avoid the area where the 'sleeping bushes' grew! She collected a fair-sized bundle as she had no idea how long they would be camping in this particular spot.

Eventually Haldriel and Tharl recovered and Ansylike and Groblic left them when they were able to fend for themselves. Fortunately, Haldriel had a potion which helped a little. It was an old remedy for 'hangovers' and tasted vile but it got them moving quickly. Tharl dangled a pot of water over the fire. He was not much of a cook, but he knew from experience that meals always started from boiling water. Their provisions were plentiful, but dwarves had big appetites and they were accustomed to large portions. Haldriel wondered what the carrion birds tasted like and wasted a few arrows trying to bring one down.

As Groblic had left his ropes in place it didn't take him long to reach the caves again. He shouted down to Ansylike who was waiting for his signal to follow. Somewhat anxiously he noted that her face was flushed with colour and she was unsteady on her feet.

"Are you all right, Spud? Are the bushes affecting you? Are you feeling sleepy?"

Ansylike uncrossed her eyes and peered at him. "I'm fine!" she shouted, in a much louder voice than was necessary. "Are you ready for me to climb the rope?"

Groblic realised that it was the wine that he had made her drink that was to blame. She was drunk! "Tie the rope around your waist and I'll haul you up! Try to clear your head and concentrate. Make sure you tie a good knot, Spud, and tie an extra one to be safe!"

Groblic shouted his orders and hoped that she was in a fit state to understand. She was, but her feet were not entirely under her control and she lost her footing twice as she climbed up. By the time she reached Groblic her leggings were torn and one of her knees was bleeding.

"Well, you certainly can't drink a lot without feeling the effects! I thought that elves enjoyed ale and wine. Are you well enough to explore the caves or shall I have to leave you here?" Groblic intended that his words would spur her into action. Instead she raised a very pale face towards him and waved him to go on without her. He shrugged.

Groblic satisfied himself that there was nothing of value in the caves and lowered Ansylike back down the rope. She had difficulty untying herself and lay sprawled on her back, gasping for breath and rolling from side to side. Groblic adjusted the knots on the ropes and joined Ansylike who was looking somewhat dejected. He waved his arms in the air as if he was about to perform some magic trick, then pulled hard on the rope. It detached itself from the rock at the top and slid down to his feet in an untidy tangle. He scooped up the coils without saying a word and started to walk to where he had left Haldriel and Tharl.

Ansylike gazed on in speechless amazement. She looked at the cliff and up to where the rope had been tied. How had Groblic done that? If the rope had not been tied fast, he could not have climbed down it, yet he had pulled it down with just a tug.

She realised that Groblic had a few skills that she had not even imagined and promised herself that she would learn as many as he was willing to teach her. She got to her feet and weaved her way after him.

Tharl's cooking was dreadful, but all ate their fill. It was somehow better to eat outdoors and their spirits soon rose again. Haldriel collected more wood for the fire and there was a merry blaze for them to huddle around.

Ansylike missed most of the conversation as she fell asleep. Groblic spread his cloak over her again and hoped that she would be sober when she woke. There was little point in going any further today so it was decided to rest here until the next day. Before they had posted a guard and determined who was to sleep first, Groblic had something of importance to say.

"There was nothing of value in the caves," he began. "There were bones, of course, scraps of clothing, and remnants of leather armour, but not a trace of anything metal." He picked at his teeth with a little twig to remove some of the tough bits of meat that had lodged between them.

"So what of that?" interrupted Tharl gruffly. "You're just telling us that we have gained nothing from your exploration!" He was more than a little cross at his own failure. Having to be rescued was a serious blow to his pride.

"There was nothing of any value there! That's the point," replied Groblic, keeping his temper firmly under control. "There was not so much as a button! Whoever perished in those caves did not go in unarmed. Who goes anywhere without a dagger in a belt, a sword in a scabbard, or at least a few coins jingling in a purse? No-one! Those caves have already been searched!" He paused for the meaning of his words to reach his friends. He could tell by the expressions on their faces that they understood what he meant.

"Someone loots the caves and probably know when there is a victim to be robbed. The birds are a good enough signal. They swarm around when they think there is a meal and they have been active today!" Haldriel said. "We had better keep a careful watch and sleep with our weapons close by."

The others nodded in agreement and all congratulated Groblic on his assessment of the situation.

Further talk followed and Groblic turned his attention to Ansylike, who was sleeping soundly. He gently eased off her boots and tucked his cloak, which he had spread over her, under her feet. He remembered the grazing of her knees and resolved to make sure that the wound was not infected before they left in the morning. He didn't wake her as she had earned her rest.

During the night Haldriel thought about the caves and wondered who had removed the loot! Groblic was right. There should have been something there apart from bones. He and Tharl were on guard and he decided to test out an idea. He told Tharl that his bladder was full and that he would have to relieve himself, which was true, and wandered off to find a secluded spot in the rocks. He walked a hundred paces or so before he found a place where he would be hidden from the campsite and looked carefully around. He didn't want to be surprised by a wolf with his trousers round his ankles! Before returning he left an iron dagger on the top of a boulder. The night sky was clear again. The moon rose and lit up the valley with an eerie, blue light, then disappeared behind the crags. An owl hooted nearby and wolves howled in the distance.

The fire burned low, but Groblic, who was by then on guard, put more dry wood on it. There was plenty to last until morning. Ansylike stirred as the first rays of sunlight were streaking the skies in the east. Distant clouds began to flush a rosy pink, bringing the threat of rain later in the day.

"Awake at last?" said Groblic. "No more wine for you, Spud, or you'll be spending half of your life asleep!" His tone was mocking, but gentle. "You certainly seemed to enjoy the mead. It's made with honey, you know? It doesn't taste strong, but it's got quite a powerful kick! I'll make sure that there's some to go with dinner tonight."

Ansylike grinned and shook her hair. She seemed alert and more like her usual self. She apologised for falling asleep and asked if she'd missed anything important. Like Haldriel she needed to relieve herself, urgently. Quickly she pulled on her boots and stood up. Then she opened her backpack, took out a small sack and a water flask and headed off into the rocks. She wished that there was a proper latrine with running water like the one at the inn. This was one aspect of life in the wilds that she did not enjoy!

Ansylike inspected her grazed knees and saw that there was probably nothing to worry about. She wiped the blood away with a cloth and fresh water from her leather bottle and pulled on a clean pair of pants. Unfortunately they were tight against her skin and she realised that they would rub her knees as she walked and make life difficult! She took them off again and cut the legs off her old pair. They would have to do for now. The clean pair that she was going to wear had bloodstains on them from her knees. She bundled them up crossly and stuffed them back into her sack. Life was certainly awkward sometimes! As she returned to the campsite, she saw that Haldriel was laughing at her.

"You do look comical!" he said. "Is this some new fashion or are you feeling the heat?"

She looked down at her legs and smiled. She did look a little ridiculous. She hadn't cut the cloth of her pants very straight and they were jagged and uneven. She tried to roll them up further so that they'd look less amusing, but the material was too tight. Groblic volunteered his services and fetched a small metal box from his pack. He unscrewed the lid and produced a needle. It was a thorn of some sort with a small hole drilled in the thick end.

With a flourish, he produced a wooden bobbin around which was wound a length of the finest thread that Ansylike had even seen.

"It's spider's silk!' she exclaimed. "I've heard of it but I didn't think it really existed. Where did you get it from?"

"A family heirloom, passed on to me by my great grandmother," replied Groblic proudly. "I've used it many times but the thread never seems to run out. Now will you allow me to make you look a bit more respectable? I am quite skilful with the needle and I promise not to prick you with it!" Ansylike looked a bit dubious, but it was modesty rather than fear of Groblic's needle that made her hesitate. She was not used to being touched by anyone, but didn't know how to refuse Groblic's kind offer. She had a sudden inspiration.

"Could you alter the clean pair?" she asked, taking them from her sack. "I've already got blood on the knees and I doubt whether it will wash out anyway. I can wear these ones that amuse you all so greatly until they're ready. I can make our breakfast while you're sewing."

Tharl went off to find more wood, Haldriel went to see if his dagger was still on the boulder and Ansylike gathered some rations together. Groblic sat down, crossed his legs and began to thread his needle.

"I'll have to measure these against you, Spud, so that I'll know where to cut them," he remarked, as he held up her new pants. To his surprise she frowned, but then nodded in agreement. "Here, hold them against your waist and I'll mark them with this little white rock." Ansylike did as she was asked and soon Groblic was sitting down again with his needle and thread, expertly making a pair of shorts! He was careful not to betray his thoughts, but he was wondering if Spud distrusted all men or whether it was just dwarves.

Haldriel returned with the news that his dagger had gone. Ansylike declared that she hadn't seen it. Groblic seemed to miss the point and told him that it was his own fault for leaving it lying around so carelessly.

"Finish your sewing, rock-head, and leave the thinking to me!" replied Haldriel. "Don't you see? None of us touched the dagger and the only things we've seen moving are those birds."

"Nothing to worry about," Groblic replied without glancing up.

"I got a good look at one from quite close range and they're bigger than I thought. They're easily capable of flying off with a dagger or even a sword!" Haldriel continued.

"I don't see what a carrion crow would want with a dagger!" stated Groblic who had paused in his work to scowl at his friend. "I'm prepared for anything in these strange lands, but birds armed with knives is a bit much!"

"Perhaps the crows collect them for someone ... someone who can control animals, like a magician! Remember those wolves and the one with the chain round its neck? I'd hate to think that there were more of those after us!" Ansylike shuddered as she finished her words.

"Now see what you've done! There was no need to frighten the poor girl. Can't you keep your worries to yourself, at least until after we've eaten!" Groblic was cross and Haldriel realised that he had understood perfectly well the significance of the missing dagger from the start. He just didn't want it discussed.

Haldriel was ashamed of himself and resolved to make amends. He hadn't thought to keep his news from Ansylike.

"You needn't worry. I doubt that there's any connection between the wolves and the crows. I was going to say that the birds probably collect bright objects. That would explain why all the metal had gone from the caves. Remember that not even a button was to be found there? If I didn't think that we were safe I wouldn't be joining you for breakfast right now. By the way, is it ready yet?" Ansylike seemed to accept this and looked relieved. She started to serve the food as she could see Tharl returning with more firewood.

After a good meal, the dwarves voiced their satisfaction and congratulated Ansylike on the quality of her pancakes. They had each eaten a dozen and had been forced to loosen their belts to make more room for them! She flushed with pride. She had spent a long time cooking at the inn, but rarely received any compliments. She was more used to being told to get her 'skinny tail' moving as the customers were impatient! Groblic held up the pants that he had altered for all to inspect. Ansylike felt the blood rising to her cheeks again, but could not help admiring the workmanship. Groblic was certainly an accomplished tailor! She took them from him and went off to find a more private place to change.

"Before she returns I think we should discuss our present predicament," began Haldriel.

"Our what?" asked Tharl who was not used to such long words.

"We could be in a tricky spot here. That's what I mean by a 'predicament'. We have a problem." He waved Tharl to be silent before he could interrupt again. "As I see it, we are in danger. Those birds are watching us and I cannot see how we can escape their attention."

"You're right." said Tharl. "I didn't want to mention it earlier, but one of those birds has a silver chain round its leg and I'm sure it's not just for decoration." His tone was even and almost casual. He never showed any fear and was renowned for his ability to face any foe without emotion. He had earned the title of "Wolf-slayer" when he was only a child. A pack of wolves had attacked him when he was alone in the mountains and he had driven them off. His axe had broken early in the fight and he had faced the leader of the pack with a rock in each hand and cracked the beast's skull!

"Then we must, at least, kill their leader, get out of this valley quickly and hope that there's a good place to hide on the other side," said Groblic. There was iron in his voice, but Haldriel could see a few flaws in this plan.

"I've tried shooting them down, but they are too difficult to hit. They seem to know when an arrow is coming and dodge out of the way. I can't hit one even on the ground!" He paused. "Anyway, they don't seem to be a threat at the moment so I think it will be enough for us to be extra careful and bide our time. We can wait and let whoever controls them make the first move." The others agreed. There was a problem, but they could do nothing about it yet.

The fire was burning low and only a thin trickle of smoke curled up to the skies where the winds were gradually gathering in force. There was no point being concerned about the smoke betraying their presence if the crows were spies, watching their every move! None of the dwarves could suggest a reason why anyone should be taking an interest in them. After all, they had no treasure and were not even seeking it. Their mission was more diplomatic and they were expecting to spend silver, rather than find any!

Ansylike, meanwhile, was also having problems. She changed into her new pants when she was sure that she was out of the dwarves' sight and put on her weapon belt. She found that the scabbards of her knives rubbed against her thighs and thought about binding them with cloth to stop the friction. That, she decided, wouldn't work. She was loathe to leave them in her backpack, as she had grown used to having them at her waist where she could reach them quickly. She grinned as she thought of the time at the inn when she had first met Haldriel and Groblic and pinned them with her knives. Neither of them had made any mention of that misunderstanding! She took off her weapon belt and slung it over her shoulder and looked down at her legs. There was far more of them showing than she liked, but she felt comfortable and her knees would heal faster this way. On a large rock above her, a carrion crow stretched its neck to watch her more closely. Its beady, black eyes twinkled in the morning sunlight. Around its left leg was a glittering silver chain.

"Here's Spud!" exclaimed Groblic, cheerfully as he saw her come into view. "Nothing of what we've been saying or else you'll be frightening her again," he added softly.

"Well, doesn't she look better now?" he asked aloud. The others nodded their heads in agreement and welcomed her back. Many a dwarf had secretly wished to have long legs and Ansylike's were wonderful! The cut of her pants showed them off to perfection.

"I suppose we'll have to be on our way soon," she said, as she took a place by the fire.

"Thank you, Groblic for your work. These pants feel fine and my knees are already mending." Despite her smile, Groblic could see that she was in pain.

"You start packing up," he said to Haldriel and Tharl. "I want to have a look at these knees before we leave." He pointed a stubby finger at the ground in front of him and said, "Sit!" to Ansylike.

There was no mistaking the authority in his voice and Ansylike waited for only a moment to see that Haldriel and Tharl were not paying any attention before she sat down and stretched out her legs. Groblic was not pleased at what he saw. The skin had been scraped off one knee and the raw flesh was weeping. For a dwarf this was not anything to cause any worry. He would have to treat this as if it were a more serious wound, as humans were less sturdy folk.

He bent Ansylike's leg and she fell onto her back with a gasp of pain. "Lie still and wait for a moment. I'll have to get my bag." Ansylike dreaded the thought of Groblic returning with his needle and thread and gritted her teeth. "You can open your eyes," he said. "This won't hurt. It will stop the wound from getting infected and should make it heal faster." He dropped a blob of the lotion above the wound and gradually worked it downwards until it covered the bleeding flesh. By the time that he'd finished, Ansylike had passed into unconsciousness. Thankfully she could feel no more pain. Groblic was glad of his sturdy, short legs! Haldriel and Tharl looked on with growing concern, but said nothing. They were not wise in the use of healing herbs. They could offer no help.

Tharl took Haldriel by the arm and led him away.

"She's only a child," said Tharl, "and this is no place for her. She should be at home, not here in this wilderness! I said it was a mistake to bring her! If she dies it will be because of us!"

"She seemed capable of looking after herself. Didn't you see her fight?" replied Haldriel.

"Do you know how old she is? Let me tell you. I asked the beer-man at the inn. She has not seen sixteen summers! At such an age we wouldn't let a child out of the home." Tharl paused for his words to take effect. Haldriel was stunned. He could say nothing, but cast a glance back to where Ansylike lay motionless on the ground.

"Fifteen, you say?"

"At the most. Maybe less. The beer-man wasn't sure."

"I never thought of her as a child. Perhaps we could take her back. We have plenty of time." Haldriel knew that there was no sense in his words, even as he spoke them. There was no going back. The decisions had been made and they would have to stick to their plan. Tharl knew this too and there was nothing further that he could add. Once again he assumed an air of stony silence. He would keep guard and leave the thinking to Haldriel.

Groblic finished dealing with Ansylike's injuries and saw that she had passed into sleep. Her leg was already taking on the orange tinge that was always associated with the healing process. Dwarven medicine worked on humans, to his relief.

He spread out his cloak and rolled her gently onto it, carefully keeping her injured leg from making contact with the rough fabric. Hopefully he could leave her to sleep in peace for a while.

The birds, above them, ceased their monotonous circling and swooped in for the kill. Groblic was suddenly thrown off balance by a strike to his shoulder, but he moved fast, rolled with the blow and stood to face an opponent who was nowhere to be seen. Above him the sky was dark with carrion birds and this time it looked as if they were not going to wait for their food to die of natural causes.

Groblic reached for his war-hammer and struck out. His aim was lethal and a crow spun through the air and crashed to the ground a few paces away. Haldriel's bow sent another wheeling to its death. Tharl's axe hissed as it met its target, then he twirled the shaft in his hands, and waved the blade above his head to clip another crow's wing. The birds were above them and hopping at them on the ground, deadly beaks and talons searching for warm flesh to rend and tear. Tharl sliced another that was perched on Haldriel's shoulders and about to peck at his eyes.

Haldriel saw that there was no time for loading his bow and used it to lash out at the birds that were encircling him. He saw Ansylike spring to her feet. Her daggers flashed through the air and thudded into feathered breasts. She seized two burning logs from the fire and waved them above her head until she could reach her sword.

Despite her injuries she felt ready for battle and whipped a bird out of the air with a clean slice of her blade. Haldriel looked to be in the most danger, so she rushed to his aid. Her sword, which she wielded with both hands, sung a death song and slashed black feathers into shreds. She moved over to where Groblic was standing his ground and struck at a bird above his head. It dropped like a stone, but at that moment a crow struck her from behind. Its beak was sharp and scored a long furrow across her shoulder and she winced in pain.

The sword flew from her grip. Haldriel downed another and crushed its neck under his boot. The shaft of Tharl's axe was slippery with blood, but he kept a firm grip on it and cut the head off a bird that was hopping along the ground towards Haldriel.

Suddenly a piercing cry of agony and rage rang out and the crows faltered in their attack. Groblic saw to his horror that the largest of the birds lay writhing in the dust, but it was gradually changing and assuming a human form! It was pinned to the ground by Ansylike's sword. The birds formed an untidy circle around this gruesome creature then plunged in to attack it. Ansylike rose to her feet and had hardly glanced in the direction of this ring of death before Groblic seized her by the waist and turned her away.

"Don't look! Cover your eyes."

Ansylike shuddered. She had seen enough already. She felt sick and clenched her teeth. The leader of the carrion crows was turning into a man and being eaten alive and she didn't want to see any more! Even Tharl had to gulp quickly. It had been a nice breakfast but he didn't want to taste it again! Groblic saw that the danger had passed but he took a good look around to make sure that nothing else was coming into the attack. He led Ansylike back to the fire which was still smouldering and sat her down beside it. There was blood on his wrist-guard. Ansylike's shoulder was bleeding and her tunic was ripped. He could see the gash where the crow had hit her. Hardly had she had time to recover from one injury when she'd received another!

The dwarves gathered under the shelter of the rock. There was no enemy now to fight. Tharl put the remaining wood on the fire and it burst into life again. Groblic applied his healing salve to Ansylike's shoulder and hoped that the wound was not poisoned. She seemed to be in reasonable health, considering what she had been through, but it was obvious that she could not take much more of this! Haldriel was also considering the damage that had been done to them and the deliberate nature of the attacks. Were these creatures simply lying in wait for passing travellers or had they been sent to stop the dwarves from accomplishing their mission? He wondered as he watched Groblic apply his 'magic' potion to Spud's injury and thought about how they had best go about protecting her. So far they had failed miserably. What must she think of them?

"I'd load my bow if I were you," said Ansylike. "There might be some other horrid thing coming to attack us and only Tharl seems prepared!" She winced in pain as Groblic continued to clean the gash on her back where the crow had hit her. "I hope that won't leave a scar," she added lightly and wiped beads of sweat from her brow with the back of her hand.

Tharl was impressed. He knew from experience that Groblic was no surgeon and he could guess at the pain that Ansylike must be suffering. Despite that, she managed to keep a clear head. Certainly she was brave and that was something that he admired. No wonder that the elves were such a difficult enemy to defeat and that the wars against them had gone on for so long.

"We need a new plan of action!" said Haldriel. "We must be more organised and we must be ready for any danger. It appears that we are likely to come under attack from all sides, and we haven't been ready. I propose that we work as a team and pool our strengths. That way we should be able to beat off any foes without getting injured."

"Spud and I will walk together," said Groblic. "She has keen eyes and I have strength! I will make it my duty to protect her!" There was sense in this but the other dwarves were amazed. This was a formal declaration that was only made in the strictest circumstances. A promise of protection was for life and could only be ended by death!

"Your oath is accepted and witnessed by us all! She is under your shield!" Haldriel sealed the vow. It was a promise that no dwarf could break and he couldn't believe what had happened. Elven blood under the shield of a dwarf was something that hadn't been seen since the conflict that had driven all of the elven folk away. He tried to see this as a good sign, but had to force himself to accept it. Why had Groblic given his oath to Spud? She was not his child and could never be his wife. Now it was his sworn duty to keep her from harm. Still, she would be well protected and that was the most important thing.

Ansylike's tunic was soon patched up with thread from Groblic's repair kit and she declared that she was fit to travel. She couldn't carry her pack across her shoulders, but it was light and Groblic strapped it to his own and gave her his rope and war-hammer in exchange. Haldriel made sure that the fire was out and Tharl inspected the remains of the corpse that had been the leader of the crows. It was gruesome! He didn't look for long. He was only interested in the silver chain that had been around its leg and in retrieving Spud's sword that was still stuck in the ground. He gripped the blade with one hand and pulled, but it didn't move. With both hands and all his strength he managed to heave it free and he saw, to his surprise that it had been stuck in solid rock. It was a wonderful weapon indeed! The silver chain had vanished.

He carried the sword to Ansylike and offered it to her, hilt first. As she gratefully sheathed it, Tharl asked how she had managed to throw it with such deadly accuracy.

"I didn't!" she replied. "One of the birds hit me from behind and the sword flew from my hands. I didn't aim it at anything." The dwarves exchanged glances.

"The sword saved us all," said Groblic, "and we should be thankful for that. We do seem to have a little magic on our side and that evens things up a bit. If we have to deal with someone who can turn men into crows, then I'm glad to have Spud and her magic sword with us!" The others agreed, although they were rather anxious about the whole business. Haldriel made a few scratches on a prominent boulder and they were all ready to depart.

The sun had reached its full height in the sky before they made their first stop. It was certainly time for Ansylike to rest, although the dwarves could have gone on at this steady pace for the whole day if they had needed to. It was pleasant weather for such a march. The sun was warm, but a light breeze kept them from getting too hot. Rain clouds had almost disappeared from view.

They found a few boulders to sit on and unslung their packs. Haldriel put his crossbow on the ground beside him and placed two bolts next to it. Ansylike watched with interest.

"Keep your eyes open," said Groblic. "I have business to attend to." He and Tharl picked their way carefully through the rocks and disappeared from sight. Rocks did not make very comfortable seats so Ansylike sat, instead, on the coiled up rope. It was not much better.

"What do you know of this sword?" she asked as she drew the weapon to examine it.

"Little," replied Haldriel. "Cledrin is a great one for secrets and he wouldn't say where he got it or how much he paid for it."

"Do people sell things like that? Could you actually go out and buy a magical weapon or have one made to suit you? I thought that all the wizards were in The Desolation and that they didn't make things like this any more."

"Err.. Well, not exactly! Such things are for sale, but no-one will say where they came from... or to whom they belonged!" Haldriel looked a little guilty.

"You mean they're stolen!" exclaimed Ansylike. She looked keenly at her elven leaf-blade. "The rightful owner of this could be looking for it! I could be hung for thieving if I get caught with it! Or worse. Do you know what they do to thieves in...". Her voice trailed off as she remembered the dreadful execution she had witnessed, not so long ago. It was too horrible to think about.

"I shouldn't worry about that." Haldriel only meant to comfort her, or he would never have told her the truth. "These weapons belong to the dark past and their owners and makers are long dead. Their tombs hold many secrets and treasures and where there is treasure... well, there are... ."

"Thieves!" interrupted Ansylike. "Grave-robbers who steal from the dead and sell their loot to anyone who has the silver to pay for it. That's dreadful. There can be no way of knowing whether a sword is cursed or full of magic. Why would people take such things?"

"Why not? The risks are great, but there are fortunes to be made. The dead have no need of their possessions and the living can put them to good use." Haldriel paused. "Some graves are better left alone, of course. There are the Barrows of the High Elven Lords that nobody has successfully plundered and the Caverns of Fire where the Dwarf Lords are buried."

"I don't see what the difference is," said Ansylike.

"They are better protected. That really is the only difference. If I could get hold of Krallim Dragon-Slayer's battle-axe for a fee, then I would. I would be proud to bear the axe of a legendary Dwarf Lord and it would do him no harm."

"Then why haven't you got it? Is it not for sale or can't you afford it?" Ansylike was beginning to see the logic in Haldriel's reasoning.

"No-one has got into one of those tombs and come out alive. The protection is too good. As I said, some tombs are best left alone because they are simply too dangerous to enter."

"Are the dwarven ones protected by magic then? I thought that you didn't go in for that sort of stuff. Don't you dwarves distrust spells?" She looked warily around her as she had heard a pebble fall, turned and pointed her sword at the rocks behind her. There was nothing threatening to be seen. A single, horned sheep grazing on a measly patch of grass above them was the only thing moving.

"The elves put the spells on the tombs, not us," replied Haldriel as he followed her gaze. "The elves and the wizards. Once there was a time when the wizards interfered in our ways, or so the story goes. Maybe it's the truth, but I can't tell. The Desolation is the result of their quarrels so I'm glad that they leave us alone now."

Chapter Five

CLIFFS AND CAVES

Tharl and Groblic appeared suddenly from the rocks. They'd made their way back carefully to see if they could catch the other pair by surprise.

"We could easily have sneaked up and attacked you. Can't you keep a better look-out than that?" Both Haldriel and Ansylike were startled. "So what were you two talking about that kept you so busy?" said Tharl gruffly.

"I hope your aim is better in battle!" retorted Haldriel, while Ansylike kept her lips sealed tightly. She turned her back on Groblic and Tharl and grinned.

"What do you mean by that ?"

"It looks as if you have both made water into the wind!" laughed Haldriel. "Your trousers are spattered and I can smell you from here!" Both dwarves looked down at their breeches. It rather ruined their victory and both were a little peeved.

"See if you can do better, Spud. It must be your turn to go now." Ansylike could not hide her amusement, but Haldriel was right and she opened her backpack and took out her sack and a leather water-bottle. "Don't go too far away and keep your eyes open!" advised Haldriel. "Draw your sword and keep it beside you."

"And watch out for the wind!" grunted Groblic. There was no need to remind Ansylike. She had learned from the dwarves' example and had no intention of getting wetter than was necessary!

"Where do we go from here?" asked Tharl as he surveyed the cliffs ahead of them. It looked as if they would have to climb if they were going to continue in the same direction. "Is The Desolation on the other side of that lot or are we in it?"

"I'm afraid that we have no choice. I can see no other path. We will have to spend the night at the base of those mountains and give ourselves a full day to get over them." Haldriel looked thoughtful and cradled his crossbow in his arms. He had known that they would have a difficult and dangerous journey. He suspected that the worst was still to come and it had not been easy to get this far!

"We have enough rope," said Groblic, "but there's another problem. How will Obolin and Cledrin find us?" He knew that Haldriel had been leaving signs for them to follow. "How will they catch up?"

"If Cledrin has his donkey with him he'll be able to go no further unless it can climb like one of those sheep," added Tharl gloomily.

"Sheep!" shouted Haldriel. "To arms!"

"I don't believe this!" exclaimed Tharl, but he took up a position as if he were expecting to be attacked at any moment. He and Groblic stood back to back, their weapons ready to strike out.

Ansylike was unaware of the dwarves' concern. She didn't even consider the possibility that sheep could be dangerous. Both of her knees had been bleeding despite Groblic's ointment and there were trails of blood that led into her boots. Her tunic was sticking to her back and she was not sure that the wound was healing. Vague thoughts of infection and life-sapping poisons flashed through her mind.

Her thoughts were interrupted as she heard the plaintive cry of an animal in distress. Without thinking, she pulled up her pants, sheathed her sword and looked up at the cliff. It was sheer and not possible for her to climb. There was a wide ledge on which a sheep seemed to be trapped, but it was more than eighty paces above. She looked for an easier route and soon found one. There was a way, but the rock was crumbly in places and might not support her weight. She unstrapped her weapon belt and left it where it dropped, then started to climb.

The animal bleated pitifully and spurred her on. She was under the impression that sheep were pretty stupid creatures, but she was wrong.

The one that she assumed to be in distress was merely calling to a lamb. It took one look at her as she climbed towards it, then turned and bounded nimbly away, closely followed by its offspring.

Ansylike continued upwards as she was already past the most difficult section of rock and now she could see that there was a cave not far above her. She hadn't noticed it from the ground. It might be worth exploring. Haldriel's talk of hidden treasure put the idea into her mind that there might be something useful to be found.

The ledge was quite wide and the cave was high enough to stand up in. She saw traces of wool and dung on the floor; evidence that sheep sheltered here. It was probably safe. That was just as well as she was only armed with two daggers and she'd been injured already. There was the sound of trickling and dripping in the back of the cave, but no treasure of any sort. The water, she discovered, had worn away the rock over the centuries and now it collected in a pool. It was crystal clear and very inviting.

First she filled her bottles. The dwarves didn't seem to be much bothered about personal hygiene, but Ansylike liked to feel clean. The water was very cold, but she could put up with that. She stripped to her skin quickly and climbed in. It was even colder than she'd thought. It didn't quite come up to her waist. She shuddered as she dipped her head into it, then held her breath and sat down. The wounds on her knees and back stung. Bravely she wiped the blood away. She didn't stop in the icy water longer than was necessary! Soon she was out again, dressed and ready to climb down. Her skin seemed to glow as the warmth returned and her cheeks flushed.

Much refreshed and very much cleaner, she reached the bottom of the rock wall and strapped on her weapon belt. She retraced her steps to where she had left the dwarves and found them standing on a large boulder, their weapons drawn.

"We were worried!" began Groblic. "Whatever took you so long?" The tone of his voice warned her that he was serious so she looked around. There was no sign of any danger. A few sheep grazed contentedly in the distance and some birds flew idly by high overhead.

"Sorry," she replied. "I found a pool and decided to wash my knees. I'll be able to make faster progress now. I didn't mean to alarm you." She gave them her sweetest smile to soften them up a bit. "What are you doing up there?"

"Er... nothing," said Haldriel as he took the bolt from his bow. "Well, we just wanted a better view of the way ahead. There's really nothing to worry about. Everything is fine! Isn't it, Groblic?" Groblic nodded, reminding himself that he couldn't expect a child, an elven one at that, to behave sensibly.

"I see you've washed your hair," added Tharl, but he was prevented from making any further comment by a stern look from Haldriel.

"And it looks very nice," continued Groblic. Tharl grunted.

"We can be on our way now," said Haldriel. "We have a lot of ground to cross and I want to set up a safe camp before nightfall. We all need a good rest. We have a lot of climbing to do tomorrow so we'll need to make an early start." There was no disagreement. The packs and weapons were gathered together and the party of four were on their way.

There was hardly a cloud in the sky. All that afternoon the breeze kept up and they reached the cliffs in good time. Ansylike was exhausted and her feet ached, but the dwarves were in high spirits and showed no signs of fatigue. She marvelled at their ability to travel without tiring. Soon a fire had been lit and the evening meal bubbled over it. The aroma of stew scented the still, night air.

Ansylike stirred the pot to prevent the meat from catching on the bottom. Expertly, she added a few ingredients from small leather and cloth bags which she produced from her backpack. The dwarves were glad that they had carried it for her. Haldriel had been successful in hunting and had butchered four rabbits and a large bird which he'd shot with his bow. He had cut the meat into pieces and dropped them into the simmering water. The rabbit skins, he decided, might come in useful, so he cleaned them and spread them out on a flat rock to dry. They might make a decent pair of gloves! There was no sense in wasting anything.

During the night the dwarves took turns to keep guard and left

Ansylike to sleep. They woke her when the sun rose and it was not long before they were all ready to begin the next part of the journey. As they were in a valley which was enclosed by cliffs on three sides, there was no alternative but to climb. The crags above them didn't look too difficult to scale, but it would take time and they could not spend the night up there. They must reach a safe place. There were no large ledges or caves where they could stop.

Ansylike had a surprise for them. She had cooked some pancakes and kept them warm over the ashes of the fire so that they were all able to eat before they started off.

"Could you cook so well before you started work at the inn?" asked Groblic between bites. He paused to wipe his mouth and beard with his sleeve. "These really are delicious!" Tharl and Haldriel both agreed.

"I'm glad you like them," said Ansylike with obvious pleasure. "I really only learned how to use herbs to season food at the inn. I had to cook anything that the customers wanted. I wasn't in charge, of course. I spent a lot of time carving and serving, but we all had a turn at cooking in the kitchens. I certainly don't miss it!"

Groblic had taken an assortment of small iron blocks from his pack and set them out on the ground in front of him. Each one had a hole drilled through the centre. He threaded them singly onto short lengths of rope then tied the ends. Ansylike wondered what they were for. She saw that Haldriel had taken off his boots and was banging nails with strangely shaped heads into their soles. It was all very mysterious.

"Tie this around your waist, Spud," said Tharl, offering Ansylike a piece of thin rope. "Tie it tight and check the knot carefully." She did as she was instructed. Tharl waited, then produced a large, iron, chain link. "Now clip this on to the rope," he said and waited for her reaction. It was predictable.

"You could have given me that before I'd tied the rope!" she retorted with obvious irritation. Tharl actually smiled. Groblic and Haldriel laughed. Tharl pressed one side of the chain link with his thumb and it bent in, allowing him to clip it neatly onto the rope around Ansylike's waist. He let go and once again it was an unbroken link. There was no sign of a joint in it.

"What do you think of that?" asked Tharl. Whether he had taken a dislike to girls, elves or her in particular, Ansylike couldn't tell. She sensed that there was a whole pot of ill feeling between them and he was stirring it. Keeping calm was the only way to keep it from boiling over.

"Is this another secret from the old days?" asked Ansylike, not daring to touch it.

"No," called Haldriel. "We can easily make these in the forges."

"When we have the wood to burn," added Tharl, reminding them of the importance of their mission.

"Now we tie this rope to the link and then we're ready," said Haldriel cheerfully. He walked a few paces to the rock wall and began to climb. Ansylike watched as Groblic paid out the rope. He was careful to keep it away from Haldriel's feet so that he wouldn't get tangled in it. Before long it was Ansylike's turn to climb. Both Haldriel and Tharl were sitting comfortably on a ledge high above her. She soon reached them. With her longer arms and legs she could make faster progress. She also had far less to carry. The dwarves, however, had a more important advantage. They could see which was the easiest route and which parts were unsafe. They avoided overhangs and sheer faces. They stayed away from loose, crumbling rock and skirted around the green, mossy patches that were damp and slippery. Haldriel's nailed boots gave him a sure grip and left light scratches on the rock that were easy to follow. He secured the rope every so often using Groblic's iron blocks. These he jammed in the cracks and tested for safety.

He attached an iron chain link to each one, then passed the rope, to which he was tied, through the chain. If he fell it would not be far. The dwarves had no intention of taking any risks here! There was no need. Time was not short and care was essential.

Shortly after midday the climbing was over. There was a valley between two peaks that led gradually upwards, but it was grassy. The going would be easy for a while. They all had a light snack before they set off again. Refreshed and relieved they plodded on. Before long they would have to find a good site to make camp for the night as it was impossible to tell what lay ahead of them in the mist. Although the sun was past its highest point it had failed to clear the cloud which lay higher up the valley. It would be damp and cold up there and no place to stop for long. Occasionally the snow-capped peaks could be glimpsed high above them. Groblic was glad that elves did not make their homes on mountain tops. He didn't relish the thought of trudging through drifts of snow to find them! It was bad enough to think of the woods and forests that they might have to explore.

They reached the mist without actually meaning to. Ansylike was surprised. She hadn't realised that they had walked so far. She looked around and saw that the mist was behind her too. Despite her keen eyesight she could not see very far and the sun above had turned pale and watery.

"Groblic!" she called urgently. He came to a stop and spun round to face her. "This cloud is moving down! As the sun gets lower this stuff creeps down the mountain. We're surrounded!"

"Nothing to worry about," soothed Haldriel, walking back towards them. "Just a spot of bad weather. This can't do us any harm, can it?" Ansylike looked beyond him. She couldn't see Tharl so she paused before answering.

"I'd feel much safer hanging onto the rope again. At least I'd be sure that I wasn't alone up here. I can't even see Tharl. I hope he's not lost!"

"I'm not!" came a gruff voice from no more than ten paces away. Tharl appeared. "I'm glad you'd miss me, Spud," he added as if he didn't really believe it at all.

If she caught the sarcasm in his voice she didn't react to it. Instead she gave him a welcoming smile.

"Let's use the rope. It's a good idea. We'll just clip it to our belts and keep our hands free." Haldriel waved to Groblic who unslung his rope and backpack.

"How will we know which way to go?" asked Ansylike anxiously. She was not convinced that all was going well.

"I'll lead," replied Tharl. "I've never lost my way in the mountains. I can take you to the top of this valley with my eyes closed. Now let's be off again or shall we stop here and chatter until night falls?"

The thought of being stuck here on this bleak, open moor in the darkness got them all moving swiftly. Tharl led them to the top of the valley. He was as good as his word and all were relieved to be out of the cloud. Stopping on a ridge they looked warily around. Behind them, not far below, was the bank of mist, but now they could see over it. Lying like a thick blanket of grey wool it hid everything, but no longer posed a threat. Ansylike was glad to be out of it!

To either side of them towered the mighty peaks of rock. The late afternoon sunshine glittered off the vast snow and ice fields. They did not look inviting! Before them, the mist had descended. They could see the ground for a hundred paces, then it was covered. Beyond that was a hilly, forested land with occasional jagged spires of dark rock that poked high above the trees. It was too late in the day to go any further. None of them wanted to go on. The way ahead was menacing. Thoughts of wolves passed through Ansylike's mind.

"We can take shelter in the rocks up there." Haldriel pointed. There was a gentle slope covered with loose scree, but not far from them some massive boulders had come to rest. "I can hear water running. There must be a stream, fed by the melting snows above. I doubt whether there will be anything to trouble us. We'll keep a guard posted to be sure." While he was saying this, Tharl was making his way towards the nearest clump of boulders. He had detached himself from the rope. After Groblic had taken the rope and coiled it neatly, they all followed him. The grass was soaking and the rocks dripped. There was no chance of making a dry, comfortable bed in this lot. Tharl marched on.

"I can see caves, I think. I'll go and check. We'll not find a patch of dry earth in this sodden wilderness!" So saying, Tharl walked towards the base of the cliff without waiting for any agreement.

"You follow him, Spud," urged Haldriel. "I'll follow in a moment." Groblic and Ansylike exchanged glances.

"This is the closest to privacy you'll get, I'm afraid!" hinted Groblic. "You can go behind that rock over there and I'll use this one." Ansylike took her pack and headed towards the rocks that Groblic had pointed out. At least she would have a fine view of the valley!

Exploring caves was best done with extreme caution. Tharl knew that a dry, sheltered place in a cold wet area was likely to be occupied already. Bears loved them and were not keen on sharing! A mother bear with cubs was lethal. Wolves used them and guarded their dens jealously. A host of other creatures might be found in the borders of The Desolation where magic had run wild. Trolls, ogres, even giants could have claimed a cave as their home!

He was surprised when he found one that suited them ideally and it was empty! The floor was sandy in the middle. A stream must have flowed through here at one time. Then it had found another route. Rock in these mountains was constantly being worn away by water and broken by ice.

The water flowing through the mountains formed caves which made handy places for dwarves to camp in at night. Much as Tharl hated the thought of getting wet, he couldn't help but admire the work that water did on the landscape. He unloaded his backpack and much other equipment and went to find some wood for a fire. Even at this height he was confident of finding some stunted trees and shrubs. They would be growing in less exposed sites. He would have to use his long knowledge of the mountains to find what he wanted.

Ansylike looked back over the valley they'd left. The view was breathtaking. In the distance she could almost picture Andric and the dwarves following them, but that was just wishful thinking. If they were really there, they would also have made a camp for the night and would not be out in the open. She hoped that they'd set out and were well on their way. This journey seemed too dangerous for such a small party.

Even brave and resourceful dwarves had their weaknesses. There were just not enough of them to withstand a serious attack and she was sure that one would come, sooner or later. The reputation of The Desolation was known to all, though very few people could actually claim that they'd travelled through it themselves. Rather they had met ones who had, or heard tales from minstrels.

By the time that Tharl returned with a large bundle of wood, the other dwarves and Ansylike were already in the cave, unpacking. While they had the chance, they got their spare clothes out to air them and draped them from the many ledges that circled the inside of the cave. The sun had almost set and they were all tired and, especially, hungry. Once Ansylike had taken off her belt and boots she felt weariness overcoming her. She was determined to stay awake long enough for a meal, though! After the plates were rinsed, wiped and stowed away safely, all made up their beds. Groblic would take first watch and keep an eye on the fire, which had already warmed up the cave and made them all feel more relaxed and comfortable. Somehow it reassured them and made them feel as if danger would leave them alone while they gathered their strength again. Who knew what trials might have to be faced in the coming day?

The evening air was cool and fresh. The scents of the night-blooming flowers and the gentle crackle of the fire behind him gave Groblic a sense of peace and security. He stood at the mouth of the cave looking into the night. The others, judging by their snores, were fast asleep. There was a clear, dark sky, full of stars. His gaze shifted down and he took a step further out of the cave and whistled quietly through his teeth. The ground mist was rising and thickening. He could not see anything of the boulders below, which he'd expected to be clearly visible. He wondered if it would rise up to the level of the cave. There was no need to alarm anyone yet, so he decided to wait a little longer before he woke any of the others. When he heard a wolf baying in the distance, however, he changed his mind! Looking back, he saw that Haldriel was already sitting up and reaching for his crossbow. Tharl had raised himself up on one elbow and appeared to be listening intently.

"I heard a wolf," Groblic informed them, "but not close enough to worry us yet. I doubt whether they can see any better in this mist than we can."

"What mist?" asked Tharl, rising to his feet and pulling on his boots. Haldriel put his loaded bow beside him and finished dressing before he joined Groblic. Soon the three of them were staring out, straining their eyes, but seeing very little Fortunately there didn't seem to be anything moving out there and the wolves were not coming any closer.

Groblic rooted in his pack and returned to his comrades at the mouth of the cave.

"I've brought these," he said, offering them each a smoking pipe. They were nestled in a little wooden box. He pulled a pouch of smoking weed from his belt and offered that around too, before he filled the bowl of his own pipe. Haldriel fetched a glowing twig from the fire and blew on it. Then he used it to light his pipe, slowly drawing in the smoke and blowing it in small puffs out of the corner of his mouth. Soon they were all blowing smoke rings into the mist.

"Do you think we're safe here?"

"Can't tell," replied Tharl. "Maybe." He paused and blew out. "Maybe not!" He winked at Groblic. That was the closest to humour that he could manage or was willing to.

"Are we safe, or not?" asked Haldriel.

"Be careful what you say in front of her." Tharl pointed the stem of his pipe back toward the cave.

Ansylike was sleeping soundly, oblivious of the dwarves' concern. It had been a long day and the exertions had sapped her energy. Although her dreams contained vivid scenes of swooping birds and wolves, she didn't wake and was not even stirred by the rumbling thunder that rolled about the mountain under which she lay.

A flash of lightning struck down into the rocks below the cave. The mist took on an eerie blue glow for a moment. Then the rain started. It was a torrent.

"Nearly forked us!" exclaimed Tharl.

"What?" said Haldriel.

"Forked lightning. Too close! It could have struck us. We're carrying a lot of metal. We could have been roasted!" They all moved back a few paces.

"It's lucky we decided to stop here and not press on," said Haldriel, pulling his collar tighter around his neck. "I pity anyone caught out in that!"

"Rather strange weather," added Groblic. "I wonder how the mist manages to hold in that wind."

"I've not seen anything like it," said Tharl. "If we had not had to stop to let Spud sleep, I would've gone on. The night was good for travel and I could easily have found a safe way through that second bank of mist."

"A party of dwarves would have done just that," whispered Groblic. "The first expedition might have perished in the storm!" No-one had mentioned that this was not the first attempt to contact the elves. They had hidden the fact that six of them had set off last summer and none had returned. "Do you think that this happens every night or is it just a freak of the weather?"

"Or a deliberate obstacle placed in our path?" added Tharl. With that thought in mind they moved further back into the cave and stood behind the fire. The wood supply wasn't low, but there was no sense in wasting any so Groblic put the stew pan on and poured water into it.

"I might as well make something for breakfast," he explained. "It'll be cold by then but it's better than dry biscuits and a cup of cold water." He looked at Ansylike's pack. "She won't mind if I add a few of her herbs. They seem to improve the flavour. If I can find them, they will give us a tasty start to the day." Haldriel nodded encouragingly. Ansylike's cooking was far better than their own! "I think she's used these before," he said, as he inspected the contents of a small leather pouch. He pulled the drawstrings further apart and withdrew a pinch of some pink, dried flowers. They looked very much like the bells of a type of heather that grew wild over the mountains in the north. In a way they reminded him of home.

He had always enjoyed walking in the hills. It was one thing he had in common with his wife. In their courting days they had often gone for long rambles together. Most of his kind preferred to have a solid roof of stone over their heads, but they enjoyed the open air and each other's company. It had seemed like an ideal match. Groblic sprinkled the herbs into the pan of stew and in an instant all the dwarves were fast asleep.

Ansylike woke, raised herself on her elbows carefully and looked around. She had been sleeping on a ledge, well above the floor of the cave, and the roof was not far above her head. To her surprise she saw that her three dwarven companions were fast asleep. They lay sprawled around the fire as if they had been suddenly struck dead! Their heaving chests and whistling snores proved, however, that they were, indeed, alive. She swung her legs over the ledge, ducked her head and readied herself to drop to the sandy floor. As she did so, she realised that the scrapes on her knees had gone. They had healed completely! There was not even a mark to show where the wounds had been. She arched her back, expecting to wince from the pain, but there was none. Lightly, like a mountain cat she dropped to the sand and poised, knees bent, eyes searching for danger. She felt a surge of power course through her limbs. She grabbed her weapon belt, drew her sword and stalked, barefoot, to the entrance of the cave.

The shadows of the boulders below her were long. "The sun must have just risen," she thought to herself and with a shock, realised that she was wrong. The sun was setting! It seemed most strange. How could they have let her sleep for a full night and a day and then fall asleep themselves?

She would have to check the dwarves first so she walked back and nudged Groblic with her left foot. He stopped snoring for a moment, stirred, mumbled something about rolling in the heather and turned over. She gave him a harder kick with her heel and he woke.

Sitting up, he shook his head and looked up in amazement at Ansylike, who stood over him with her sword drawn. Once again he was struck by the length of her perfectly-shaped, tanned legs, and her long, lean torso. The sword that she held so lightly in her hand could slice him in two before he could take another breath. Had it not been made specially to slay dwarves? He had a brief insight into why the elven folk and his own kin could never live side by side.

"What happened?" he asked groggily? His senses gradually came back to him, but there was a fuzziness in his head. He couldn't hear for the buzzing in his ears. He couldn't believe the thought that he'd had about elves and not living together. He was appalled at what must have been lurking in the back of his mind. How could he dream that Ansylike was his enemy? He shook his head and blinked.

Looking at Tharl and back again at Ansylike, he continued. "Did we all fall asleep? I can't believe it. That never happens to dwarves!"

Ansylike stood and waited for him to gather his thoughts and made no reply. "I'll wake them," said Groblic, as if he were asking for permission. She heard the question in his voice and nodded assent. Groblic shook the other dwarves in turn and they came to. They looked as if they'd been drinking strong ale all night. Their eyes were glassy and hooded by thick, purpled lids. Both Tharl and Haldriel opened their mouths cautiously as if their lips had been sealed for a long time and their tongues were stuck to their palettes. It took them a while to gather their thoughts. Sleep lay heavily on them. It was not easy to shake off.

Ansylike prodded the ashes of the fire which had long since gone out. The stew pot was cold. She sniffed the air and, recognizing the smell, looked closely at the breakfast that Groblic had been preparing. As she had suspected, it smelled strongly of a familiar herb. She held her breath, moved away and went over to the cave mouth to fill her lungs with fresh air.

She returned quickly, holding her breath again, and seized the stew pot. In a few long strides she had covered the distance to the cave entrance, where she paused, swivelled on her hips and threw the pot, contents and all, down the hill. After much clattering and banging, it came to rest by the clump of large boulders.

"So someone has been stealing from my backpack!" she accused, pointing a finger at the dwarves.

"I added a few herbs from a little leather pouch," admitted Groblic. "I meant no harm... ." His voice tailed off.

"Show me which ones," she said gently, putting down her sword. She was very reluctant to let anyone see what she had in the privacy of her backpack and cursed Groblic silently. He quickly found the right pouch and handed it to her. She dampened her annoyance. They had all been asleep for a whole night and most of a day and were lucky that no large, hungry animals had discovered them.

"They looked like fairly common flowers to me," moaned Groblic. "I'm sure I've seen blossom like that many a time." He had obviously not forgiven himself for putting them all in such danger.

"They are a common flower," Ansylike told him. "I suppose it is an easy mistake to make. I don't see how they can have affected you, though. Throwing a handful into a pot of stew should have done nothing except make the air smell fresh. They're a remedy for sleeplessness, but are only used for children."

"Something makes the herbs more potent!" shouted Haldriel suddenly and made them all jump. "This is the second cave where some of us have fallen asleep. It must be something in the cave itself." They all looked around, but could see nothing unusual.

"I'll leave it to you," said Tharl. "I'd better fetch some more wood. We'll need to get the fire lit if we're going to spend another night here. Have we got enough food?"

"I'll join you," replied Haldriel, taking up his bow. "I'm starving. Spud threw the last of the fresh food down the mountain, pot and all. It shows what she thinks of your cooking, Groblic!" He laughed and all the others, except Tharl, joined in.

"We'll search this place while you're gone," grinned Groblic. He waved to Ansylike. "Put your boots on and start looking in the back of the cave. I'll start outside and work my way in."

Haldriel and Tharl trudged around the mountain following a path that had been made by sheep to where there was a ready supply of wood. They walked in silence, deep in their own thoughts, but keeping a watchful eye on their surroundings. Although there was quite a strong breeze, the mist below them seemed to lie still as if the wind had no effect on it. They reached the dead tree that Tharl had discovered and he hefted his axe to cut more wood.

"Meet me here later and help to carry the logs back?" requested Tharl. "We'd better have enough to keep a good blaze through the night."

"Agreed!" Haldriel nodded, patted Tharl once on the shoulder and continued along the sheep trail. There was no need for Tharl to remind him not to go too far or to take care. Haldriel could look after himself and he was an excellent hunter.

For a dwarf, he was remarkably cheerful and he never knew when he was beaten. He could face the most difficult task with confidence and put all his energy into it, when others might have given up in despair. That was one reason why he had been chosen to lead the group. He was also an excellent shot with a crossbow. He had won cups and medals to prove it!

Chapter Six

STRELL

Haldriel's hearing was acute, so he didn't miss the sound of a pebble falling a little way above and behind him. He whirled and pointed his bow. A goat with curved horns that were longer than the dwarf's legs was preparing to charge at him. It pawed the ground with its cloven hoofs and lowered its head. Four more of the creatures eyed him intently with bared teeth. Goats and sheep usually have teeth that are made for nibbling and munching. These were designed for tearing and ripping! They looked as if they belonged in the jaws of mountain cats! He took aim and fired at what he hoped was the leader.

He knew that he would have time to reload and fire once more before the others could close the distance. If they all attacked at once he would be in deep trouble. He fired again and called out, hoping that Tharl would hear. The other three were closing. One was within five paces of him when an arrow whizzed out of nowhere and brought it down at his feet. He used his crossbow to block the attack of the next one, but its weight pushed him over and he fell backwards into the grass, with it looming above him.

Its head reared back and its lips curled, baring its deadly canine fangs. He had one glimpse of those awful teeth before it crashed lifeless on top of him. He heaved the rank-smelling carcase away and scrambled unsteadily to his feet. He was covered in blood, but grateful to be alive. The goats had nearly had him for dinner, but instead he hoped to feast on one of them!

Three stout, hairy figures were making their way towards Haldriel and each carried a longbow. They had saved his life, so he assumed that they were friendly. He didn't want to provoke them so he left his crossbow where it had fallen, in the grass. There were two men and one woman and all were clothed in animal skins and furs. From their belts they wore an array of weaponry. They had daggers of bone and horn, skinning and flaying knives and slings for throwing stones. All were broader than Haldriel and nearly twice as tall.

"What are you doing out here?" asked the woman. The men said nothing, but their hands were close to their daggers in readiness. "Are you alone?" Before Haldriel had a chance to reply he heard a shout and, looking back along the path, he saw Tharl approaching at full speed.

"They're friends!" he shouted. "They saved me from these animals." He waved an open hand to indicate that he meant the goats. Tharl realised that the danger had passed and slowed his pace. All waited until he had reached them. He lowered his axe and rested its double-edged blade on the ground. Haldriel returned his attention to the woman who now stood beside him. She was obviously bred from warrior stock! Her limbs were heavily muscled and her bearing was proud and noble.

"I must thank you. I am most grateful for your timely intercession." He bowed his head slightly in the formal dwarven attitude and hoped that his words and manner were understood.

"I asked you what you were doing here and I expect a reply!" she retorted. "Now!"

"We are looking for the elves," stuttered Haldriel. "We have come a long way to find them and faced many dangers. We need their help."

"You need their help? It's a pity then, that you drove them from your forests. I doubt that they'll give you much of a welcome, if you ever find them."

"Then you know where they are?" asked Haldriel. "Any help you could give us would be appreciated. We would pay in gold of course." Haldriel was surprised by the reaction of the strangers. The men smiled, as if amused and the woman laughed loudly.

"Gold we don't want! If you have iron or steel we can trade. Soft metal is no use to us!" She looked at him, closely. "Are there any more of you?"

"Yes," interrupted Tharl. "There are more of us in a cave close by. They'll be coming to look for us soon." He didn't trust these people and wanted to make it clear that it would be unwise of them to attack.

"In that case you'd better take one of these goats for your evening meal. The flesh is tasty, but they take a lot of cooking. We'll meet you here in the morning. You have my word of honour that we mean you no harm. Now we must leave before the mist rises. On no account must you get caught out in it. Long ago there was a battle here and the dead still walk at night. Those who hear their call may join them and walk the hills forever! Be warned."

Haldriel recovered his arrows which were unbroken and could be used again. Tharl heaved one of the goats onto his shoulders and held his axe in both hands in front of him. Then he set off. It was already getting dark and it would not be safe once the mist rose. He left Haldriel to pick up the firewood.

Groblic and Ansylike met at the ashes of the fire and sat down, facing each other. They had found nothing.

"Let's think," said Groblic and he stroked his beard. They had taken enough time to search every corner and there was not a clue as to why the herbs should be so effective. Ansylike's stomach rumbled. It was a long time since either of them had eaten and she was hoping that Tharl and Haldriel would be returning quickly with food and enough wood to keep them warm for the night.

"That's it!" she exclaimed and spread the ashes out. "It's the fire."

"I don't see how it can be," said Groblic gloomily. "There was no fire in the cave where Haldriel and Tharl fell asleep.

"What about these?" Ansylike held her left hand up to show Groblic some tiny glass beads that she had sifted out of the ashes. "Have you seen these before?"

"Yes," replied Groblic as he rolled the beads around in his palm. "The fire has made these out of the sand. I don't think they're anything special." He handed them back to Ansylike and she trickled them into one of her leather pouches, just in case! Then she filled the pouch with sand from the floor of the cave.

"I see that your wounds have healed," he continued. "Remarkably quickly, I might add. How is the scratch on your back? Do you mind if I take a look?" Ansylike nodded and swivelled around to face away from Groblic. He pulled up her shirt while she leant forward and cradled her head in her arms. It was necessary but she didn't like it! "Amazing!" exclaimed Groblic. "Either you have wonderful powers of recovery, or this is another sort of magic!" He ran a finger over the line where he had expected the scar to be. "This has totally healed. Lift your arm." Ansylike clutched her tunic closer around her chest and lifted her left arm. Groblic saw that the muscles under her skin rippled and flexed as normal. She had nothing to show that she had been injured in battle.

He pulled her shirt down again. Ansylike hadn't said a word. "I think you'd better tell me more about the healing herbs that you carry. They seem to be very effective!"

"The only thing I've had on that is the lotion that you put on. I haven't used any of my own medicine. I don't think that I've got anything that would help, anyway."

The sun had passed well below the line of the horizon before Tharl and Haldriel reached the cave again and the mist was creeping up towards them. It seemed to Haldriel that there were figures moving in it. They were just slightly darker patches in the grey, but he had learnt to take no unnecessary chances. He paused only for one final glance, then hurried on. The dead goat lay on the floor and Tharl was regretting his decision to carry it.

"I'm covered in blood!" he moaned. "It will rust the links in my armour and my tunic is stuck to me. It's even dripped down my leg into my boot. I'll stink like a slaughter-house in summer!"

"Quiet! You moan like an old woman with a flea in her drawers!" scolded Haldriel. "I want a guard on the entrance."

"Now?" asked Groblic.

"Now!" came the swift reply. "I can't be sure, but I think there may be something other than mist out there." Before he had finished speaking, Groblic had seized his war-hammer and positioned himself in the shadows at the mouth of the cave where he could peer down into the mist. "I'll take my bow and watch with Groblic. Tharl, get the fire sorted, but don't light it yet. We don't want to attract attention, but we may need it if there are prowling animals intending to have us for supper."

Without saying a word, Tharl started to do as he had been instructed. Ansylike waited. "You can do something with that. We're getting hungry." Haldriel pointed at the goat. Ansylike scowled, then shrugged. Perhaps it was for the best. Haldriel didn't know that she was fit to fight again and she did not want to question his authority. He had not treated her like a kitchen-girl so far and he seemed to respect her. Besides, she had already proved what she could do in battle. Then she looked at the bloody goat and wondered how to begin. She didn't suspect that Haldriel wanted her to keep away from the mist.

"I don't like the idea of butchering this thing in here," she said, to no-one in particular. "Can't I drag it out of the cave. We'll be awash with blood and guts otherwise." Tharl looked back at her. She stood over the animal with a dagger in her right hand, clearly unsure as to how she should proceed.

"She wouldn't know what to do with a rabbit, let alone a goat!" he declared. "Fetch your sword, Spud, and take my place. I've not seen any sign of danger." Ansylike looked to Haldriel. He seemed uncertain for a moment, but then he nodded his agreement, so she took up her sword and joined him.

"There are people out there," he whispered. "I'm sure of it! Listen!" Faintly, Ansylike heard the sound of a cry, eerie and forlorn, like a lonely bird searching for its mate, soaring on the high winds, with no place to land. It could have been her brother's flute, but he would never play such a sad song. She felt drawn to it. In the same way that she had gone to the rescue of the sheep that was only calling to its lamb, she felt that she had to help.

"What do you hear?" asked Haldriel, gently.

"It's like an elven song of doom, of pain and broken hearts. It beckons me," Ansylike replied.

"I hear the sound of dwarves marching towards their homes. It's like the end of the day and we're all coming home. The more I look in..." Haldriel jumped back and clutched his leg. There was blood oozing from a gash above his ankle. "You clumsy girl!" he shouted. "You've cut my leg with that sword of yours! Why can't you be more careful?" Then he recovered his composure. "I was on the way to join my comrades out there! If you hadn't... ." He looked at Ansylike. She stood as if she was listening to a far call. Her sword was clenched in her hand, but her eyes dreamed into the darkness. "Groblic, take a hold of her and..." Groblic was nowhere to be seen. "Tharl, we're in trouble again. Be ready with your weapon. Come and stand by me. Pull Spud back and keep her here. I'm going after Groblic. He must have wandered off."

"Wait!" said Tharl. "You're not using your head. We could get lost out there. It's better if we're roped together and we leave one end of the rope in here." He slapped Ansylike, none too gently. "Snap out of it," he insisted.

"I suspected that it would affect her, but I thought we'd be safe!" moaned Haldriel.

"We need you to keep your head clear. No more dreaming!" urged Tharl, glaring fiercely at Ansylike.

"I'm fine now," she replied and Tharl could tell by the tone of her voice that she had shaken off the enchantment of the mist. "I'll light the fire and hold the rope from well inside the cave. That way I won't have to look out."

"Sound thinking," complimented Haldriel. He wrapped the rope tightly around his waist and set off with his crossbow at the ready. Tharl followed and Ansylike paid out the rope. It was not long enough for them to go very far, but it would have to do! They found Groblic easily. He was standing at the end of a ledge, muttering to himself about the silver in the mines and how he was going to make his wife rich. Below him there was a long drop on to jagged rocks. Haldriel could see their cruel points poking through the swirls of cloud and thanked his luck that Groblic was not already spiked on one of them.

He untied the rope and attached it to Groblic's belt, then gently hauled him back. He had nearly got him to the safety of the cave when he saw the dim figures in the mist take shape.

"We'll not have an easy time fighting that lot!" he said. "I don't know where they've come from, but there are plenty of them and few of us. We can't escape, We'll have to make a stand out here. We can pick them off as they climb towards us. I'll warn Spud." He helped Haldriel bring Groblic back, then ran on ahead to the cave where Ansylike was taking in the slack rope.

"To arms!" he exclaimed. "We could be in for a serious attack! Get your weapons and stand fast!"

"Have you found Groblic?" she asked anxiously as she dropped the rope and drew her sword.

"Yes. He's babbling, but that's nothing new! They'll be here soon. They're not far behind me. These ghostly warriors won't catch them."

Even as he spoke, Haldriel appeared with Groblic who was quickly brought to his senses by a few sharp slaps on his cheeks. Ansylike was relieved to see that he had come to no harm. She had grown to like him and they had become friends. She wondered, however, what Tharl had meant by the words, 'ghostly warriors'.

The three dwarves and Ansylike stood at the ready and took turns to stare into the mist below them. It was thicker than on the previous night, but didn't seem to be rising as high. Each of them could make out the forms of people. Ghostly figures passed in procession. Then it was over.

"I've not seen anything in a while," whispered Ansylike. "Do you think there is still some danger, or has it passed?" She clutched the hilt of her sword nervously and ran her tongue over her lips.

"I think we can take turns to guard," replied Haldriel. "There's no need for us all to watch. The main danger is being taken unawares and now that we know that it's a sort of illusion, we won't be tempted to investigate. Will we, Groblic?"

"Certainly not!" stated Groblic, who felt a little foolish at having almost wandered off.

"Then we'll eat, sleep and keep our appointment at dawn. We have a long way to travel and an early start is always a good idea."

Dawn came and the mist receded. After a good breakfast and the usual preparations, the dwarves and Ansylike were ready to be on their way. Before she left she raked out the ashes of the fire and collected a few more glass beads. Popping them in her pouch, she wondered whether they had any use. Time would tell. She noted that the sky was heavy with clouds. To the east it was streaked pink, but elsewhere it was a sullen grey. There would be rain before long. The air was cool and a light breeze made the fine hairs on her arms stand up.

They reached the dead tree, but there was no sign of anyone so they continued to the point where Haldriel was attacked by the goat. All kept a careful eye on the hills in case there were any other animals which liked dwarf for breakfast!

"So, you have a girl with you! Is she your guide?" The voice seemed to come from nowhere and all the dwarves were startled. From out of the heather and undergrowth the people of the hills appeared. There were six of them and none was smiling. They seemed more like an ambush party than a group of traders. Haldriel addressed the one who had spoken.

"I must thank you again for saving me last night," he began diplomatically. "Without your timely intercession I would not be here now to offer you our terms of trade."

"What's he saying?" whispered Ansylike to Tharl who happened to be standing beside her.

"Talking from his bottom!" muttered Tharl. "Plain speaking does not come naturally to that one." Ansylike stifled a giggle and tried to look serious.

"What do you have for us?" said their leader. He seemed unimpressed by Haldriel's speech. "We want iron weapons. In return we offer you bows and food. We can also tell you of the dangers that lie ahead and how to find the safest route through the valley."

The dwarves were, of course, prepared for this and took out their surplus weapons and metal equipment. Ansylike watched in amazement but made no comment.

"How," she thought, "did they carry so much?" Each of the dwarves must have more than his own weight in metal alone!

Stacked on the ground in front of her was a formidable collection of weaponry. There were hammer-heads, axe-heads, knife blades, short swords and jackets of chain mail. Amongst these were buttons, buckles, bracers and combs. The hill-men showed no reaction until the woman who had talked to Haldriel on the previous night appeared. None of the dwarves had seen her approaching and all were sure that she'd not been in the original party.

"Good enough," she said. Then her eye caught Ansylike's sword. "Show that to me, child. Don't worry, I won't take it." She held out her hand, palm upwards. Ansylike drew the blade that Cledrin had given her and offered it for inspection.

"My name is Ansylike," she said. "My friends and I are strangers in these lands and we are grateful for any help that you can give us. You are welcome to my sword if that is what you want."

"And my name is Strell. We have little love for strangers and even less for dwarves. You, however, have elven blood. That makes a difference. These are odd companions for you to travel with. Have you no man to share your journey and your love with?"

Ansylike blushed slightly and lowered her eyes. It was a rather personal question!

"No. I've never been in love and never... well, been very close to any man. It's difficult to know whom to trust...and...." Her voice faded as she spoke, but Strell continued to regard her intently.

"This is an elven leaf-blade," she replied. "Have you any idea what these runes speak of?"

"None." Ansylike shrugged. She'd guessed that the strange writing on the sword was an ancient elven script, but she really had no idea what the words meant. "I can't read ordinary elven writing. These strange letters are a mystery to me!"

"Then heed my warning," began Strell. "The old books tell of a time when an elven maiden will come into The Desolation. She will bear a sword of power. This is such a sword. You are a maiden." She waved a hand to silence Ansylike and linked her arm. She led her to one side and lowered her voice. "There are powers of darkness all around us. They can be defeated, if only we can stop fighting amongst ourselves."

"Fighting?" asked Ansylike. "Who's fighting?"

"Perhaps the sword and you can bring an end to the wars and heal the wound that has opened between men and elves. The runes on the sword speak of the destruction of the High Elf Lord. He is the cause of all the grief that we suffer. The sword can kill him, but I doubt whether you have the strength."

"How could a sword, made long ago, have anything to do with what's going on now? I can't see how this is possible! Why would elves make such a thing, anyway?" The tone of Ansylike's voice and the look on her face clearly showed her disbelief.

"Questions that I cannot answer!" laughed Strell. "In seeking answers for yourself you will learn much. If I were to tell you what I know, you would only doubt my word and it would make it harder for you to reach a decision when the time came."

"This is too much for me to take in at once," began Ansylike. She felt a little calmer since Strell had laughed. "I'll have much to think about. Oh, there is one question you might answer for me."

She unlinked her arm and slid her backpack off her shoulders. She explained how the dwarves had fallen asleep while she rooted for the pouch in which she'd stowed the glass beads from the fire. "I wondered whether these might be the reason," she said, rolling three of them in her open hand.

"I was afraid that the dwarves might have discovered the secret of the 'healing-caves'," whispered Strell. "I need not have worried!" She looked carefully back to where the men and dwarves were standing. They seemed busy and were not taking any notice. "Let's move a little further away to make sure that they can't hear us." She linked Ansylike's arm again and led her towards a group of large boulders where they could also shelter from the wind. Ansylike appreciated that, as she was feeling chilly, standing on the mountain-side in the cool breeze. "We can talk here," began Strell. "First you must promise never to tell a dwarf of this secret. Do you?"

"I promise," replied Ansylike sincerely, as she made herself comfortable on a conveniently flat rock.

"The beads are nothing. It's something in the sand that has a sort of magical healing power."

"The sand?" asked Ansylike, as she poked a finger into the pouch. "How can that be? It looks ordinary enough to me. It's just common sand." She raised her head to look at Strell who was watching her closely.

"You do have a lot to learn!" she stated plainly, but without intending to hurt Ansylike. "Truth is not always to be found in appearance, You will do well to remember that, if I can teach you nothing else. Often it's the fairest of flowers that hold the deadliest poison, while a humble weed can cure disease."

"Well, I've noticed that," she agreed.

"Somewhere high in the mountains is a great power of healing. The rains wear it away slowly and it trickles through the stone. A little of it is deposited in certain caves in the sand. And there it stays for us to use when we need it. None of the men in our tribe know of this. Only the women are told, and only when they are wise enough to keep a secret!" Strell laughed again. Ansylike grinned. She was beginning to get the idea!

"That's why you're in charge, and not a man!"

"Exactly!" Strell laughed again. Then she composed herself and continued. "The important thing is that the dwarves never know. If they hear of it, they'll want to mine it and you know what that would mean. They would dig a tunnel into the mountain and tear out its heart. We know exactly what sort of people they are. The source of healing is in the rock and it can be mined in the same way that they rip out gold and iron, There would be nothing left. The mountain itself would die!" Ansylike thought of what her own friends had admitted to. They had destroyed their lands in the search for silver and now they had to seek help from the elves that they had driven out. She lowered her eyes and felt confused. Strell laid a hand on her shoulder to comfort her. "I can see you understand me. Can I rely on you to keep our secret?"

"Of course you can," said Ansylike quietly, raising her eyes.

"Then let's go and see what the men are doing. We've talked enough."

Ansylike tidied the contents of her backpack and fastened the ties. Then she slung it onto her left shoulder and nodded to Strell to show what she was ready to leave.

"Can you use a bow? I see that you've worn bracers before. Is that what you still call the wrist-guards that archers wear?" Strell's voice was even and casual and betrayed nothing of the urgency that had been in her tone before.

"Yes," answered Ansylike. "I am pretty good with a longbow, but I had to sell mine and the bracers that I'd worn since I was a child to pay for food and lodging. Money has been a bit scarce for a while and I ended up working as a skivvy in an inn. That's where the dwarves found me."

"Lucky that you didn't sell the sword, then, isn't it? That would have really made a mess of the prophecy!"

"I didn't have the sword to sell. A dwarf gave it to me at the inn. He seemed to take a liking to me. That reminds me! They should be catching up with us. You could keep an eye out for them. Andric should be with them. He's half elven, like me, but much taller and..." Ansylike realised that Strell was no longer at her side.

She looked over her shoulder. The wind blew the hair across her face and she raised a hand to keep it from her eyes. Strell stood many paces behind her, gazing into the darkening skies. "You didn't hear me!" called Ansylike in annoyance.

"I heard, child. I heard only too well! This does change things. Maybe I should go with you. The prophecy has spoken of this! I'm not afraid to die, but I also have to look after my people. I'll have to think." Ansylike ran towards her and gripped her by the shoulders. Strell stood, her eyes unblinking, as rigid as if she were a stone statue. "The sword was really given to you by a dwarf?" she hissed from between clenched teeth. "This could be very bad. Very bad indeed!" As she turned her head to look at Ansylike, the muscles in her neck seemed to twitch and her eyelids fluttered. Her face became suddenly pale and she stumbled forward as if she would collapse to the ground. She steadied herself and took a deep breath and put a hand on Ansylike's shoulder. Her grip was fierce and her knuckles whitened. Ansylike put an arm around her waist. The dwarves and hillmen rushed towards them as Ansylike lowered Strell to the grass where she lay with her eyes closed.

One of the men spoke, his eyes on the body of his leader.

"She is a Seer of the futures, a prophetess and a reader of dreams. She has these strange turns occasionally. They are nothing to worry about. She will recover soon." His voice was calm and he seemed to think that there was nothing unusual in his leader collapsing without warning.

"These people must go soon," sighed Strell weakly. "Help me up. We must make haste." The men obeyed. "Get my bow and the best arrows you can find. Run!" The man whom she addressed turned and sped across the hillside, climbing steadily upwards. Soon he was lost to view. "Ansylike, I must warn you again. The prophecy also gave us knowledge of a darker future. I fear that this is coming to pass. It tells us that the man you love most dearly will take your place on the throne. He will lead the elves, not you! The sword is a gift from the dwarves and this makes all the difference. Success may prove to be very bitter for you! Even if you win there will be a heavy price to pay and you may find yourself banished from the kingdom that should be yours. The man you love most dearly will cast you from his side and favour another. It's so cruel!"

"Not really a problem," replied Ansylike lightly. "I love no man. I don't trust them. I know what they're like." She thought of the loyal dwarves, standing beside her. "These are my friends." She pointed to Groblic, Haldriel and Tharl. "They've been my loyal companions for only a little while, but I trust them far more than any human." She noticed out of the corner of her eye that Groblic's cheeks reddened slightly and Haldriel smiled happily at her. Tharl furrowed his brow and cast his eyes upwards. "All of them have helped me and I'll stand by them if they're in trouble!"

"May I have a word with you, in private?" asked Haldriel. "I'm the leader of this party. If you are well enough, I'd like to ask your advice before we leave." Strell nodded and walked back to the boulders, followed by the dwarf.

"I wonder what he wants," said Groblic.

"All this talking is getting us nowhere," replied Tharl. "I wish we could be on our way! The clouds are getting thicker and the wind is rising." Ansylike shivered and folded her arms. It was certainly getting colder and she decided to get her cloak from her pack and find some warmer clothes.

"I must explain that Spud is just a child. She doesn't always understand what's going on. Ansylike, I mean." Haldriel paused. "We are doing our best to look after her, but I didn't realise that she was so young when I asked her to join us. If you think that the way ahead is too dangerous, then could we leave her with you?"

"You cannot." Strell considered her words carefully before going on. "We are no longer safe here and I will be calling a War Council tonight. Ansylike's sword will not pass without being noticed! You must all go on together. There is no safe way. You will stand no chance in the mountains. The wolves will soon hunt you down in the mists. There are not enough caves to hide in at night. The only way for you to go is through the valley. Beware of the swamps! The rain from the hills drains down and the ground is treacherous. There are many strange creatures there and none of them is friendly. On the other side you will find a farm where you will be made welcome. Few of my tribe have been there, but all who have tell of unusual hospitality! Is there anything else that you wish to say?" This was all spoken in gasps and some of the words were taken by the wind before they could reach Haldriel. He caught the general gist but missed much of the detail.

"Indeed there is." Haldriel explained how Obolin had been injured and how they were hoping that they would catch up and join them. Strell listened patiently until his tale was told before replying.

"I was going to join you, at first, then I realised that I was needed here because my own people may be under attack before long. Now I see that I must look for your friends and guide them to you. I'll try to bring them safely to you at the farm on the other side of the swamp. I will find the other dwarves and this minstrel you speak of. I must admit that it seems odd that you have two half-elves travelling with you. They are as rare as six-legged sheep!"

I must have forgotten to mention it," returned Haldriel lightly. "Andric is Spud's brother."

Nothing could have prepared him for Strell's reaction. She seized him by the arms, lifted him into the air and kissed him firmly on his hairy lips. He was stunned and could not even splutter a protest at this indignity.

"Her brother! All is not lost! For once I think I may be on the winning side!" exclaimed Strell as she lowered Haldriel gently to the ground. "Ansylike is too young, as you said, to appreciate the meaning of my questions. I hope it all turns out for the best. Now let's return and see you off on the next stage of your journey."

So saying, she strode off, leaving Haldriel bewildered and totally unsure as to what he'd said to provoke such a startling reaction from Strell. It was not the first time that he had wondered why women were such a strange people! The differences between elves and dwarves were great, but the differences between men and women were far greater! He remembered asking his father once, why it was so difficult to understand the dwarven maidens. His father had given him a pebble and told him to suck it until it was dissolved. By that time he would be old enough to understand!

As Haldriel trotted after Strell he wondered whether any dwarf had ever lived long enough to suck a pebble until it had dissolved! As he reached the rest of the group he saw that Ansylike was holding a long-bow and admiring it. On the grass in front of her was a quiver, full of arrows. They were presents from Strell.

It took little time for them all to say their farewells. Parting was best done swiftly. The dwarves and Ansylike made their way steadily downwards. Only Ansylike paused to look over her shoulder, but there was no sign of the hill people. They had vanished into the mountains and would, no doubt, be preparing for the attack that Strell had foreseen.

Chapter Seven

GRUND AND CHARRIE

Tharl was in the lead, some ten paces ahead of the others. Then came Haldriel, ever watchful. Behind him was Ansylike. She was more intent on watching where her feet were going, oblivious of danger. She felt secure in the presence of the dwarves and was sure that they could spot any hazards before she could. At the rear was Groblic, who took his duties seriously. He looked from side to side and, at regular intervals, looked over his shoulder to see that no-one was following. As time passed he began to take a closer interest in the bow that Ansylike had strung over her shoulder. It slipped off occasionally and she had to keep hitching it back into place. It was not easy to carry a full backpack, a quiver full of arrows and a bow on one back. Ansylike's shoulders were not broad and her muscles were not that well developed and it was clear that she was having difficulties.

"Stop a while, Spud," he called. She halted and turned to face him. Haldriel also paused and shouted to Tharl that it was time to take a break. "Strap your pack on to mine," insisted Groblic. "If we're attacked you will need both hands free. I can carry it easily. We need your bow and your sword to be ready in an emergency. The way we are going is no good. We're not ready for a fight." He looked to Tharl to confirm his words.

"The path has been easy so far, but you're right. We had better be more careful." Tharl looked up the hill that they had descended. He could easily see the tracks that they'd left. Anyone wishing to follow them would not have to try very hard to see which way they'd gone.

"We are not far from the trees. When we reach them we'll change direction."

"I'd like a look at Spud's bow, before we go on," said Groblic. "If I may?" He addressed the question to Ansylike.

"Certainly," she answered unslinging the bow and handing it to him. She was also glad to part with her backpack. It seemed a lot heavier, with an extra supply of food in it. "Why do you want to see it? It's far too big for you to use!" She laughed.

Groblic smiled as he notched an arrow in the bow. He held it at a slant and wedged the bottom end under his left boot. Then he drew the string under his chin, brushing his beard aside with his outstretched fingers. He paused only to wink at Ansylike, then let the arrow fly. He caught a rabbit in mid-hop and it spun once in the air before it came to rest. Ansylike stood with her mouth open and her eyes wide with astonishment.

"Right between the ears!" exclaimed Haldriel. "Your aim gets better all the time. You'll be giving me lessons soon!" He took the bow from Groblic's arm and gave the string a tentative twitch. "Well strung! This is a fine bow. I'm surprised that Strell didn't ask us to pay for this in silver." He looked carefully at the wood and the filigree of metal that adorned its centre.

"Gold wouldn't have made her part with a weapon like this!" replied Groblic. "Spud has another relic from the past to add to her collection. See the lettering in the metal? It matches the runes on her sword. I think that there's more going on here than a band of weary dwarves in search of an elven gardener!"

He looked at Ansylike, but she was not willing to say anything. She merely took her bow and slung it over her shoulder. There would be time, later, to tell the dwarves what Strell had said. Groblic understood that it was not the time to talk and tied Ansylike's backpack on to his own without further comment. He fetched the rabbit and returned the arrow to Ansylike's quiver.

"Let's get to the trees before the rain starts," suggested Tharl. "The sky is promising us a good soaking and I think that thunderheads are gathering around the mountains.

Ansylike followed the direction of his gaze and saw that the place where they'd left Strell was shrouded in dark, heavy mist. Even as she watched, lightning forked the ground and she saw a plume of smoke rise into the crackling air. The trees seemed even more inviting. All thoughts of caution and hiding tracks were lost in a mad sprint for the cover of the tree-line. With her long legs and the advantage of having little to carry, Ansylike reached the first tree well ahead of the dwarves. She steadied herself with one hand against the bole of a twisted oak and caught her breath. The dwarves were running as if they were being chased by wild dogs or wolves. It seemed as if their very lives depended on reaching the trees. It did!

Suddenly a bolt of lightning arced down from the skies and frizzled the turf behind Groblic. Steam and smoke rose in a burst from the grass. All the dwarves ran even faster and joined Ansylike. They crouched down in the roots of the massive oak and waited for the storm to pass.

"That last one was aimed at me!" complained Groblic. "It made my hair stand on end. My boots are still hot and I'm sure that my armour is scorched."

A light rain began to fall and Ansylike fastened her cloak tighter around her neck. The wind was getting stronger and it brought an icy coldness that chilled their limbs and made them huddle closer together.

"We can't stop here. Let's get moving and we'll see if we can find some better shelter in the woods," urged Haldriel. "No-one has been through here in a long time and there are no traces of animals. We should be safe for a while." He took a few steps further forward and sank to his knees in slush. All the others laughed. Tharl came to his rescue and hauled him out of the mire.

"I'll go first," volunteered Ansylike. "I'll check the ground with my sword."

"Not without the rope," added Groblic. He slipped both of his packs to the ground and started to uncoil the rope that had come in very handy on several previous occasions. "If you fall into anything we can soon pull you out. but be careful. Swamps are always dangerous places. Keep an eye out for leeches and snakes."

"And marsh-flies," added Tharl helpfully. "They carry all sorts of diseases." Groblic shushed him before he could go into detail. He took the hint and shut up which was probably worse. Ansylike was already regretting her offer to go first. She tied the rope round her waist and drew her sword, then set off.

The forest was open and light. The trees didn't grow too closely together and there was little vegetation on the ground. It was, however, very wet and Ansylike was glad that her boots didn't let in any of the water that squelched up every time she put a foot down. Progress was slow as each bit of the route had to be checked and Ansylike soon tired of prodding the earth with her sword. When they came to a fallen tree she decided that it was time to stop for a rest. The dwarves caught up and climbed on to the trunk, which made a convenient bench. Ansylike sheathed her sword and joined them.

The rain had stopped and the sky was brightening. It looked as if the rest of the day was going to be more pleasant. Even the cool wind had dropped and the leaves, high above, were unstirred.

"Have we anything to eat?" asked Tharl. "I'm getting hungry. We must have been travelling through this forest for ages." Ansylike retrieved her pack from Groblic and began to sort out the rations. There was plenty of meat that they had cooked on the previous night and stowed in a clay jar. All the dwarves had worked up healthy appetites and were soon tucking in. Their packs would all be a lot lighter. "The best way to carry food is in your stomach!" remarked Tharl, between munches. "I'm always happier after a good meal!" All agreed with him and continued to eat.

"Look at the mushrooms down here!" said Haldriel, leaning over to inspect the other side of the tree trunk. "I think I've found our supper." There were three white puffballs and a host of creamy-yellow fungi that looked like ears.

"Can you eat that stuff? It doesn't look very tasty to me!" Ansylike regarded the mushrooms from a safe distance and didn't go any closer.

"I thought they were poisonous."

"Not at all!" replied Groblic. "These are a great delicacy. I'm surprised that you've not come across them before. Did you never see them when you were working in the kitchens?" Ansylike shook her head. The only mushrooms she had cooked had been ones with little stalks and flat white caps. These strange things looked like something from a nightmare. She kept guard while Haldriel collected this unexpected harvest.

"Which way do we go from here?" she asked. "I can't even be sure which way we came from. We don't seem to be leaving any tracks." She looked around. "We'll have to get out of this swamp and on to dry land before long. I don't fancy the idea of spending the night in a tree!" She peered up into the forest canopy above her and realised, with a start, that a brown, furry face was peering with unblinking eyes back down at her. "I don't want to alarm anyone, but there's something in that tree and it seems to be taking an interest in us!" she whispered, under her breath.

The dwarves looked up, following the direction of her gaze, and saw the creature moving down the tree trunk towards them.

"Danger!" hissed Tharl.

It was human in shape, but much smaller and covered in thick, orange-brown fur. It had a long, curling tail that it seemed to be using like an extra arm to aid it in the long climb down. Its face was black, although it had white streaks across its cheeks. Its eyes were like dark, purple pools of liquid, ever rippling as if stirred by the wind. Haldriel gently took up his crossbow and popped a bolt onto the shaft.

"It doesn't look dangerous," he explained, "but it's wise to take no chances. I didn't think that goats were any threat until I almost got eaten by one." He didn't point the bow at the creature in case that was considered to be an unfriendly gesture.

"There may be more of them up there," Tharl advised them, "but I can't see any. Look around on all sides."

"Don't draw your weapons," insisted Groblic. "Let's see what it wants before we do anything rash." He was confident that the creature posed no real danger and it was sensible to avoid trouble whenever possible. Besides, they might be out-numbered!

The animal stopped, still high in the trees and threw a round, orange fruit towards them. Without thinking, Ansylike reached out and caught it in both hands. The dwarves dived for cover as if a missile had been fired at them. They were not taking any chances! Ansylike inspected the fruit and recognised it as a rare, rather delicious type of melon that she hadn't tasted in many years. She waved gratefully and sunk her teeth into it to break the rind. Then she split it and bit into the succulent flesh.

The dwarves gathered themselves from the mire and looked at her in disbelief while the creature scampered across the ground towards them. They could not believe that she had simply waited for the object to reach her. It could have exploded! Travellers had told tales about the fruit that grew in The Desolation. They had earned a reputation for blowing holes in people or spiking them with thorns. Once you had been nipped by a crab-apple, you didn't take fruit lightly! Trees and bushes, flowers and shrubs had all developed offensive capabilities that were unpredictable and potentially lethal to the careless and unwary. One sniff of the wrong flower and you were compost! ... Or so the stories told.

Before the dwarves had time to react, the hairy creature had reached them and joined Ansylike on the fallen tree. It chattered to her and waved a paw, as if it were sure that she could understand every word that it was saying if she only paid close enough attention. The juice from the melon dribbled down her chin and she spat out a pip. The offer of the fruit seemed to be a gesture of friendship. That much she understood. The rest of the message was a mystery to her. It was certainly urgent and the creature kept jumping up and down as if it was keen to be on its way.

"I think it wants us to follow," said Haldriel. "It keeps pointing to the trees over there. It's time we were going, so let's see if that's what it wants. There are bound to be plenty more of these things in the trees and I'd prefer to have them on our side."

There was no dissent so Ansylike slipped off the tree trunk and gathered the few belongings that were scattered around her. Groblic was to carry her pack again so that she would have both hands free to use her bow.

They set off with Ansylike's new friend chattering at her side. The dwarves kept well away, although they accepted that the creature meant them no harm. She hoped that it was leading them out of danger and not into it! Her bow hung across her shoulders, but she kept her sword in her right hand.

Before they reached a clearing, the creature stopped and seemed unwilling to go any further. It jumped up and down, chattering wildly, and pointed fearfully ahead. Ansylike stopped and looked carefully at the clearing which seemed to be shrouded in mist. It was hard to make out the tree tops, although the ones behind her were clear enough. She wiped her left hand across her face. Something seemed to be tickling her. She blew out and rubbed her face again.

"What do you make of it?" she asked Tharl who was the first to join her. He looked up into the trees and the blood drained from his face.

"To arms!" he shouted and before Ansylike had time to twitch her sword-arm the dwarves were bristling with weapons. "Look at the size of that!"

A spider of monstrous proportions was nestled in the branches above them, carefully weaving a cocoon around a small figure that was evidently destined for its larder. There was no doubt that it had already seen the approach of the dwarves. Pairs of glittering, beady eyes fixed them with a malicious intensity. A silk thread suddenly lashed out, as if from nowhere, and caught Groblic around his waist. He was pulled off balance and raised off his feet before Ansylike had the presence of mind to slash out at the air above him and release him from the deadly grip that was pulling him to his doom. The furry creature waved its paws wildly and Ansylike understood that it was urging them to rescue its friend that had been captured by this loathsome beast.

Haldriel's bow twanged and he reloaded while his bolt sped towards its mark. He doubted whether one crossbow-bolt would have much effect on an animal the size of a wagon. Groblic and Tharl stood, poised to repel any attack, so Ansylike put her sword away and unslung her long-bow. By the time that she had loaded an arrow, Haldriel had fired again. She took careful aim and her shaft sped with deadly accuracy to its target. Its body was a huge bag, covered in hair, but Ansylike guessed that it would, like normal spiders, be highly vulnerable from underneath. She was right. The spider dropped, legs curled, into the ground and sank!

The clearing was a lake and the leaves that covered its surface parted only for a moment before reforming. Appearances were indeed deceptive. It looked solid enough, but it was a pool with a layer of leaves and weed on top of it. Bubbles rose to the surface and ripples spread out from the point where the spider had landed. The cocoon that the spider had been weaving had come partly free and dangled above the dwarves, but it was still too far to reach. Haldriel raised his bow and fired, severing the thread, and the spider's captive fell to earth and lay wriggling on the leaves. Fortunately it didn't plummet into the water! The furry one chattered with glee and capered around while Ansylike used one of her daggers to cut through the gossamer casing. To her surprise she saw that it was a human child, a young boy, and certainly one of the ugliest children that she had ever seen in her life.

"Can you talk?" she asked gently, while the dwarves kept guard. "You're safe now. The spider's dead. Is this a friend of yours?" She pointed to the creature that had led them to the clearing to rescue the boy.

"I can talk perfectly well," came the reply. "Spiders like their dinner to be moving." He seemed to be unworried at the thought of the fate that had so nearly befallen him. He brushed off the cobwebs and turned to regard Ansylike. "My thanks to all of you. You must join us tonight. The forest is not a safe place to be in when darkness falls." He waved a hand. "Come, Charrie! We're going home! With that he set off through the trees.

"Rather an ungrateful brat," commented Groblic. "You'd think that his life was rescued every day."

"My thoughts exactly," returned Haldriel.

"Quite well-mannered for an ogre," suggested Tharl. Ansylike started to grin, then remembered that Tharl was not in the habit of making jokes. Ogres ate people and they had been invited for dinner. She hoped that she was not going to end up as the main course!

"Are we really going to follow him?" she asked, as she trotted after Groblic. Clearly they were, but Ansylike wanted to express her reservations. She was also hoping to be reassured. She desperately wanted someone to tell her that all would be well. She waited in vain.

None of the dwarves was willing to make a promise that he couldn't keep.

An appointment with an ogre was more dangerous than trying to tickle a bear under the chin. She splashed after the others and hoped that she would be spending the night under a warm blanket and not under a sheet of pastry!

"I think we're heading for the farm on the other side of the swamp," said Haldriel. "It's in the right direction, I think, and we don't want to spend an uncomfortable night in the trees, now do we?" He marched steadfastly on and talked to Ansylike out of the corner of his mouth. Ahead of him the ogre-child and his strange companion wound their way through the trees taking a route that went this way and that, as if they were trying to confuse any that might try to follow them. In fact he was avoiding the swamps and pitfalls and this he did with unerring skill. He seemed to care little for the other dangers in the forest.

It was quite late in the day before the ground began to slope upwards and the dwarves felt that they were on firmer land. Their boots were soaked and only Ansylike had dry feet.

Charrie, the furry humanoid creature, seemed to have taken a liking to Ansylike and pranced about in front of her as they went on, or dangled from the trees above her and reached down to stroke her hair.

The first time that this happened, Ansylike shrieked and ducked to a crouching position. She was thinking of the spider in the branches and feared for a moment that she was going to be whisked up on a silk thread!

This only caused Charrie to chatter with increased happiness. He was under the impression that Ansylike was joining in the fun and took every opportunity, after that, to ambush her. The fact that his pet had found another friend did not seem to bother the ogre child. He had struck up a conversation with Tharl and they found that they had a lot in common. They moaned on together about the misery of life, complaining of this and that and getting cheerfully depressed in the process. Groblic and Haldriel walked together, keeping a wary eye on their surroundings. They said little but squelched ever on, occasionally having to break into a trot to keep up. With a sigh of relief, Haldriel noticed that Tharl and the little ogre had stopped for a rest. It was not before time. The sun was beginning to set and the forest had taken on a gloomy air.

"My name is Grund and this is Charrie," said the ogre by way of introduction. "Our home is not far from here, but Tharl tells me that you need a break so here we can rest for a while." He looked at Ansylike. "Your females are very different." He regarded Tharl with a keen gaze. "I would not have thought that you were of the same race."

"Indeed we're not!" replied Tharl. "We are dwarves and she is a half-elf. Our kind are very different from hers."

"I see my mistake," returned Grund. He looked again at Ansylike, who was sitting on a rock and had her legs stretched out in front of her. Charrie was in the tree above her and was preparing to launch another surprise attack, but Ansylike knew exactly where he was and was preparing a little surprise of her own! As he dropped towards her she flicked a stick and caught him neatly on his nose. She laughed as he scampered off in defeat to plan his next move. "An elf. I always wondered what they were like. We see few travellers and never any elves, although I have heard enough about them. Dwarves and elves in one day. Whatever will I see next?" Without waiting for a reply, he strode off. "Nice legs," he said over his shoulder. Groblic and Haldriel exchanged glances, but Ansylike seemed not to have heard.

Chapter Eight

AN UNEXPECTED WELCOME

There was less than an hour of daylight left before they came in sight of the farm. It was unmistakable. A fence had been constructed with living trees as posts and mighty slabs of stone as buttresses. It was more than twice the height of Ansylike and seemed as if it was designed to keep dragons out. "Wolves," explained Grund briefly, and Groblic shivered, looking warily about him. The gate was secured with a metal chain and a solid lock. Grund produced a brass key that he wore on a woven thread of spider-silk around his neck and let them in. The door creaked open and gave them sight of the ogre's farm. It was obvious that it was managed on very efficient lines. The lambs were neatly penned, the cows grazed contentedly and the chickens pottered about as if they hadn't a care in the world. In a large paddock, a group of horses chewed the turf and did no more than twitch an ear at the approach of the strangers.

"Father is home. That's his stallion," stated Grund, indicating the largest of the horses. "I'll be in trouble for being late."

"Large buildings," added Groblic as he looked at a barn that was still stacked with hay. "There's enough fodder to stable an army here. Are you expecting guests?" Grund made no reply, but made his way to the central building. As he approached, the door was flung open and an enormous woman bore down on him.

"What time do you call this?" she bellowed and seized him by an ear. "Playing with your friends in the forest while your work remains undone! You scamp!" She whacked him mightily with a huge hand across his bottom and the force of the blow carried him through the door. "The rest of you can help him with his chores or there'll be no dinner for you and you'll feel the back of my hand before bed-time!" She gathered her skirts and marched in to the kitchen muttering dire threats under her breath. She left a trail of flour behind her as she moved away. She ignored the dwarves, closing the door behind her with a mighty thud! Charrie was unperturbed. He was obviously used to this sort of treatment. Taking Ansylike by the hand he led her round the side of the building to another door. The dwarves followed. There was nothing else to do. The side-door was on a latch and Ansylike paused before opening it, wondering whether she should knock first.

"Get on with it, Spud," insisted Tharl, "or we'll be here all night. In case you hadn't noticed, it's getting dark. I don't wish to sleep with the chickens!" The other dwarves muttered their agreement so Ansylike lifted the latch, pushed open the door a little and peeped in. The door swung suddenly inwards pulling her with it. A giant arm seized her round the waist and hauled her in.

"Look what I've got for supper!" boomed the voice of the ogre as he held Ansylike tight and peered at the dwarves. "Yum! Yum!"

"Let me go!" screamed Ansylike, as she pounded at the monster with her fists. He shifted his grip so that she dangled over his shoulders while he held her around her knees. The dwarves were horrified and were just drawing their weapons when Grund appeared.

"Stop teasing them. That's no way to treat our guests. Put her down." The ogre did as his son had told him and lowered Ansylike to the ground. She was relieved and extremely annoyed. She looked up at the ogre who towered above her and grinned at her displeasure.

"I didn't think that was funny!" she protested. She looked to the dwarves for support and was surprised to see that they were sharing in the joke. Groblic was leaning against the door frame, his face convulsed with laughter. Even Tharl seemed to find the episode hugely amusing and tears of mirth rolled down his cheeks and into his whiskers.

"Well!" exclaimed Ansylike. She was lost for further words.

"You'd better straighten your pants before we go any further," advised Haldriel. "You're showing far more of your bottom than usual!" Ansylike blushed and pulled the hems of her shorts back down while the dwarves continued to enjoy her embarrassment. Grund waved for them to come in and took Ansylike by the arm. Charrie appeared and capered in front of her. He was obviously delighted that they were to be staying at the farm. He was a strange creature, but not as strange as the ogres.

"I'm Drole," said the ogre, pointing a massive finger at his hairy chest. "My son in Grund. This my wife." He waved an arm in the general direction of the room from which the smell of baking bread was coming. "And you," he added to Ansylike, "are very tasty indeed!"

"Pleased to meet you," replied Haldriel, but the ogre seemed to be only interested in Ansylike.

He regarded her with a beady eye. "I wouldn't mind seeing you wrapped in pastry!" Ansylike shivered and lowered her hand to the hilt of her sword. She took up a defensive position and prepared to attack. The ogre found this hugely amusing and laughed aloud again. "I'm forgetting my manners," he apologised. "You are welcome here and we don't eat people!"

"Father has a warped sense of humour," explained Grund. "We have never eaten any of our visitors. Would any of you like to help me in the kitchen? I've an enormous amount of vegetables to peel." Ansylike began to volunteer, but Drole silenced her and pointed at the dwarves.

"These little fellows can peel and scrub to earn their meal. This tasty one is coming with me."

Ansylike looked anxious, and cowered further back into the corner to which she had retreated. This caused Drole to laugh again.

"You'll not come to any harm with me. I'm only going to show you around the farm before the sun sets." Ansylike look unconvinced, but the dwarves were all watching her and she didn't want to seem like a coward. Reluctantly she agreed and accompanied Drole. Charrie bounded after them.

Groblic had seen the inside of many a kitchen, but nothing had prepared him for the state of this one. There were many times that he'd been unable to pay for his drinks at the end of an evening and been forced to wash the plates and ale-pots. His arms were well used to hot water and soap suds. He stood aghast, however, at the pools of water on the floor, the grease-stained ceiling and the pile of pots and pans in the sink. There were three mighty fireplaces and huge cauldrons bubbled over each one, sending bursts of steam towards the roof. Grund's mother was kneading dough on a wooden trestle table that was the size of a double bed. Clouds of flour surrounded her. Groblic rolled up his sleeves and set to work.

Fortunately, the other dwarves decided to help, preferring the horrors of the kitchen to the company of Drole! They stripped off their armour and weapons and set to work cheerfully, knowing that there were worse ways to earn a meal.

Eventually it was time for dinner and the dwarves were pleased to see that there was even more than their appetites could manage. After they had all eaten and come close to bursting point, Groblic got out their clay pipes and the smoking-weed that he had stored so carefully. Drole accepted a pipeful, then produced some of his own which he had grown himself. The kitchen was large, but the air was soon thick with smoke and Ansylike decided that a walk in the fresh air before she went to bed would be a good idea. She would have liked some company, but everyone else seemed to be occupied. Charrie was curled up in front of one of the fires. Grund had also fallen asleep and the ogres and dwarves were swapping stories of their adventures. She made her way into the night air, having promised not to go far, and looked up at the sky. It was clearer than it had been all day and there was now no sign of the heavy rain clouds. In the mountains on the other side of the forest was an occasional flash of lightning. Other than that it seemed to be a peaceful, quite unremarkable night.

When he was sure that Ansylike was out of earshot, Grund became suddenly more serious.

"And now to business!" he said. "I could do with some help to deal with a problem that we've been having. A creature has recently moved into the swamp and it's scaring the deer away. I don't suppose you saw any, did you?" The dwarves all said that they hadn't. "That's just what I mean," replied Drole. "They've taken to the hills and I'll have no meat for the winter if they don't come back before long."

"What sort of a creature are you talking about?" asked Haldriel. He couldn't imagine that there was any animal that an ogre couldn't deal with. Unless it was a dragon!

"A sort of worm," continued Drole. "Or maybe a snake. It disappears under the ground when I go after it. I've tried to sneak up on it, but it always knows where I am." Drole rubbed his stubbly chin thoughtfully. "It doesn't belong here and I've an idea that it's been sent to cause mischief."

"Deliberate, you mean?" asked Haldriel.

"Elves!" answered Grund. "It's the work of the elves. They want us out of here. Gromixillion. He's a nasty one!"

"There ought to be enough of us to catch one worm," stated Tharl confidently. "We can set out in the morning after breakfast. Spud's bow should prove handy."

"This is no work for a girl," insisted Drole. "Even an elfling. I'll not see her put in danger.

"She can look after herself in a fight!" retorted Groblic. "As long as she isn't being dangled over someone's shoulder." They all laughed at the memory of this indignity and prepared to turn in for the night.

The dwarves made their way, as quietly as possible, to the barn and found that Ansylike wasn't asleep. She was sharpening her throwing knives on a special stone that she always carried with her. Briefly they explained about the worm that Drole wanted them to kill and tried to work out a strategy. Clearly they would have to tackle it when it was on the surface and Ansylike suggested that they could use a goat or a sheep as bait to lure it up. This was agreed upon. What they would do when the thing appeared was another matter and best left until the morning when they had rested and the effect of the ale had worn off.

After a suitably large breakfast they followed Drole and Grund towards the swamp. The sun shone from a clear, blue sky and helped to keep their spirits up, but it was soon blotted from view as they walked down from the hill. Soft, spongy earth replaced the firm turf and pools of foul-smelling water splashed and squelched under their feet. Groblic led a goat on a rope and before long they had reached the clearing where they'd killed the spider on the previous day.

"It lives in there," said Drole, indicating the leaf-covered floor, "but it must come out at night to hunt. Tie the goat to that tree and we'll see what happens." He lifted his club and moved a little further away. The dwarves got their weapons ready. It was a nice day for a fight but a worm was not really an exciting challenge.

"So that's why you were here yesterday?" asked Haldriel, turning to Grund.

"I thought I might get a better look at it from the trees," he replied, "but I didn't know that there was a spider in the branches. I won't make that mistake again."

"That's not a bad idea," added Ansylike. "If one of us was to climb a tree we would have warning of when the worm was moving."

"Go on then," urged Tharl. Ansylike looked to Groblic for support, but he only shrugged his shoulders.

"I'll give you a lift up," offered Drole, but Ansylike declined graciously. Being seized by an ogre was not an experience that she wanted to repeat. He laughed aloud at her refusal and watched as she scrambled into the nearest tree. On one thing, he and his son were in complete agreement. She did have lovely legs! If he had been less intent on watching Ansylike's acrobatics and more attentive to the work in hand he might have noticed the gradual movement in the leaves. As it was, he was unaware of the danger until a snake-like tendril wrapped around his leg and pulled him off balance. He crashed to the forest floor with a mighty thump and a splash and slid towards the swamp. Haldriel had loaded his bow, but there was nothing to shoot at. The sudden burst of noise startled birds from their perches in the trees and they flew off, squawking loudly.

"It's attacking!" exclaimed Groblic, wielding his war-hammer and running to help the ogre who was suddenly waist deep in water. A tentacle whipped up from the leaves, wrapped around his waist and bore him to the ground. It was clearly not a worm that had taken up residence in the swamp, but something far more deadly!

Tharl's battle-axe flashed through the air and cut Groblic free, but Drole was having a more difficult time. He was floundering in the water, unable to find any firm footing, and Grund was trying to pull him to safety. Tharl had, however, wounded the creature and it raised a head to see what had caused it so much pain. Then it raised another head... and another. Before long each of its five heads had reared above the surface. In each head was a single eye and this enabled it to see all around. It did not, however, look up and only Ansylike was free of its gaze.

Trying to make the most of this small advantage she continued to climb, as quietly as she could, towards the tree tops. She doubted whether an arrow was going to make much of an impression on this foe, but she intended to give it her best shot and trust to luck. She was encouraged to see that a bolt from Haldriel's crossbow sped towards one of the heads and blinded its eye.

Another tentacle darted towards the dwarf as he reloaded, but he spotted it and moved out of its reach.

Grund had managed to pull his father free, but neither one of them could do much to help. A head darted toward Tharl and he severed it cleanly from its neck, getting showered with greenish blood in the process.

Without going dangerously close to the water, Groblic couldn't find a target and he could only stand and watch. Then he had an idea. He moved away and searched his backpack for an oil flask and his tinderbox. He uncorked a flask of oil and ripped a piece of cloth from the corner of his cloak and soaked it, before stuffing it back into the neck of the bottle. Then he lit it with a spark from his tinderbox and threw it towards the creature in the swamp. It landed in the water, fizzled briefly, then went out and sank.

Ansylike had reached a wide branch from which she could safely fire an arrow without losing her balance, so she unslung her bow and took aim. "Get the one with the chain!" shouted Groblic. He pointed and

Ansylike changed her target and unleashed one of Strell's arrows. It had an instant and drastic effect.

The entire swamp creature shuddered, writhed briefly in a spasm of agony and vanished. The level of the water dropped, giving the dwarves some idea of the size of the monster that they'd faced. Clearly there was a pattern to the incidence of the threats that faced them. The silver chains proved that. There was a deliberate series of obstacles in their path and Haldriel resolved to have a war council before they went any further. They had been lucky so far, but how much longer could their luck hold out?

The dwarves marched sombrely back to the farmhouse. None of them felt much like celebrating. Only Drole and Grund seemed particularly happy, and the goat that had been given a fortunate reprieve. The smoke pouring from the chimneys did cheer them up a bit as all felt that they had earned their dinners. The smell of cooking drifted towards them and Tharl licked his lips in anticipation. Their speed increased!

Drole was the first to reach the house, followed closely by his son. As he flung back the door, he was greeted by a cloud of steam and smoke that seemed essential to all ogreish cooking. He was also welcomed by the voice of his wife who was stirring a stew pot that hung over one of the fires that she'd lit.

"Back again, are you? I suppose that you're all hungry and no-one has thought to bring any more wood for the fire." She shooed away a couple of chickens from beneath her feet and strode to the sink, where she assumed a defiant posture with her hands on her hips.

"My love!" exclaimed Drole and seized her about her waist. He planted a wet kiss on her lips and she squirmed in his grasp as if she wanted to escape. To Groblic it was obvious that she did not. She felt left out, excluded from the main business. Groblic knew the symptoms well and had learned that women were not to be taken for granted. Their place was not in the kitchen and it was a foolish man, or ogre, who thought otherwise! He caught Ansylike's eye and offered his hand to her.

"Let's wash before dinner. I think that we could all do with a good scrub and a change of clothes."

"I think you have a point there," she replied. "Tharl smells like a dung heap and I don't suppose that I'm much better." The dwarves made their way back to the barn where they had spent the night. They collected a few essentials and trudged off to the well to wash, leaving Drole to make peace with his wife.

"I'll bring you a pail of water," said Groblic to Ansylike. "You can wash in here. I'm sure that you don't want to see Tharl without his trousers!" He shuddered in mock horror. "You can close the door and I'll see that you're not disturbed." There was no hurry so the dwarves and Ansylike took their time. There was a lot of dirt to clean off! Eventually Drole shouted out to them that dinner was served and on the table and he was going to start without his guests if they were not ready to dine soon. They hurried up and made their way to the kitchen. The aromas of roasting meats, baked bread and braised vegetables greeted them.

The meal was enormous, as they had all expected. The cooking of ogres was legendary and, if one wasn't actually on the menu, it was a feast to remember. Fortunately they all had appetites to match it! Even so, eating it took up most of the afternoon. When it was over, and the pots and pans had been cleared away, the dwarves settled down in comfortable chairs and Haldriel decided that it was time to discuss their progress and the dangers that they'd faced together. There was much that needed to be talked over.

"I'll fetch the pipes," offered Groblic, then he looked at Ansylike who wrinkled her nose in disapproval. "Well, maybe later." Ansylike smiled at him in gratitude. She didn't want the room filled with smoke again. It made her cough and she was sure that it did no good to her health.

"You've something of importance to say," reminded Tharl and Haldriel leant forward and rested his folded arms on the table. It was a gesture that always signalled that a speech was on the way so Groblic settled himself in his chair and waited for it to begin.

"The wolves, the crows, the goats and the swamp creature all had silver chains. None of those were random attacks by wild animals. All the dangers that we've faced have been prepared to stop us. I want to know why! Our mission is very important to us, but who would want to stop us? It's not of any significance to anyone here. Who would go to all that trouble to put enchanted monsters in our way? It doesn't make sense." Ansylike felt that it was time to tell the dwarves some of what Strell had told her, although it was difficult to know where to begin. She cleared her throat and looked at Haldriel. He nodded to encourage her and Groblic patted her arm.

"Tell us what you know, Spud. We're a team now. We're sticking together despite the danger."

"I'm really not sure how to tell you this," she began, "but Strell said that there was a prophecy. An elven maiden would carry a sword of power into The Desolation and she would use it to kill the elven warlord." She paused and lowered her eyes. There was a moment of silence as the dwarves considered the weight of her words. "I don't know whether it's important and I don't see how I can have got involved in all this."

"So you've got on the wrong side of the elves, have you?" said Drole. "You're in for a hard time!" He looked at Ansylike. "But she's an elf!"

"Hush yourself!" said his wife. "These people have important things to talk about." She grunted in annoyance and poked him in the ribs. "Let the girl speak. Let them tell us how they came to be here. I've heard their tales in bits and pieces, but I took them for the stories of wanderers whose exploits grow each time they are told."

"I'll tell you then of how we come to be here and how we first met Spud. Then she had better fill in the details in case there's anything that I've missed. Or anything that she knows and I don't!" Haldriel told their story and this time explained that they were not the first party of dwarves to explore The Desolation in search of the wisdom of the elves. This was certainly news to Ansylike and she wondered why the dwarves that she had come to trust had kept such a vital piece of information from her.

"Occasional travellers pass this way, but we have seen nothing of dwarves or elves before. None have stopped here," added Drole.

"Could they have gone by without you noticing?" asked Tharl.

"I suppose so," replied Drole. "If they wanted to avoid us, then they could have sneaked past. Not everyone wants to sample our hospitality. They don't realise that some ogres are friendly and won't eat them." He scowled at his guests, then grinned and winked at Haldriel as if it were a huge joke.

"To be honest," added Ansylike, "I'm inclined to agree with them. I thought all ogres ate people! I thought I was heading for the stew-pan when you slung me over your shoulder." The memory of the incident made her check that her pants were not riding up again.

"We are still no nearer to finding an answer," reminded Haldriel. "If this elf-lord that you speak of wants to stop us from going further, then he must know that we're on the way and I don't see how that's possible. Unless he uses magic to track the sword! Now there's a thought. Strell said something about the sword not passing without being noticed. I wonder if that's what she meant."

"Not a very comforting thought," commented Groblic, "but I admit that it would explain a lot."

"There's not much we can do about that, except leave the sword behind," suggested Tharl, looking at Ansylike. "What do you think, Spud?"

"I'll leave the sword if you think that we'll be safer," she replied, although she was reluctant to part with it.

"There's no way to be certain," said Haldriel, "and I feel safer with Spud's sword around. Leaving it is no guarantee that we won't be attacked again. We've come this far with it so I think she should keep it at her side. Anyway this is not entirely news to us. I heard Strell talk of this prophecy and the sword. Did she say anything else that we ought to know?"

"Not that I can think of at the moment," returned Ansylike. "It's still a mystery to me. I don't know what we ought to do."

"I have a suggestion," offered Drole's wife. "There is one person that you could ask for advice, but her price is always high and sometimes a little strange." She had said so little that all the dwarves and Ansylike were surprised at the sound of her voice. "First I must tell you our own story." She looked to Drole for encouragement and he gave her an enormous grin and a pat on the shoulder that would have broken the back of a horse. "We have not always been like this," she began. "I don't suppose any of you have ever stopped to wonder why ogres are so rare?" She searched their faces, but there was no response. "Let me tell you then. There is no creature with a worse temper than an ogre. Except perhaps a troll."

"Or a dragon," added Grund, who had never seen one in his life.

"Let me get on with it!" she insisted and gave the table such a thump that Haldriel's elbows collapsed from under his chin. She had their attention and began again. "It is one of the misfortunes of our race to be cursed with dreadful tempers." There were no interruptions. "This causes great problems when a male ogre and a female ogre take a fancy to one another. They simply can't get on and one of them usually ends up killing the other!"

"I see!" said Ansylike. "So how...?" She caught a nudge in the ribs from Groblic and said no more.

"So I went to the sorceress on the mountain and asked for her help. Drole followed me."

"At a safe distance!" he added, under his breath, but loud enough for all to hear.

"And what did she do?" asked Ansylike. She skilfully avoided Groblic's elbow and continued, "What exactly is a sorceress, anyway?"

"She enchanted us both. That's what she did. She made us give up eating people and made us better tempered so that we could get on with each other. There was a price to pay, of course. My price was that I could never be called by my own name. Even my son doesn't know it. Drole, of course, suffers the same fate. If he even calls out my name in his sleep, the spell will be broken and we will go back to our old ways. It is a cruel price to pay, but we think it is worth it."

"Cruel indeed!" said Haldriel. In the moments of silence that followed, the dwarves pondered whether it was a price worth paying and cast sympathetic glances at Drole and his wife who must be forever nameless.

Would it be wise to seek the help of such a heartless person? And such a powerful one! Casting spells was not easy and this must have been very tricky to do. The price also seemed very peculiar. Why had she simply not asked for money?

Ansylike's mind wandered on to another track. "Couldn't anyone say your name just by accident?" she asked. "What if your name was 'Spoon', for instance and someone just happened to say, 'Pass me the spoon.' Would that mean that the spell was broken?"

Groblic wondered what he had taken on when he had promised to look after Spud as if she was his own child. She was innocent of the ways of the world and it was surprising that she had lasted so long! He shook his head and sighed dramatically.

"Ogre's names are long and unusual," explained Groblic patiently, "and they have their own language."

"I see," replied Ansylike. "So we don't have to be careful of what we say?"

"Not unless you can speak ogreish!" laughed Drole. "Very few people get the chance to learn it, for obvious reasons! Now let my wife get to the point of the story before we all forget what we're supposed to be talking about."

The ogress looked at him blankly for a moment, still wrapped in the thoughts of her own painful memories. Her heavy, hairy arms rested on the table and her fingers twitched. Clearly the subject was one that disturbed her. Then she seemed suddenly to snap out of it and continued.

"Zileika is a strange girl. She lives in a high tower on the top of a cliff and practises her magic. Her guards are all enchanted creatures and she allows no humans or elves to stay with her. She is the only sorceress in these parts so people go to her when they have a problem that needs to be solved by magic. They take her food and clothing in part-payment, but she always asks for something else. No-one who goes to her can tell what she will want in return."

"Are you suggesting that she may be able to solve our problems?" asked Haldriel. He had his doubts. Magic was best avoided. Still, if it was already being used against them, maybe they should have a little of it on their side!

"I'm sure that she can tell you a lot more about what goes on here than we can. You already seem to be in great danger so it may be worth the risk. What do you think, Drole?"

"It's the only thing that they can do if they want advice and she may be able to tell them how to make the trees grow again. That would save them having to ask the elves who seem keen to kill them."

"It sounds like our best course of action," said Haldriel thoughtfully. "There can be no harm in giving it a try."

"She sounds really interesting!" added Ansylike with enthusiasm. "I can't wait to meet her! How far is her home from here?" Groblic sighed in desperation. There was no hope for this girl! He had thought that Haldriel had a rare ability to ignore the danger that was under his nose, but Spud was amazing!

"No more than a day's travel from here. I'll take you when you're ready to go, if that's what you want," offered Drole. "You can stay here and think about it for a while. I'm off to my bed." His wife pushed her chair back and stood up as she got ready to leave. She reminded them that there was still plenty of food for them to eat and ale to drink. They were welcome to as much as they could manage. Then the ogres departed.

The dwarves talked long into the night and lit their pipes after Ansylike had made her way to the barn. She was eager to have a long sleep after such an eventful day.

So it was that she missed the arrival of Strell, Andric, Cledrin and Obolin. Strell had been as good as her word. She had found the missing members of the party and guided them to the ogre's farm where they were made welcome by their friends. There was much to talk about. Over mugs of ale and bowls of stew the dwarves boasted of their exploits. There was much laughter and merriment.

Eventually the conversation turned to their present position and Haldriel recounted the tale of the ogres and their advice. All agreed that consulting the sorceress, Zileika, was worth a try. By the time that the stories had been told it was dawn and they were ready for some sleep.

There was no need to wake early. They could all lie in and have breakfast at noon.

Ansylike woke to the sound of a cockerel crowing somewhere in the farmyard and was surprised to find that Strell was asleep, a few paces from her. To her delight she saw that the number of huddled forms on the other side of the barn had increased. Cledrin, Andric and Obolin had caught up with them after all! She took some things from her pack and made her way to the well to wash. She was careful to move quietly and woke no-one as she left. There would be plenty of time to greet them later.

As she washed, Ansylike had another thought. Drole and his wife had been put under a spell to make them less like ogres, but what of their son? He certainly didn't seem to be dangerous. He was a bit grumpy and not very well-mannered, but he certainly didn't seem to be like a real ogre. She wondered whether he was also enchanted. She made up her mind to ask Drole when she got the chance.

The farmhouse kitchen was back to its usual state of chaos when Ansylike let herself in. She shooed a few chickens out of the way and offered her help to Drole's wife who was stirring another mighty pan of stew which bubbled gently over the fire.

"You could set the table," she replied. "I hear that some more friends of yours have turned up. I dare say that they'll all be hungry. We won't wait for them, though. We'll have breakfast as soon as it's ready. There'll not be room for us all to sit down at once!" She wiped her hands on an apron that had once been white. "And you can call Drole and Grund when you've done that. I'm surprised that they're not here already. My man is never late for his meals. Here, taste this." She held out a spoonful of golden, vegetable soup.

"Delicious!" Ansylike told her after she'd slurped the liquid off the huge spoon. "Your own recipe?" The ogress nodded happily. "Is it safe to call you by something that isn't really your name?" asked Ansylike. She was not sure that she had been heard in all the general hubbub and considered whether she should repeat the question. There was no need.

"What do you mean exactly?" came the reply.

"I don't think it's right that I should not call you by any name at all.... Everyone needs a name." It was difficult to explain exactly what she meant and Ansylike gazed into the fire as she struggled to express her thoughts clearly.

"What would you like to call me, child? Have you thought about that?"

"Well..." hesitated Ansylike as the ogress loomed over her. "Mother. Is that...?" For an awful moment it seemed to Ansylike that she had broken the spell of the sorceress. She was suddenly seized, pulled up into the air and almost smothered in the enormous folds of the ogress's apron.

"You called me mother!" The words were whispered as Ansylike was lowered safely to the ground. "Mother! How long have I waited to be called that? Drole!" she roared in an ear-splitting call that made Ansylike put her hands over her ears.

"What have I said?" exclaimed Ansylike. "What have I done?" Her arms were still caught firmly by the ogress and there was no way of breaking free. Was she for the pot this time?

Apparently not. Drole appeared at the kitchen door as his wife let go of Ansylike and wiped her eyes with her sleeves. "The dear child called me 'Mother'," she explained. Ansylike backed a little further away. She darted looks from the corners of her eyes to prepare her escape route in case it looked like she was in danger of being hugged again. Drole comforted his wife, but he was grinning widely and Ansylike realised that his wife's tears were of pleasure, not pain. "After all these years a child has called me mother!" This was quite enough for Ansylike who could not understand what the fuss was about. She edged closer to the door keeping a wary eye on the ogres.

"You have brought us great happiness!" said Drole, who had noticed her after all. "Part of the enchantment is lifted. One of the conditions that Zileika put on us was that we could never have a daughter of our own until a girl-child called my wife 'Mother'. We were, of course, forbidden to tell anyone of this. There were the usual restrictions to stop us from hurrying up the process."

Ansylike had no idea what the 'usual restrictions' might be. She was very glad that she was not in danger and that the ogres were happy. She decided to continue with her work and set the table for breakfast. Older heads than hers could sort out what the ogres were on about. When they woke up! Which reminded her! She peered out of the window to see if Andric was up and about yet. It was rather too high for her and she had to strain her neck to look out, but she managed to get a clear view of the barn and the well. There was no sign of her brother nor her friends.

Breakfast was enough to set Ansylike up for the day. She had a glass of fresh milk, two savoury pancakes, fried eggs, mushrooms and meat, toasted bread rolls with lashings of butter and honey and another glass of milk to finish.

She was well and truly full and doubted whether she would ever be able to eat again. For a horrible moment she wondered whether she was being fattened up like a pig for the slaughter. A swift glance at the expression on Drole's face reassured her. They were strange folk, but she trusted them. Their appetites were huge and the meal that Ansylike had struggled over would have been nothing more than a snack to them, but they did not seem to regard her with anything except affection. They really were not threatening. She finished her last glass of milk and wiped her lips.

"The others can wash up," said Drole. "After they've eaten. Mother can do with a rest and I can show you a little more of the farm. He stressed the word 'mother' and patted his wife gently on the arm. She burped contentedly and nodded. "How would you like a stroll around the estate to wear off some of that food?" This seemed an excellent idea to Ansylike and she readily agreed. She would only fall asleep if she sat at the table and she was no longer afraid of the ogres. They were like any other couple really and she remembered Strell's advice that she should not judge by appearances. Dark intentions were often hidden behind fair faces, while rough exteriors housed kind hearts.

"This is where we keep the cows." Drole waved an arm and indicated a pasture. "Everywhere is fenced in, of course. We have to keep out the wolves and the other creatures." He marched on. "Have I shown you this bit before?" He didn't wait for an answer to his question, but strode along. It was obvious that he took great pride in his farm and it pleased him immensely to show it off. "The pigs are here, in these sheds. They have a bad reputation, but they're lovely creatures." Ansylike reached over a fence to stroke a browsing sow, but Drole seized her collar and pulled her quickly back. She protested and he continued, "They have teeth like razors! You can look at them but you must never let your hands go near them. Even the piglets could take off your fingers! I always wear a stout pair of boots and a leather apron when I go in the pens. They might bite off something that I can't replace!" He winked confidentially at Ansylike and smiled. She didn't appreciate his joke and Drole found that a lot more amusing.

"I expected them to smell a lot worse than this," she admitted.

"Cleaned out regularly," the ogre informed her. "The manure makes my rhubarb grow. Let me show you."

Andric woke and rolled over in the hay where he'd been sleeping. His head was heavy from the ale that he had drunk the night before. His eyelids were gummed and he wiped them on his shirt sleeves. The dwarves were all snoring and he could make out the huddled form of Strell on the far side of the barn. She hadn't stirred either. Noticing that the sun was high in the sky, he decided that it was time for him to be making a move.

At this moment Ansylike appeared in the doorway. She laughed at the sight of her brother and told him that lunch would be ready soon and he had better hurry if he wanted to eat. Drole stopped behind her and asked casually if she needed some pails of cold water to help them all wake up. This had the desired effect and soon all the dwarves were trooping to the kitchen.

The rest of the day passed without them doing much except talking and planning. The dwarves were taken on a tour of the farm. They asked polite questions, but were not really interested. They liked their meat on plates, not still mooing, oinking and bleating! Even Haldriel, who tended a little garden at home, missed the vital lesson that Drole's farm could have taught him.

Chapter Nine

THE TOWER OF THE SORCERESS

The next morning they were all awake early and ready to leave just after dawn. Their farewells were brief. Drole's wife had made up packs of food to last them through the day. Haldriel remembered about the mushrooms that he had collected in the forest and handed them over to her. They were not in the best condition, but still edible. Then they were on their way. Drole led, as he knew the route, and he set a fast pace. The farm was soon out of sight behind them as they took a path that wound along the side of a mountain, climbing ever upwards.

At noon they stopped for a rest. The view behind them was stunning. There was time to admire it as they tucked into the food that they were carrying. Ansylike wandered off a little way to find a secluded spot where she could empty her bladder and discovered a blue berry bush that was covered in fruit. She knew it wasn't the right time of year for them to be ready, but she sampled one and found that it was ripe and very tasty! Soon she was picking the berries and eating them happily.

"Didn't you hear us calling?" Strell's voice startled her, but she kept stuffing her mouth. "It's time we were on our way!"

"Right," replied Ansylike and she got up to follow. It seemed a pity to leave all the berries behind. There were loads still on the bush.

"Look at your mouth!" exclaimed Groblic, as if that were possible. "And your hands! What have you been up to?" Ansylike looked guiltily at her hands that were now stained a delicate shade of blue.

"She's been eating magic blueberries!" laughed Drole. "We'll be making a few more stops than I'd intended." He set off again, still laughing and Ansylike trotted after him to find out what he meant. He continued to laugh and would only reply, "You'll see. It won't be long. You'll see!" Groblic marched at her side, scolding her for her foolishness and saying that he shouldn't have let her out of his sight.

"You just can't be trusted," he complained.

Strell and Andric walked along together. "Will she be all right?" he asked.

"Oh yes, but it will slow us down a bit. There is much magic in these hills. A little of it occasionally rubs off on the plants. The blue berries have their own system for spreading. The berries are very sweet and people can't help eating them, but they have a dramatic effect on the guts. Soon she will be looking for a sheltered place and...."

"I see," interrupted Andric. "The seeds go through the body quickly and are passed out again in a quiet spot."

"In their own little supply of manure!" added Strell tactfully.

"That's not too bad then."

"Unfortunately the process is repeated at regular intervals," laughed Strell.

"How regular?" asked Andric suspiciously.

"About a dozen times before the sun sets!" replied Strell. Andric whistled through his teeth.

"That'll teach her not to eat things that grow on these hills."

"Indeed it will!" chuckled Strell. "Indeed it will!"

It was dark before they even caught a glimpse of the tower and it was still a long way in the distance. They wouldn't have noticed it at all if Drole hadn't pointed it out. Stark and bare against the skyline, it rose like a twisted stump from the ruin of rock on which it perched. Menace seemed to ooze from the air around it and even Tharl shuddered as he clutched tight hold of his axe.

Ansylike had spent more of the afternoon squatting in the heather than walking and their progress had been seriously slowed down! Groblic had forgiven her quickly and his anger had turned to concern. His charge was not in the best of health and was looking weaker, paler under her tanned skin, and more tired as time went on. Heather, twigs and rocks made her stumble frequently and it seemed to be only a matter of time before she fell flat on her face. She was also drinking far too much water. She had only the small flasks that she kept in her pack for washing. All the rest were empty.

"We can camp at the base of the cliff and go to the tower in the morning. There's a stream of fresh water and we can light a fire and have a comfortable night under the stars," Drole told the weary travellers and volunteered to stand guard. Groblic was relieved to hear that there was a supply of water. He didn't want Ansylike to be drinking wine or beer in her delicate condition.

"Did you hear that?" he asked her. "I think that you can drink the water in your bottles now and we'll fill them up from the stream." She was sitting with her head in her hands and looking most dejected. He rooted out one of the flasks and held it to her lips. Andric looked on with obvious concern, but there was nothing that he could do.

"This is better!" said Ansylike raising her head and taking the flask from Groblic. He knelt in the heather in front of her and saw that she was visibly brightening. The blue stains around her lips were disappearing and her hands were returning to their normal colour. She finished drinking and even managed a smile.

"Where did you fill this?" asked Andric, taking the empty flask from her.

"In a cave," she answered. "I went exploring and I found a rock-pool. I filled the bottles, then had a bath."

"And your wounds healed!" added Groblic. "I wondered why you made such a swift recovery! A pool of healing! If only we had known about it then."

Ansylike felt a little guilty. "You'd been waiting for me and you all seemed cross. You were standing on a big rock. I didn't want to mention it again. Anyway, I didn't know that it was a pool of healing at the time."

"Don't worry yourself," soothed Groblic. "I didn't mean to upset you. What's done is over with and we're all learning from our mistakes. If you're feeling better we can get on. We'll soon be snug around a roaring fire and having our dinner. I could eat a horse!" Cledrin scowled at him. He had walked over to see how Spud was doing and he was a little annoyed that Groblic was taking such an interest in her. He was jealous and sad that his elven friend seemed to be ignoring him. It wasn't fair and there was no sense in him complaining. That would only make matters worse. He said nothing and kept his thoughts to himself as he turned and followed the ogre towards the cliff.

Ansylike had not forgotten Cledrin's kindness and she did her best to renew their friendship at the camp. They all sat around the fire after they'd eaten, except Drole and Tharl who stood guard. Strell had told them of the worries that she had for her own people and decided to leave them in the morning and return home. Drole would not visit Zileika again so he volunteered to return with Strell as far as the farm. There was no point in him climbing the cliff for nothing.

Only the original party would go to the tower of the sorceress. Groblic wondered how many of them would leave it. He was not keen on magicians, witches, sorcerers and seers. Magic was best witnessed from afar or read about in storybooks!

Night passed and the dwarves insisted on having breakfast before they began the climb. The cliff rose ominously above them. In places it leaned out and it looked as if parts of it were ready to come crashing down. None of them relished the thought of starting on that!

Ansylike wandered off to the stream after she'd said her goodbyes to Strell and Drole. She was hopeful that she would see them again soon. Standing on the bank of the stream, she leaned down to scoop up a handful of water. To her astonishment she saw that the reflection in the water was not her own! She made sure that there was no-one standing behind her and peered down again. The face that looked back at her was that of a young girl with piercing blue eyes. Her skin was tanned and her hair was gathered back away from her face. For a moment Ansylike thought that there was a real body in the water, perhaps a girl had drowned. She recoiled and stood up again.

"You've come a long way to see me. Don't you want to talk?" The voice came from the face in the water and Ansylike knew that she had just met Zileika! She knelt down again and looked closer. This time she saw the lips on the image move. "I thought I'd better tell you that the stair is in the cave behind you. There is no need to climb the rocks although you can if you want! Dangerous, though. Even for dwarves. Pretty, aren't you? I can't wait to find out why such a fair maid should be walking through The Desolation."

"Thank you," replied Ansylike as she gazed down with wide eyes.

"No trouble. I'll expect you before lunch. That's it for now. See you later." The face faded and the water was normal again. Ansylike was still not sure whether she was dreaming. She looked in the direction of the cave. That was one way to check. If there was a staircase in there, then Zileika had really spoken to her. If there was not, then it had all been in her imagination. She could wash later. She had to see the inside of the cave before she did anything else.

"Are you ready to ascend?" boomed a deep voice. Ansylike was not a coward, but she took one look and fled. She didn't even think of drawing her sword or throwing a dagger. She was running back to where she'd left the dwarves before she had time to even shout a warning! They could see that she was not being followed, but she was clearly alarmed so they were prepared for trouble before she reached them.

"What's the matter?' asked Groblic as she skidded to a halt behind him and put her hands on his shoulders. She was positioning him between her and whatever she thought was following. There was still nothing to be seen.

"I don't see what all this trouble is about. There's nothing there, Spud! Are you seeing things?" She stood behind him with her hands gripping his shoulders hard enough to turn her knuckles white. Andric stood to one side with his sword drawn. The rest of the dwarves moved cautiously towards the river. "Get a hold of yourself," urged Groblic. "Unless there is some invisible monster out there, you've nothing to fear. We'll protect you, won't we, Andric?" He was aware that Ansylike's teeth were chattering and she was too terrified to reply.

"There's nothing in the water that I can see," stated Haldriel.

"Nothing on the cliffs," added Obolin.

"Then it must be the cave!" suggested Cledrin. "I'll take a look." He walked cautiously forward with Tharl at his side while Haldriel and Obolin kept a watchful eye on the stream and the cliffs that rose above them. They all knew that Ansylike was not spooked easily. If she was frightened out of her skin then there must be something dangerous and they intended to find out what it was and see it off.

Cledrin was the first to enter the cave and he was taking no chances. He was, however totally unprepared for what followed. He had gone some way in and was only five or six paces from the back wall when a strange thing happened. A pair of giant eyes opened and stared at him without blinking. They were formed of the very stone of the mountain. Beneath them the rock crinkled suddenly and opened to form a mouth.

"Are you ready to ascend, or are you going to scamper off too?"

Cledrin scampered! "It's a stone-giant and it's a big one!" he shouted to Haldriel as he ran past.

"Granite!" added Tharl who was not far behind Cledrin. Haldriel didn't hear him. He was already in the stream and trying to swim to the opposite bank keeping one foot on the bottom! Obolin managed to keep his head. He knew that there was no point in trying to out-run a stone-giant. There was no point trying to hide, either! He stood his ground. Legends told of the power of the stone-giants. They were formed of the earth and were said to have built the mountains upon which all things now stood. They had lain down to rest when their work was done and slept under the ground keeping the world in place.

They were said to dislike the work of the dwarves who burrowed into rock to extract the ores and build their homes. Obolin reminded himself that creatures of legend did not suddenly pop up out of nowhere. The other dwarves must have been in a state of panic. He had to set a better example! He marched after them, trying to whistle a tune to keep up the appearance. He didn't succeed for long and broke into a trot that then became a headlong dash.

As the dwarves came running back, Andric saw that a real problem faced them. He was unsure of what it was, but he knew that it could be overcome if they faced up to it. From what he had heard of Zileika, the sorceress, he had already got the impression that she liked to play nasty jokes on people and this was probably one of them.

"Pull yourself together, Spud, and follow me!" he commanded and waited for the response.

"There was a face in the wall," she stuttered, but at least she had managed to stop shaking. "The rock suddenly spoke. There were huge eyes and teeth!"

"Why did you go into the cave? You knew it wasn't safe on your own!"

"Zileika, or I think it was her, said the stairs were in the cave. Instead I got stared at!"

"You had better explain from the beginning. Are you calm enough, now?" Ansylike was more composed and was just telling Andric and Groblic her story when the other dwarves arrived. She waited for Obolin to reach them and began again.

"We'll have to go back, anyway," said Groblic. "There's no sign of Haldriel. He must be still there!"

"He dived into the stream," offered Tharl, and he smiled. The thought of a dwarf willingly trying to take swimming lessons was hugely amusing. There was no point in them waiting any longer. If the giant had to be faced then it was best done soon.

Andric was first into the cave. Once again the face appeared and the giant's voice rang out.

"Are you ready to ascend or are you just here to waste my time?" The eyes regarded him coldly, but he stood his ground.

"What do you mean by the word 'ascend'?"

"I can see it's going to be one of those days!" came the reply. "Do you want to go to the top of the cliff or not?"

"Yes, we do. But not just yet."

"Typical! Well, tell me when you're ready."

Haldriel didn't manage to get very far in the water. Dwarves in metal armour carrying weapons and heavy packs of equipment do not float! Even though he was as frightened as any dwarf can be, he could not get across the broad stream. He lay gasping on a sandy bank and that was where Groblic found him.

Andric suggested that they wait until Haldriel had a chance to put on some dry clothes before they went back into the cave. Although Haldriel was keen to make up for his cowardice, he was not given the chance yet. Ansylike told him that she was not going to see the sorceress until she had made herself more presentable. She was going to have a wash and brush down her clothes. If he wanted to stand around dripping that was his decision!

Andric and the dwarves waited by the cave and Haldriel put on some dry clothes that the others had given him. They could not see Ansylike, but they could hear her splashing happily in the stream. That did nothing to improve Haldriel's mood! When all were ready, they went to see the stone-giant. Haldriel led the way.

"Ready now?" asked the giant, as a massive eye opened.

"Ready," replied Andric. "What do we do now?"

"I open my mouth and you all climb in. Then I stand up. When I open my mouth again you all climb out. Simple really, isn't it?"

"I hope you'll remember not to swallow!" said Ansylike.

"I'll remember. Even a tasty morsel like you will be safe with me!" His mouth opened and they scrambled in quickly. There was a strange rumbling as the giant rose through the mountain which simply parted around him. It was as easy for him to move through stone as for a bird to fly through air. Then the mouth opened again and sunlight streamed in. They got out and stood on the grass, thankful that the ordeal was over.

The mouth closed behind them. Ansylike turned to thank the giant and saw that only his head poked above the ground.

"That was a most comfortable journey. Thank you. I am Ansylike and I'm pleased to have met you."

"Not many people have thanked me," came the reply. "In fact, you are the first. I'll be glad to assist you anytime. Just call if you need me."

"I'm sorry, but I don't know your name. What shall I call you, if you don't mind telling me?"

"Granite. It's not my real name, but it will do." The giant regarded her with interest. "I must say," he added, "you have charming manners ... and lovely legs!" He winked, then sank back through the mountain. Ansylike could only turn to the dwarves and shrug her shoulders.

"You're blushing!" laughed Groblic. "Now let's get on our way. We're expected!"

Above them rose the tower of Zileika, the sorceress. It was impressive. It appeared to be unguarded, with no sign of the enchanted guards that the ogress had mentioned, and there was a large, open door at the bottom. They made their way to the door and wondered whether they should knock first, or just go in. There was no need. As they got close, a figure emerged from the doorway and she came out to greet them.

"So you're here at last! I was expecting you ages ago. Not had any little mishaps, I hope." As she said this, she looked directly at Haldriel. It was clear to them all that she knew what they'd been through to get here and was having a little fun at their expense! "Let's all go inside, shall we? It might rain soon and we don't want to get wet, do we?" She laughed lightly and threw back her head.

Ansylike recognised her face. It was the one she'd seen in the stream. She also recognised her behaviour: that of a spiteful brat! She could have warned them of the giant in the cave instead of just telling them that the stairs were in there. She must get her pleasure from seeing other people in trouble. It would not be easy to get help from this girl and Ansylike wanted to warn the dwarves before it was too late.

"Such cloudy looks, my pretty one! Tell me what's bothering you." Zileika's voice was soothing and innocent as she addressed Ansylike. "You don't want to scowl at me. Let's be friends. I've been waiting for a girl of my own age to play with in such a long time."

"Like a cat plays with a mouse," thought Ansylike. She pretended to smile and let Zileika link her arm and lead her inside the tower. There was no point in showing her true feelings. Zileika might have a warped sense of humour, but she was clearly powerful and there was danger in annoying her. The dwarves and Andric followed. If they suspected that anything was wrong, they showed no signs.

"This is where your friends will be staying," said the sorceress, indicating the ground floor. "It's very comfortable. As you can see, I was expecting you." That much was obvious! A welcoming fire burned in the hearth and the air was pleasantly warm. A long, wooden table had been laid for lunch and it was laden with food. "There's roasting meat, vegetables, sauces, bread, butter, honey, fruit, wines, ale in that barrel, mead, and there are the cups. I thought you'd like a meal and a rest after your travels."

As she pointed to each stacked platter of food, the dwarves grew more hungry. "There are smoking pipes, of course, and a box of the finest pipe-weed. I've arranged some chairs by the fireside. The beds are over there. I hope you will be comfortable." Even Ansylike was impressed and some of her earlier fears evaporated. She unlinked Zileika's arm from her own and went over to the fire to get warm. Zileika followed her. "You will have your own room. Would you like to see it after you've eaten?" Ansylike nodded.

Lunch lasted for ages and the dwarves seemed to be at their ease as they ate and ate. Each of them had loosened his belt three or four times before finishing. The fright that they'd had in the morning when they first met the stone-giant appeared to be forgotten. Even Haldriel was in high spirits!

"Would you like to see your room, now?" asked Zileika. "I'm sure that the men would like to try the pipe-weed and I'm not fond of the smell. They can relax without us. You don't smoke pipes, do you?" She nodded in approval when Ansylike assured her that she had no intention of picking up such a filthy habit.

"Don't you want a hand to clear some of this away first?" Ansylike indicated the dining table, and hoped that the answer was no. They had made a terrible mess. She'd noticed that Obolin's table manners had not improved and the remains of his meal were scattered before him. As he sat with his arms resting in front of him and his head forward, his beard was soaking up some of the ale and wine that he had spilled.

"No need to worry. Just sit here and watch," she whispered. "We are going to see the room I've got ready for Ansylike," announced Zileika, in a louder voice as she stood up. "Perhaps you'd like to move closer to the fire and smoke your pipes?" The dwarves rose to their feet, thanked her for the excellent feast and made their way to the chairs round the hearth. Zileika waited until she was sure that none of the men were watching before she stretched her hands over the table, twiddled her fingers, and uttered a spell. In an instant the remains of their meal had disappeared. There was not a crumb on the table, not a drop of ale and the wooden surface gleamed as if it had been freshly polished! "I'll need a rest after that," said Zileika, as she rubbed her hands together. "Doing the housework always tires me out!"

Ansylike started to laugh, but the sorceress shushed her and pointed to the dwarves. "Let's slip off before they notice," she whispered. Stifling a giggle with her hands over her mouth, Ansylike followed as Zileika sneaked up the narrow, stone stairs.

"This is it," said Zileika after the girls had reached a room, high in the top of the tower. They had climbed hundreds of stairs, but their legs were not tired and they weren't out of breath. Zileika explained that she had put an enchantment on the staircase to save her legs. She didn't want to suffer with unsightly veins in her old age! "Your own private bathroom!" she continued proudly. "Sink, lavatory behind that door, bath... it's all here. And the water's hot. I have a water tank on the roof and I put a 'hot-water' spell on it. It's never empty, of course. What do you think?"

"Wonderful! I've never seen such luxury. What's in all those bottles?"

She pointed to the rows of jars, carafes, pots and glasses. No herbalist that Ansylike had ever visited had such a fine collection of coloured liquids!

"Scents, oils, lotions and balms. If they don't get you clean, then nothing will. Now would you like to see the clothes?"

"Are they magic? The bottles, I mean."

"No," replied Zileika. "Have I disappointed you? Never mind. I can make them magical for you, but it'll take a little time.... I'm sure you'll enjoy looking in the wardrobe. Here. These are some of my finest creations."

Rather reluctantly, Ansylike followed her, remembering to watch her manners. It would not do to offend her hostess.

"There are plenty of clothes in here," said Zileika, pulling open a door. "I guessed you would be the same size as me. A little less developed, perhaps, but the same height and build. This one is special. Accept it as a present." She held up a green, silk catsuit. "You wear it under your ordinary clothes and it'll keep you warm. On its own it can change colour to match its surroundings. Watch." She held it against the stone wall and it quickly became grey. "It only works properly when it's worn. It needs body heat to have its full effect. It took a while to get that spell right and I had a lot of bother finding the material."

"It's amazing." Ansylike accepted the suit and draped it over her arm. She looked at the array of clothes that hung, by some magic, in the wardrobe. There were styles to suit every occasion. "Do you do a lot of entertaining, then? These are your clothes, really, I suppose."

"No, they're not my clothes. They're for you. And I don't have many guests. It gets really lonely up here and my visitors don't stay long. I try to make them feel welcome, but they never trust me. They leave as soon as they've found out what they want to know!"

"Maybe that's because they have to. People come here because they urgently need to know something, don't they?"

"But they like it here. They're safe and well fed. I sort out their problems. What more can they want?" She took a striped silk dress in pure white and held it against her. It glittered a metallic blue as it changed to match the rest of her outfit.

"Everyone has a life of their own to lead. I suppose they want to get on with it. Perhaps they'd like to stay, but there are other things that they have to do."

"I don't think it's fair!" Zileika stamped a foot, folded her arms and pouted. She looked like a child that was about to have a tantrum. She scrumpled the silk dress and threw it on to the bed. "You'll stay for a while, won't you? Or will you be just like all the others?" Tears trickled from the corners of her eyes.

"I can't say that I'll stay, but I can promise to come back. If I'm alive, that is. Shall I tell you of our mission and why I must leave soon?"

"Later. There'll be time later." Zileika sighed unhappily. The thought that her new friend would be leaving, and didn't want to stop with her, gave her a sudden idea. A nasty idea! She was contemplating what horrid fate she could devise for her latest acquaintances when her chain of thought was broken.

"Why don't you come with us?" offered Ansylike. "You could help me, I'm sure. I'd be glad of your company." Zileika forgot her nasty idea for the time being.

"You'd really like me to come with you? You're not just saying that. I can tell when you're lying, you know. Are you serious?"

"Of course! You might enjoy some travel and different company. I thought the dwarves were a bit strange, at first. Now I really like them. They've been good friends to me. I don't think that you really get to know people until you've had to live with them. Travel with them, I mean. Share the same food and look after each other. Groblic is a bit like a father. He fusses a bit, but I know that I can trust him. When that giant of yours frightened me, he was the person I ran to for help."

"Really?" Zileika looked thoughtful.

"What are you thinking about?" asked Ansylike. She moved over to a bed that was big enough for three and sat down on it. The mattress was soft and springy. She curled up on the eiderdown and rested her head on an elbow, then pulled her legs up behind her. "I'm tired. Didn't you say that you needed to rest after tidying the kitchen? I need a snooze." She laid back on the bed and closed her eyes.

"Oh, I meant to tell you...." It was too late. Ansylike was fast asleep. Zileika gazed out of the window at the lands beyond and wished that she could visit them. She knew that Ansylike could not hear her so she said what was in the back of her mind.

"I can never leave here. This tower is my prison and here I must stay. I want someone to stay with me, but they all leave. I'm afraid and so alone!" Her words were carried off by the wind. "I cannot leave my magic behind. It's the only thing I'm good at. How would I live out there? Without my magic I couldn't even grow a carrot."

"Perhaps you are wrong!" said a gentle voice. Andric stood in the doorway behind her. Zileika turned and raised a hand in a magic gesture that could have turned the minstrel into a toad. How had he got up the stairs without her hearing him? She didn't allow anyone up here without a personal invitation. She was peeved! Her anger showed as her cheeks and neck flushed. Andric was alert to the warning signs and held up his hands to show that he carried no weapons and meant her no harm.

"Wait just a moment and hear what I have to say. I want to talk to you in private. She might wake and I want this to be just between the two of us." He had one or two spells of his own and he had been ready with this one! It cast an air of peace and calm. It made people less inclined to attack him. He nodded his head towards Ansylike as if in question.

"She can't hear us. The bed has a 'rest' spell on it." Zileika pointed to Ansylike. "Say what you have to and prepare yourself for a life in a lily pond!"

"I think you're wrong. Listen!"

"I hope you like water! A life on the lily-pads would suit you well!" She raised an arm and pointed a menacing finger. "I only have to say the words and you will hop off!" She meant it quite literally! "Toad!"

Andric realised that he had to speak convincingly. He had to get his words just right and explain to the sorceress that there was no need for her to feel angry.

"You are in need of our help. We need yours. Spud meant what she said. She will come back to see you. Why shouldn't she?" His spell hadn't worked. Despite the power and energy that he'd put into it! Clearly he had no chance of using magic as a defence against this one!

"She has you, doesn't she! I've seen the way that you exchange glances. I saw you looking at each other across the table when we ate. She'll want to settle down and have a family of her own. She'll have no time for friends!" Zileika had worked herself into a rage and she took a pace forwards. "All that talk about the dwarf being her best friend was to deceive me. I see through your lies now. She's just like all the rest!" In her anger, she spoke through tightly clenched teeth. The skin on her forehead was taut, drawing her eyes into slants of blue fire.

"I'm her brother," replied Andric. "That's all." He watched the sorceress closely. "What she said was true. The dwarves are her friends. All of them seem to look after her in the best way that they can. Some of them have grown fond of her. Spud has no plans for settling down! She likes her freedom too much." He paused, desperate, waiting for a reaction. It was sudden and unexpected. Zileika's expression changed to one of pain and longing. Crackles of blue fire escaped from her finger tips, but they fizzled out before they'd gone far.

"That's what I' d like! Freedom. I can watch other people going off on their adventures, but I never have any of my own." Her voice was calm, but her eyes filled. Although she blinked a few times, tears escaped and rolled down her cheeks. Turning away, she wiped them with the backs of her hands.

Andric swallowed nervously, but said nothing.

"I'd better wake her up, unless there's anything else that you don't want her to hear?" continued the sorceress. Now her voice was even and measured and she managed a small smile. Andric shook his head, so Zileika went over to Ansylike and gently raised her off the bed, cradling her limp form in both arms. It was effortless and Andric had no doubt that the sorceress could lift him up just as easily. She walked a few paces and placed Ansylike in a chair. "She'll wake soon. You can forget about being turned into a toad. I cancelled the spell."

"Could you really do that?" asked Andric.

"Easily! I'd have made you a little pond, though. I'm not heartless!" She did not appear to be joking.

"You're very skilled in the arts of magic. I don't see why you don't think you'd be safe in the outside world." He was ignored.

"Oh good. She's awake." Zileika addressed herself to Ansylike. "That was rather rude of you to fall asleep when I was talking to you! Some friend you'd make!"

She laughed and stopped Ansylike's apologies by explaining about the bed. "I was telling Andric here, why I can't leave and join you on your adventures. I won't bore you with the details. The essential thing to know is that I offended some rather important people and they banished me to the tower and here I must stay. If I go far from here I'll lose my magic powers for ever."

"How long must you stay here for?" asked Andric, forgetting to be cautious. "Will you be forgiven one day?" It seemed a rather harsh punishment. He didn't like to ask exactly what she had done to deserve it. He didn't like to think of how powerful the magician must be to put a spell on this mighty sorceress!

"If you come back here I will tell you how you can help me. You are on important business now and that must come first. I knew that from the start, but a girl must live in hope."

"I'll do my best to return," promised Ansylike. "I really will!" She stood up and put her hands on Zileika's shoulders. The girls were of equal height and their eyes were on the same level.

"That's good enough. Now we had better see what those dwarves are up to and what sort of a mess they're making in my kitchens. Shall we go down?" She smiled, then led the way. Soon they were re-united with Haldriel and the others who were still sitting by the fireplace. Obolin spat into the flames and a long, juicy strand of spittle dribbled down his beard.

It took a long time for them to recount what had happened to them all, but Zileika sat and listened patiently. Occasionally she interrupted to ask questions and to quiz them on details that she thought were significant. Haldriel told much of the story, but the others all added bits here and there, until Zileika had a clear picture. She examined Ansylike's sword and the bow that Strell had given her and studied the runes carefully. When they'd all finished, they waited for her reply, but she seemed deep in thought and said nothing. The dwarves blew smoke rings. It occurred to Ansylike that the smoke never drifted towards her. She hadn't coughed once and her eyes hadn't even started to water. The hearth or the chimney must have a spell to draw in the smoke. She looked carefully, almost expecting to see a little demon sucking it all in. There was, however, nothing unusual!

"There is a complicated problem here. I think I'd better deal with it cautiously. There's always a price to pay for advice. I'd better tell you that first." Zileika looked at Haldriel, then Groblic. "Do you agree to pay?"

"Aren't you going to tell us what the price is, first?" asked Ansylike.

"Not this time."

"When we set off on this quest," began Haldriel, "we knew that we were putting our lives at risk. We will pay whatever price you ask."

"You speak for all the dwarves?"

"I do." The dwarves nodded. Haldriel was their leader and he'd given his word. That bound them all.

"Andric. Do you agree to pay whatever I ask?"

"Indeed I do," said the minstrel. "I didn't trust you at first, but I understand you a lot better now. I hope it isn't anything weird, but I'll do whatever you ask."

"Good enough. Then you are all agreed." Zileika settled herself back into her chair and joined her fingertips. Andric hoped it wasn't a magic gesture.

"What about me? Don't I have a price to pay?" asked Ansylike timidly, leaning forward.

"You have already agreed," replied Zileika fixing her with deep, blue eyes. "One day you will come back and help me with a few problems of my own. You have promised. And that was before I offered you anything except friendship. I can ask nothing more of you."

Ansylike relaxed and settled back in her chair. She grinned. She was most relieved. Zileika didn't seem so bad after all and she was looking forward to a little holiday in the tower. It would be nice to forget about all this adventuring for a while. Maybe she could learn from the sorceress. A bit of magic might come in handy! Her own education was sadly lacking.

"Now, Groblic. You have promised to look after Spud. You will treat her as if she were your own daughter. She is under your protection, but she needs her freedom."

"That I agreed to willingly. It's a pleasure as well as a duty."

Although the dwarf smiled as he spoke, there was no doubting the sincerity in his words.

"It's never easy to look after someone that you love. Yours is, perhaps, the hardest task. All of you share in this." She noticed that Cledrin nodded vigorously. "The rest of you must accompany her until her work is done. You must not leave The Desolation until she's safe. I hope that means that you can deliver her back to me. I'll be waiting. That's all."

"The trees," reminded Haldriel after a moment. "Do the elves have the power to replant them?"

"Certainly!" replied Zileika. "And not only the elves. You have already passed many people who could have helped you, but you were unwilling to learn."

"Who?" asked Groblic in astonishment. "Who could have helped us? Do you mean that we've come all this way for nothing?" All of the dwarves were taken aback by this bit of information and they sat in stunned silence, waiting for the sorceress to continue.

"Not for nothing. You will have an answer. It is easy to replant a forest if you take a little time over it. The trees look after themselves, but you don't have the patience to wait. You root out the saplings and stick them in where you want them to grow. Nature doesn't work like that! Forests grow up slowly. It takes time. Have you ever thought of using a fertiliser on the land?"

"I don't understand," said Haldriel. "We've already tried everything that seems logical. It doesn't work!"

"You will never understand," Zileika replied slowly. "Dwarves will not have their woods to themselves. They need to be lived in and looked after. Animals need to live there and so do the elves. You must persuade the elves to return."

In the stunned silence that followed, the dwarves had time to ponder over the words of the sorceress. She was giving no more advice. She simply scanned their faces, noting the impact of her message. It was like telling ogres to stop eating people! They didn't like it, but they eventually realised that it was for their own good!

"I'll leave you to think about it. It's time for a rest." Zileika stood up and headed for the staircase.

"Good idea!" agreed Ansylike. "I could do with finishing the snooze that I started. It makes a change to be sleeping in a bed instead of a barn!" She got up from her chair and waved a cheery goodbye to the dwarves who were still sitting in silence. Andric, she noted, had started to fill a smoking pipe. She scowled her disapproval and left.

Ansylike locked the door of her room behind her. It was more from habit than anything else. She was sure that the dwarves wouldn't disturb her. They'd been careful to respect her privacy so far. Remembering that she'd left her sword downstairs, she hesitated, then decided that it wasn't worth bothering about. It must be safe here. She went over to the window that Zileika had left open and pulled it shut, thinking of the crows that had attacked them. The latch on the window was secure. It would not do to be caught napping on a 'bed of rest'. Before she snuggled down under the covers, she promised herself a hot bath and a trial of the lotions and oils. All those bottles of coloured liquids looked really exciting. Then she fell asleep and resumed the dream that Zileika had interrupted earlier in the afternoon.

As the dwarves seemed to be in a state of shock, Andric was the first to break the silence. He offered Haldriel the pipe that he'd filled.

"What do you think?" he asked. "Can you live with the elves again?"

"I suppose we'll have to! Many of our people have suggested that we invite them back. We have had long talks about it. Nothing firm was settled."

"I'm not in favour!" growled Tharl. "They are enemies. How many of our kin have perished under elven blades? How many burial mounds are filled with the heroes that died in battle driving them out?'" He spat into the fire. "Their kind will never live in peace with us. Never! They're not to be trusted. I'd rather see our people move to other lands than invite our enemies back to live on our doorsteps. I'll hear none of it."

"Groblic, what do you think?" asked Haldriel when Tharl had finished.

"I am in favour of inviting them back. I know that what Tharl Wolf-slayer says is mostly true and I respect the wisdom of his opinions, but I cannot agree with him. There were many elves killed in the old battles. We won, after all. They were defeated, not us. We must have killed more of them. How many of their kind lie under the turf?"

"I agree with Tharl," said Obolin when it was his turn to speak. "We fought for the land and it's ours. Pay them with silver, if we have to, but don't ask them back!"

"I vote with Tharl and Obolin," said Cledrin. "Personally, I don't mind elves, but I'm afraid of the trouble that would be caused if they came back. It might mean war again. That couldn't help them or us. Ask for their help, but don't invite them to do the job for us."

The other dwarves and Andric looked at him in surprise. Haldriel had assumed that Cledrin would vote the other way. Then it would be for him to decide. He and Groblic were in the minority. He was their leader, but he couldn't make the offer to the elves now! This was a mess that he couldn't see a way out of. Zileika had been quite emphatic and she'd offered no alternative, but if they rejected her suggestion....

Andric poured himself another glass of wine and looked at Haldriel. "Do you have the authority of the High Council of Dwarves?" It was intended to help, but it had the opposite effect.

"No, he doesn't!" stated Tharl. "He speaks for us, that's all. As far as I'm concerned that means nothing. It's time for us to have a new leader if the best he can come up with is to invite us to disaster! Our people fought hard and for many years to drive the accursed elves from our lands. How much blood was spilled then? Haven't our fathers told us of the treachery that the elves were guilty of? Didn't they try to bring the wild magic of The Desolation to our mountains? They tried to wipe us out! Invite them back? Never!"

"I speak for myself, not the Council," replied Haldriel, crossly. "If that's not good enough for you, then I'm sorry! All this talk of the past can't help us now. Isn't it time for peace? How much of it is true, anyway? I'll tell the elves what I think and you can do whatever you like. If you don't want me as your leader, then you can vote on that as well." He stood up and glared at them, daring them to defy him.

It didn't work. Tharl stood up to face him. Half a dozen paces separated them and neither carried a weapon so there was no immediate danger of them coming to blows.

"I'll follow you no longer! You've led us from one disaster to another, It's time to have another leader! I challenge you. Who is with me?"

"You can count on me!" declared Obolin, moving to his side.

"Me too!" said Cledrin and he stuck his jaw out aggressively, before he too moved to Tharl's side.

"Does this mean that you won't come with us?" asked Andric. "Is this the parting of our paths?"

Zileika was fast asleep in her own room which she had decorated tastefully in various shades of blue. As she lay still, a crackling web of magic fire gathered around her and arched into the air, spiralling out and down the stairs. Her eyes flashed open.

"Oh no!" she exclaimed. "I've really done it this time!" She pulled back the covers and whipped her feet onto the deep carpet. She stood and waved to her gown which flew from the cupboard and draped itself around her. Then she moved to the door which opened in front of her. She sped to Ansylike's room and found that the door was locked. In her anger, she kicked at it with a bare foot. It hurt! "Open!" she commanded.

"Chip off!" replied the door. She'd forgotten about that particular spell. And it had been one of her favourites!

"Open!" she insisted. She was getting more and more irate. "If you don't open, I'll batter you down with my fists!"

"It'll hurt you more than it hurts me," advised the door.

"Take that!" she shouted and thumped her knuckles on the wooden panels. The force of the blow was enough to take a few layers of skin off, and her knuckles started to bleed.

"You wait!" she screamed. "You just wait!"

"You wait," replied the door calmly. "I''m not opening until the sleeper wakens. Those are my orders. You should know."

"I'll..." Zileika gathered her thoughts. "Awake," she commanded. She could not undo one of her spells, but nothing stopped her from starting a new one. She could not open the door, nor could she cancel the spell on the bed. This might work instead.

"Who's there?" came a slurred voice from inside the room.

"Unlock the door, Spud. I've made a mistake. Those dwarves are in deep water and I'm to blame. Let me in!"

"Very well then," said Ansylike as she turned the key. "I hope you've not been playing one of your tricks on them." She held the door open and stood, holding it wide. She was wrapped in a sheet.

"I left a nightdress in the wardrobe for you. Young ladies should not sleep in their skin and nothing else! Modesty is a virtue, you know!"

"Is that all you came to tell me?" Ansylike gathered the folds of the sheet tighter around her. She was never in the best of moods when she first woke up.

"Dress and follow me down the stairs. I've done something terrible. See you later."

Haldriel stared in horror. In the place where Tharl, Obolin and Cledrin had stood was a pond. Three toads crawled about in the water, trying to reach the sides. He went over and peered at them closely.

"They broke their promise," explained Andric. "They swore to follow Spud and look after her. They couldn't stand the thought of elves living on their land and they paid the price. They should have followed the decision of their leader, not doubted your judgement." He didn't leave the chair. "Sit and wait. The spell may wear off. It might be to teach them a lesson. There's nothing you can do anyway."

The three toads reached the edge of the pond and squatted in the short grass that fringed it. They croaked and looked towards Haldriel.

Despite the seriousness of the situation he grinned back at them. Then he laughed. At first it was a giggle, but soon it grew in volume. He couldn't help himself. He stared at his friends and thought of his own hatred of water. Soon he had rolled back in his chair and given in. He clutched his sides, but he couldn't stop laughing. He didn't notice Zileika and Ansylike rushing down the stairs.

"Shouldn't we grab them in case they get too close to the fire?" asked

Ansylike. The toads looked at her and croaked miserably. Or so it seemed.

"They're safe enough," replied Zileika. "They still have their intelligence. Their minds are intact. I only altered their bodies."

"Well, alter them back!" urged Ansylike. "It must be terrible for them. How could you do such a silly thing?"

"I can't change them back. Once I put an enchantment on something it stops. I didn't finish at college. I was thrown out. I never got to the bit where you learn how to undo spells. They are like that until the spell wears off." Her voice trembled slightly.

"How long will that be?" Ansylike seized Zileika by the shoulders. "Think, can't you?" She could see the sadness in Zileika's eyes. Tears had already begun to flow down her cheeks. "Do you know? Do you know how long the spell will last?" The sorceress raised a tear-stained face and shook her head. Shoulders heaving, she put her arms round Ansylike's waist and held her tight. Tears soaked Ansylike's collar and dripped down her neck. Her new friend regretted what she'd done, but didn't seem to know how to put matters right.

"I think you speak for all the dwarves, now!" whispered Andric. Haldriel heard, but made no reply. The minstrel looked at Zileika who was still sobbing, then back to Haldriel whose face was equally wet. But the tears on his face were from laughter!

Andric explained why Haldriel was coping with the situation so well. This news cheered her up. She described how the spell worked automatically. It wasn't her fault really. With this, they all agreed and she began to see the funny side of it. She went back up the stairs to wash her face and to dress properly and Ansylike went to keep her company.

"This makes things rather awkward," said Groblic looking at the unhappy toads. "We can't take them with us in that state."

"We'll have to leave them here, unless the spell wears off soon," decided Haldriel. "From what Zileika was saying I think there's little chance of that. Still, I'm sure we'll manage somehow."

"That depends on what lies ahead," added Andric. "There is much that Zileika hasn't told us. She made no mention of the creatures that attacked us and the silver chains. I think that we had better have another word with her before we leave. We don't know what we're up against."

Ansylike was surprised at the size of Zileika's room. It was not actually one room, but a series of chambers with strings of glass beads separating them instead of doors. The beads were strung on fine silver threads. She had never seen anything like them. There were several windows which gave a wide view of the lands around. The furniture was simple, but comfortable. Although the walls were mostly bare stone, there was a series of bright pictures that caught her eye and she moved closer to inspect them.

They were made of some material, like very thin carpet, and the strands were woven to form the images. Obviously the threads, of different colours must have taken ages to get into place.

"This one looks like me!" she said aloud. In fact, it looked very like her. In the picture, she was standing alone on a hill. Her hair blew in the wind. She caught her breath. It was so life-like. It seemed as if her hair was actually moving. It was strange to look into her own eyes. She moved to the next one. "This has to be Andric." Her brother was playing his flute while he watched the girl who danced at his side. She was laughing and her piercing, blue eyes gazed back at the minstrel. "Zileika!"

"Yes? You don't have to shout. I'm not deaf!" Zileika said as she parted a bead curtain and returned to the room. "Oh, you're looking at those. What can you see? Nothing horrible, I hope. Don't worry. They're not real. I call them 'magic carpets'. They do have a proper name, but I never found it out. They show a different picture to whoever looks at them. They show parts of your future as it might be. That's not a lot of use. If they showed what was really going to happen then it would be worth knowing."

"Then you could do something about it? If it showed you in danger in a particular place, you could avoid that place."

"In which case the picture would be wrong! Then you'd think that there was no reason to avoid the danger because the picture lied anyway!"

"Complicated," said Ansylike, thoughtfully. "It must have taken a lot of magic to make them. Did you do it yourself?"

"No, it's beyond my power. A group of magicians worked together to produce them. I won them as a prize for coming first in my class. I've got a certificate too. That was just before they kicked me out!"

"How long ago was it?"

"I don't know. Ages, I expect."

"How long have you been here, then? You must know that?"

"I'm afraid not." Zileika went sadly over to a chair and sat down. "It's part of my punishment. They told me that I would stop here until I grew up. The exact words were: 'You will stay there until you grow up a bit and stop behaving like a spoilt brat!' and I thought they meant a season or two. I didn't imagine that it would be for so long!"

"The ogres!" exclaimed Ansylike. "They came to see you before Grund was born. He must be nearly my age. Well not far off it. You must be a lot older than I am. You can't be a young girl at all." She gazed at the sorceress in horror. Was she really an ancient, old witch? Had she deceived them all? Ansylike couldn't believe that. Zileika was pathetic and she certainly had her faults, but she wasn't evil!

"Time only passes for me when I have company. I don't grow older when I'm alone. I don't need to eat, drink or sleep unless there's a guest in the tower. It has to be someone who wants to be here. I can't even kidnap someone. Of course, nobody comes here unless they're desperate! I'm not allowed to help people without asking them to pay a price. So everyone is afraid of me and thinks I'm mean and spiteful.... I am, a bit, I suppose."

"The price you asked the ogres to pay was mean, wasn't it?"

"Actually it wasn't. I couldn't really do anything to change their natures. Instead, I frightened them. It wasn't easy. They have to concentrate on being good."

"So do you!" laughed Ansylike. "So do you!"

Zileika smiled and felt a bit happier. She wondered whether it was possible to feel miserable for long in the company of her new friend.

She would miss her when she was gone and hoped that she'd return swiftly. It was sensible to stop brooding and feeling sorry for herself.

"I saw you in one of those wall-pictures," said Ansylike changing the subject. It was best, she decided to try and take Zileika's mind off her problems. She was looking depressed. "You were with a man. Shall I tell you who it was?"

"Anyone I know will probably be old before I get out of this prison!" Then she paused and thought for a moment. "Was I still here in this tower?"

"No. Outside, dancing on the grass, I think. I could see a village in the distance. Should I have another look?"

"Yes, do! Please!" The voice of the sorceress was urgent. Any chance of an end to her solitary confinement was wonderful news. However remote the possibility, she clutched at the dream of freedom.

"I don't recognize the village," said Ansylike, as she looked at the picture again. "They are rather strange buildings. Tall, with small turrets, like little castles, but made of wood, I think. There are trees, but they are arranged in rows. They might be an orchard."

"What am I doing? Am I still dancing?"

"Yes. You are dressed in blue. The man plays a flute and you are looking into his eyes."

"Go on!" urged Zileika.

"That's it, really. I can't make out the rest. It's fuzzy at the edges. I don't think it's grass after all. Not where you are. More like a wooden stage."

"Who am I dancing for? Who's playing the music?" demanded Zileika in increasing excitement.

"Oh, sorry. My brother, Andric. He's playing..."

"Andric! I don't believe you. You're making this up!"

"I wouldn't!" protested Ansylike. "I don't torment people or play nasty jokes on them. How could you say that?"

"Sorry. It came as a bit of a shock. I didn't mean to....Honestly, I'm sorry." Zileika looked genuine, so Ansylike forgave her.

"What's wrong with Andric, anyway? He's not that bad! Looking, I mean. Isn't he good enough for you? Prettier girls than you would be flattered!"

"He's an elf. Elves live a lot longer than us. I'd be old and wrinkled before he had one grey hair!"

"I'm sure that you could do something about that! You came first in your class at magic!"

Zileika looked a little pale and her expression suddenly changed. She went back to her chair and closed her eyes.

"That's what I was punished for. I made old people young again! They didn't like it. Not at all! I wouldn't dare to try it again." She opened her eyes. "He is a handsome man, though. It might be worth the risk!" She grinned and winked at Ansylike. "If I was using the spell on myself, no-one could complain. I was very good!"

"This is a wonderful place," said Ansylike, smiling. "I can believe all things are possible when I'm here. It's a shame that it seems like a prison to you. Have you changed your mind about coming with us? I suppose you've got even more need for your magic now."

"I've also got to stay and look after the toads!" She giggled. Ansylike joined in. The sight of the three dwarves in the pond was just too much! "You'll be leaving in the morning, I expect. The sooner you go, the sooner you'll be back. I'll have to make sure that we eat well tonight. What shall we have? Think of something that we can have for a change."

"Worms," replied Ansylike.

"Worms?" Zileika looked at her in disbelief. "I can't eat worms!"

"No, but the toads can!"

The two girls collapsed into fits of laughter.

Zileika was the first to recover and she wiped the tears from her cheeks.

"Let me show you some more of my stuff, then I'll show you properly round your own room. You obviously didn't find the nightdresses!"

"It was nice actually to take my clothes off. Sleeping without a knife strapped to my leg is a change in itself! I felt safe here. I haven't been able to sleep between sheets in such a long time."

"At least you've put on some different clothes. What did you do with the old ones? Lying on the floor in a scrumpled heap, I suppose?"

"Certainly not!" said Ansylike pretending to sound angry. "I left them to soak in the bath."

"You didn't?" asked Zileika. "I don't believe it! The bath is for you, not your clothes! I'll bet that you haven't been in it. I really must teach you how civilised young ladies are meant to behave. You might be invited to a castle, one day. People are often judged by their manners. You won't make a good impression if you leave your clothes in the bath and sleep bare!"

"Who'd know? Why should I care?"

"They have maids, you know, who notice these things and they gossip about the guests. You can't afford to put a foot wrong. Too many nights sleeping under the stars will ruin your chances if you ever meet a prince." Ansylike wrinkled her nose.

Zileika showed Ansylike through her rooms, pointing things out, opening drawers and cupboards and offering her trinkets to examine. She showed her the books of spells that she was studying and warned her not to touch them. They were protected by magic. It was all very interesting, but tiring. She was exhausted by the time that they'd finished. In her pockets she had an assortment of things that the sorceress had insisted that she keep as 'presents' and what she was going to do with them, she didn't know.

"Now let's see your room!" insisted Zileika. "You haven't finished yet."

"I need a rest. I'm worn out," complained Ansylike.

"That's fine by me." Zileika didn't sound disappointed in the least. They walked to the door which opened instantly on command and went in. "You just make yourself comfortable and I'll see to your washing."

When she returned from the bathroom, Ansylike was fast asleep. There was a pile of clothes by the bed. Clearly, she'd just stripped off and curled up under the blankets. There was no point trying to teach some people! Zileika sighed and made her way back to her own room. Nightdresses were wasted on her!

Dinner, as expected, was something special. Ansylike was not always sure what she was eating, but it was delicious. As they intended to make an early start in the morning, they didn't spend too long in conversation after the meal. Zileika, in answer to their questions, told them what she knew of the silver chains and the animals that had attacked them. Only the elven war-lord used such devices.

She had heard of the prophecy, but could add little to what Strell had already said of it. If Ansylike was destined to slay the most powerful individual in the whole of The Desolation, then so be it. However, they would be well advised to avoid trouble, not go seeking it. There was no point knocking on his gate and calmly announcing that they had come to kill him! His magic was not as powerful as Zileika's, but it was enough to defeat the lot of them. "Gromixillion!" she whispered. He was old and cunning!

Once again it was time for bed. At Ansylike's door, Zileika reminded her to have another bath before she left. It might be her last chance to relax in hot water for a long time. She promised that she would.

They all slept soundly and awoke refreshed in the morning. After breakfast, they said goodbye to the toads, who would have to remain in the tower until the spell wore off. At least they would be safe, but that didn't stop them from croaking miserably!

Zileika waved a tearful farewell from the doorway of the tower, then ran after them and made Ansylike promise to take care. She reminded them all of their duty to look after her.

Andric, she seemed to have grown a particular fondness for and she hugged him so tightly that the dwarves turned their heads away. Only Ansylike watched as she clutched his tunic and apologised for threatening to turn him into a toad. He laughed and thanked her for the hospitality that she'd given them all. Then they were on their way. Ansylike glanced over her shoulder and saw the sorceress walking slowly back to the tower. Her shoulders were hunched and her head hung dejectedly forward. She was crying bitter tears of loneliness.

Chapter Ten

GLADE

The weather was good and the ground was firm and not too rocky, so they made fast progress. They were heading for the nearest elven village, but it was more than a day's travel. It meant that they would have to spend a night in the open before they reached it. As the sun was setting, they looked for a place to make a camp. They had a fair choice. There were woods below them and a rocky escarpment above. The site they were on was level and dry.

"I think we should stop here," said Andric. "We can keep a watch and nothing can sneak up on us."

"I prefer the cliffs." Groblic peered up at them as he voiced his opinion. "There are bound to be caves and I like the comfort of stone above my head."

"It's an escarpment," observed Haldriel. "I doubt whether there are many caves! We might find shelter in the rocks, though. We'll certainly need to keep out of the wind. It's getting cool already."

"Then I suggest the forest," interrupted Ansylike. "At least we know that there will be wood for a fire. There's more likely to be a stream, so we can have fresh water. We can't be too far from the elven village and they are sure to keep the forests safe."

"The forest it is then!" declared Haldriel.

"I can see someone moving down there. Just at the edge of the trees. Look! Crawling in the grass!" Ansylike pointed.

"Careful, now," warned Groblic. "Keep together and have your weapons ready!" He took a cautious pace forward. "Aren't you going to load your bow, Haldriel?"

"What sort of creature is that?" came the reply. "A child?" He screwed up his eyes as if that could aid his vision. "It looks to be the size of one of us, but it can't be!"

"Are we going down or not?" asked Ansylike. "We're not going to find out much from here!"

She marched down the hill, knowing the others must follow. Her eyesight was keen and she scanned the trees for any sign of danger. There was none so she didn't slow her progress. She didn't draw her sword either.

The figure in the grass stood up and looked towards them. He was holding a basket over one arm which was full of mushrooms. He appeared to be unarmed and not worried by their approach. He stood where he was and waited.

"We mean you no harm," called Andric. "Wait awhile!" He also checked the trees for a possible threat, while Groblic and Haldriel made sure that they were not being followed.

"Hello, I'm Glade, apprentice wizard and pupil of Lon-Y-Eskrit, the powerful magician. Although his sight is fading, his powers grow by the day. He can weave any spell that you can pay for." He extended a hand in greeting. Ansylike bent down and took it. She shook hands with the tiny man. He seemed friendly enough. "And you are . . .?"

"Ansylike, a traveller in these lands. These are my friends." She introduced them all.

The man before her, or below her, was human but half her size. He was clearly not a dwarf, even smaller, and too slightly built. His hair was as long as hers, but of a coppery brown colour. Green, twinkling eyes glittered below his fringe and his smile seemed to be a permanent feature of his face.

"We're looking for a safe place to spend the night, actually," began Ansylike. "As I said, we're travelling and we were thinking of sleeping in the forest here. If you could offer us . . . ?"

"Think nothing of it," replied Glade. "Just follow me and be careful not to tread on the herbs. Keep to the path or I'll have to tend them all again tomorrow."

"You look after the trees?" asked Ansylike as she followed in his footsteps. It was not easy as his legs were short and hers were long. She had to keep her eyes on where she was putting her feet and she hoped that the dwarves behind here were being as careful.

"No. The trees look after themselves. I pick the herbs and gather the edible mushrooms. As you see, I have a basket of them." He held it up for her inspection.

"Where are we going?" called Groblic.

"Just a little bit further. And here we are!" replied Glade. He stopped and pointed to a wooden building in a clearing. "The inn. It's a bit rough, but it's cheap. And it's almost empty at the moment so there's bound to be plenty of room for you. Let me take you inside." He offered Ansylike a hand.

"I'll lead, if you don't mind," insisted Haldriel, pushing his way forward. "I think we'd better be on our guard." Groblic nodded and kept a tight grip on his war-hammer. Andric stood alert with his right hand on the hilt of his sword.

"It's not that rough!" insisted Glade. "We have our own rooms, of course, but no-one has complained even in the communal rooms. There have been no robberies. No fights. Pretty boring really!"

"It looks safe enough to me," called Haldriel as he peered into the gloom. He had opened the door and looked inside. There were no customers. Other than that, it seemed ordinary. Except it was dark. They filed inside, carefully.

A man behind the bar smiled and offered them a drink. There was no-one else, except an ancient figure in long robes sitting in a corner. On the table in front of him was the remains of a meal. He must have lost his appetite as it was mostly uneaten. He was reading a big, leather-bound volume by the light of a single candle.

"That's the magician," explained Glade. "He's a bit deaf. You can book your rooms at the bar and order a meal. The wine is quite good, but I'd go easy on the ale. It's a bit strong!"

"What's that about my ale, Master Glade? I hope you're not giving these fine people the wrong impression!" The serving man scowled from behind the bar.

"I was telling them that the drinks are not watered down here. They're good and strong," lied Glade.

"Hmm, well, that's all right then. Now what can I get for you all?" He wiped his hands on his apron and nodded towards the display of barrels and bottles behind him.

"Brewed them all myself. Only the finest ingredients. Can I interest you in some pipe-weed?" Pulling the stopper from an enormous, clay jar he passed it over the bar.

"We want rooms for the night. How much do you charge?" asked Haldriel. The price seemed fair to him so he accompanied the innkeeper to check them. The others moved over to a table by the only unshuttered window. It was the only light spot in a very murky tavern. Glade poured drinks, measured out the pipe-weed and brought it over. Then he decided to join them and climbed on to a stool opposite Ansylike. They didn't object as he had helped them and asked for nothing in return. Besides, he might have information of use.

"It's very dark in here!" complained Andric. "That chap is having to read by candlelight. Why don't they open some of these shutters?"

"Or light a fire?" suggested Ansylike.

"Not much point, really," replied Glade. "We are the only customers and you weren't expected. There's only Flegg here now. He has to do everything himself. Prepare the food, gather the firewood, serve the drinks, tidy the rooms . . ."

"Yes, I get the point," interrupted Ansylike. "Don't you do anything to help?"

"We could, of course. We've offered, but he won't let us. It's a matter of pride. We're paying guests and guests are not expect to serve themselves, although I just did."

"It must be very quiet, then. Where is everyone?"

"There's been a lot of trouble, recently. Men fighting elves and so on. It's like a lot of little wars, rather than one big battle. It's been going on for years. The two sides are wearing each other down. I can see no end to it!" He looked sadly at Ansylike, then past her, out of the window. His eyes widened. "Here's trouble!" he shouted and startled them all. "Close the shutters! Bar the door!" He was off his stool in an instant and running to the foot of the staircase. "Flegg!" he shouted. "The bears are back!"

Andric took one look outside before he closed and barred the shutters.

"He's right! They're big ones and they've not come to picnic in the woods!" He saw that Haldriel had already shut the door. He had dropped the heavy bar across it and was busy sliding the bolts into place. Behind him stood Groblic with his war-hammer in his hands.

Ansylike suddenly realised that it was no longer dark in the room. The magician's candle had brightened until its radiance lit every corner. He might be deaf, but he knew when trouble was brewing. She was just thinking that they would all be safe, when there was a loud crash at the door. The whole frame shook and splinters of wood burst inwards. That would not last for long! The shutters were less strong. The bears could be through them in no time! They would have to fight for their lives. She drew her sword and moved into the centre of the room. Glade had scurried up the stairs. That left her, Andric, the magician and Groblic to face the bears.

"How many did you see?" she asked anxiously.

"About six," replied Andric.

"Oh, scrollions!" cursed Ansylike. "We're in it now!" She rested her blade on her left shoulder, holding it with both hands.

The door could not stand such a powerful attack and burst in, shattered, followed by a bear that had to crouch to pass through the opening it had made.

Groblic's war-hammer crunched into its gut, ripping through the thick fur. He braced himself and pulled it free. The bear staggered, bellowing with rage and pain. Then it came forward again. Haldriel fired from the stairs and his bolt struck it between the eyes. It was enough. Before the bear hit the floor, another had charged in and it brushed Groblic aside with one sweep of a paw. Ansylike ducked and parried as it swiped at her. Another came in and Andric engaged it in ferocious combat. Then another lumbered past them. By this time, the magician had finished preparing a spell and a jet of flame sprang from his outstretched palm and incinerated the bear which was coming towards him. Then he composed himself to prepare another spell and slid under the table, out of harm's way!

Flegg charged down the stairs past Haldriel, carrying an axe and a shield. He judged that Groblic needed help the most and came to his aid. He had only delivered a few blows when another bear bore down on him and he had to give that his full attention.

Ansylike held her sword in both hands, ducked, crouched and thrust upwards. The blade bit deep into the bear's chest and stuck there. It fell back, mortally wounded, taking her sword with it!

Defenceless she flicked her eyes around for another weapon as a new foe waved its claws at her and approached with arms outstretched. Its lips curled back in a grimace, to reveal its dagger-sharp teeth. There was no escape. She saw that it would soon gather her into its deadly hug and bite her face off! Help came unexpectedly. Glade dodged in front of her and struck with a short sword into the groin of the crazed animal.

"Run!" he urged, as the bear clawed down at him. There was no help that Ansylike could give so she dived for the ground and rolled out of reach.

Groblic was used to the sort of fighting where he stood face to face with an enemy and pounded away. Dwarves had a reputation for standing fast and not giving ground. To retreat was considered to be an act of cowardice. He was, therefore, not having much success with an opponent that kept backing, feinting blows and delivering mighty swipes from either paw! His armour had taken so much damage that his chain shirt was ripped into shreds and hung uselessly from his shoulders. His arms were both bleeding, scored and gashed. He didn't have the reach to deliver a blow to the bear's head and it seemed to be unworried by the damage that was being done to its body.

Andric started with an advantage as he was standing on a table when he began battle. He managed to get in a few deadly slashes with his sword before the bear kicked the table so hard that it overturned, sending him hurtling to the floor. Agile and well-used to battle, he rolled and sprang to his feet before the bear had the chance to maul him. He was evenly matched and it took all his skill as a swordsman to keep his opponent at bay. Flegg was also holding his own and he was sure that time would give him the chance to get in under the bear's guard. All were kept very busy, so there was dismay when another two bears lumbered through the door.

A bolt from Haldriel's crossbow sped through the air and pierced the eye of one of them, but the other came in unchallenged and made its way, purposefully, towards Ansylike. She had both hands on the hilt of her sword and was trying desperately to pull it free from the bear she'd slain. Even with a boot on its chest, she couldn't move it. This time there was no sign of Glade to help her.

"Oh, Mother!" she exclaimed as the yellow fangs menaced her.

"Coming, dear!" came the instant reply.

A bear-hug can crack a man's ribs in seconds. An ogre-hug can crack a bear's ribs even faster! Drole's wife linked her mighty arms around the bear's chest and squeezed once, then she hauled the lifeless animal to one side and smiled at Ansylike, who gazed at her in astonishment.

"Let me," she continued and drew Ansylike's sword with ease. "You won't need this just yet, so you'll not mind if Mother borrows it for a moment." She made her way heavily towards the bear that Groblic was having problems with and tapped it on the shoulder with the blade. It whirled and caught the full force of her left fist under its jaw. Its head jerked back as its neck snapped and it lifted off its feet and crashed on to Groblic. She went to help Flegg and the result was the same. Before long, the bears were ready to be made into rugs!

"Now take this sword, dear, and be more careful what you stick it into." She pounded at her apron and sent clouds of flour into the air. "I can't stop long," she explained. "The spell only allows you to have my help for a short time."

"What spell?" gasped Ansylike. "How did you get here?"

"You called on your mother for help," the ogress replied. "Now I'm your mother. It was part of the deal with Zileika. She does have her good points. Unfortunately you can't ask for my assistance again until after the next full moon. I hope you'll manage on your own."

"Thank you," was all Ansylike could think of. It was clearly not enough so she put her arms, as far as she could reach, round the ogress and hugged her.

"My child!" soothed Mother, stroking Ansylike's hair gently and dusting the flour off. "Such a gentle child. Such a dear!" She gazed sternly at Groblic, who was still flat on the floor, although he'd managed to crawl free of the bear. "You'd better take good care of her, now, or you'll have me to deal with!" The dwarf nodded as he ran a hand over his chest to check that all the vital bits were still there. A loud pop followed and the ogress was gone. Ansylike staggered forward and braced herself against a table.

Lon-Y-Eskrit peered at her and wondered what sort of magic enabled this slip of a girl to summon such help when she was in a tricky spot!

"I think we could all do with a drink. I'll pour us some ale," offered Flegg returning to the bar. "I can assure you that this doesn't happen often."

"Where's Glade?" asked Ansylike. The others looked about them and over their shoulders, but he was nowhere to be seen. Then she saw a tiny arm hanging out from beneath the body of a bear. "Help me, quickly!" she demanded as she ran towards it. "He's under here!"

They rolled the bear away and Glade was indeed under it, but unconscious. Even the magician showed concern and shuffled over to see if his apprentice was still alive. He was, but only just, and his chest fluttered lightly. A claw had ripped down his face and the wound continued over his shoulder. He'd been knocked unconscious by the weight crashing down on him and this had also squeezed out much of his blood. His face was pale and his lips were tinged with the blue coldness of death.

"Get him onto the table, before it's too late," said Lon-Y-Eskrit. "I have some healing powers. I might be able to save him. It'll be close, though."

"Let me try first!" ordered Ansylike. "I might be able to do better without your spells." She went to fetch the flask that held the healing water while Glade was being lifted onto the table. The magician waited. He knew that there was little that he could do. His energy had gone into the fire spell and he had few reserves.

"Pour this down his throat. I'll hold his head. Don't spill any." Ansylike issued instructions and the magician obeyed.

Haldriel stood by the door, his crossbow loaded and watched for any fresh attacks. Groblic stood behind him, ignoring the blood that was trickling down his chest. Andric went outside to see if there was any danger round the back. Flegg poured the beer.

"He's coming to! I think he'll be all right. Keep pouring. Give him as much as he can drink." Holding his head back, Ansylike saw that Glade was beginning to swallow. His lips were returning to their usual colour and the blood stopped flowing from his wounds. Gently, she laid him back to rest and thanked her luck that she had filled both of her flasks with the water. Glade had saved her from certain death and almost lost his own life in the process.

"A survivor, this one," said the magician as he saw the life returning to his apprentice. "He killed a troll once! Sneaked up on it from behind while his friends were having a really hard time. He's no slouch when it comes to battle. Pity he's so little. He would have made a fine warrior."

"He is a fine warrior already!" stated Ansylike. "He saved me when I thought that all was lost. I can never thank him enough for that."

"You already have," came the unexpected response from Glade. Then he slipped into the deep sleep of recovery. Ansylike draped her cloak over him and sighed.

"That's a relief."

"You're not going to like this!" called Haldriel. "We've got more company!" He looked out of the door at the troop of riders approaching. It was a full-sized war-band, perhaps fifty men in light armour. They did not look like a party of sightseers! They meant business! Haldriel took the bolt from his crossbow and loosened the string. Best to look friendly and avoid trouble. Groblic lowered his war-hammer.

Flegg began pouring ale. This was good for business, if they were willing to pay. They might slit his throat instead, but that was an occupational hazard. He whistled a cheery tune, a little off-key. It was annoying enough to wake Glade, who dangled his legs off the table and dropped to the floor. Ansylike helped him up and placed him in a chair. His eyes were still hooded, but he seemed to be recovering remarkably well.

"Ho!" commanded the leader of the riders and the troop behind him reined in their horses. He dismounted and strode towards the inn. "We're on the track of some bears. They're dangerous and might be heading this way. Have you seen any signs of them?" He addressed Haldriel, but his gaze was drawn, halfway through his speech, to the scene within. He didn't wait for a reply, but walked past the dwarf. He couldn't believe what he was seeing! "All dead. All of them!" He motioned for his Lieutenant to witness the carnage. "Well done!" he boomed. His troops gathered around him. "You killed them?" The tone of his voice was full of disbelief. "I have 200 men with me and we've tracked these creatures ever since they left their lairs. I wasn't sure that I could defeat them. How many of you are there?"

"Just us," replied Ansylike, "but we had a little help."

"My name is Ar-Vang. I lead these men in our war with the elves. I can see that you're an elf, of sorts, but your actions tell me that you are on our side. How did you overcome the were-bears?"

"As you heard, we had a little help." Ansylike was unwilling to tell this stranger the full story. She merely nodded in the direction of the magician who was reading another of his books.

"Him? He can only manage one spell a day, if he's sober and that's a rarity! You must have more magic than that. Or else you have powerful magic of your own." He waited for an answer, but there was none. He then noticed Ansylike's sword on the table where she had left it. He made no attempt to touch it, but stared at it in fascination. "So, it's returned! The Rune-Blade! As was promised! No wonder the bears lost to you." He faced Ansylike and bowed his head. "We will serve you, Lady. Wherever you lead us into battle, we will follow. My men are at your command and they're a fine troop. No cowards ride behind me. Our swords have tasted elven blood."

Ansylike watched as he knelt before her. His Lieutenant did the same. Outside, a cheer went up as the news spread. "The elf-slayer has returned! Victory is ours!" The noise continued to rise in volume until it became more like the sound of battle itself. Ansylike turned in horror and went to Groblic for support. He'd patched up his wounds and rubbed a healing balm over them to stop the spread of infection. His chain shirt, however, was ruined and lay on the floor beside him.

"Problems, Spud?" he asked gently.

"They think I'm going to lead them in the war against the elves! It's something to do with the sword. I really wish I knew where Cledrin got it from!"

"I doubt whether he could tell you himself. He's not a grave-robber. He doesn't spend silver on weapons that he can't use himself. It must have been given to him by a wizard. Someone who wanted it passed on to you. A powerful magician, a sorcerer . . . Why else would he have carried it so far and then given it to you?"

"Why me?"

"I wonder how many people have asked that? It must be the most popular question in the . . . Why you, indeed? You are not entirely human and not really an elf. You have no sympathy with either side. Nor have we. Dwarves are not fond of humans or elves."

There was no time for further discussion, Ar-Vang was too close. He was supervising his men as they carried the bodies of the bears off the premises. Even four men were not enough to heave one body off the ground and they had to drag and push them. As one passed Ansylike, she noticed the silver chain around its neck. She had a close look at the rest of the bodies and found that they all bore similar chains. Haldriel had noticed too and he nodded to Ansylike to show that he was aware that this was another planned attack on them.

Flegg eventually set the table for dinner. He was well assisted by the cook of the war-band and his quartermaster and their servants. They knew how to cater for large numbers of hungry people. The meal was adequate, but not very tasty. There was enough, but it didn't do much except fill them up. Zileika's table was far more satisfying. Before Ansylike had finished eating, some of the men had begun to fill their smoking pipes.

That was too much! She made her excuses and left the table to get some fresh air. Her plate was half full, but she had no appetite for it. Better food was fed to pigs.

Outside the inn there was a small group engaged in conversation around a table. She decided to join them. They all stood up when she approached. That was a bad sign! It was not only courtesy, it was because she was a girl. She kept her anger under control and took the seat that was offered to her. There was silence.

"We were talking about you." Ar-Vang stood and, putting his knuckled hands on the table, he leant over to face Ansylike. "Will you fight with us or not? The battle may be won with your help, but we will win without it. It will just take a little longer." There was iron in his voice and determination in his eyes. He was prepared to fight to the death for his cause.

Ansylike accepted the pot of ale that was held before her and took a sip. It was horrible and she had to restrain herself from spitting it out. Bitter, sour and strong enough to make the blood rush to her cheeks, it was a strange brew.

The men around the table were looking at her with unusual interest. She was just waiting for one of them to ask her if she was a frequent visitor to this inn. A messenger appeared and whispered into Ar-Vang's ear and that was the end of the conversation. He called his men to arms and bade Ansylike a hasty farewell. Within moments he was back in the saddle and his troops were hard on his heels. She sipped her pot of ale alone and watched them trot off. It took some time for the procession of riders to pass her and she was almost at the bottom of the glass before Groblic joined her.

"They've put an armed guard around this place," he began. "We'll not get out of here without an escort. They expect you to stand at the side of Ar . . . what's-his-name in the big battle that's planned." He looked at her carefully, but he was sure what her reply would be.

"We're not on the side of anyone," she began. "We don't know who's right and who's wrong. How can I fight for Ar-Vang? Can't we just sneak off?" She looked into Groblic's eyes and saw that he was smiling. She had expected him to have a much more serious demeanour. He grinned and patted her on the shoulder.

"You're learning!"

"Then let's chip off when we can. Perhaps tonight when the guards are asleep?" Ansylike whispered, but her words reached other ears. Glade stood unnoticed in the shadows. He went to pack his possessions and to say goodbye to the magician who had taught him very little. This was an adventure that he didn't want to miss.

"Has Andric been in touch with you? He was outside when the soldiers appeared and I've not seen him since."

"No," replied Ansylike. She looked carefully around. "He must be hiding in the trees. He's very good at avoiding people if he doesn't want to be noticed. He'll wait until he's sure that we're safe."

"It won't be easy to get out of here. These soldiers are not likely to be snoozing when they're on guard. We'll need a plan. I'll have a word with Glade. He must know the woods and he'll show us where we can hide." Groblic then left and made his way inside, leaving Ansylike to finish the dregs of her ale. It wasn't too bad after all and she decided to have another one. She licked her lips.

The torches on the walls were all lit and a fire burned in the hearth, giving the inn a much jollier atmosphere. Flegg was behind the bar, whistling again and pouring ale. Ansylike settled herself on a stool and waved her empty tankard at him. Soon he had filled it and she was sipping the strong, bitter ale. Ar-Vang's Lieutenant came over to join her and asked whether she minded his company. She noticed that he wasn't drinking. Probably he was still on duty and needed to keep a clear head.

"Where did your commander go?" she asked. "He certainly left in a hurry. Are there more bears around?"

"My name is Gunsel and I am second-in-command. My sword is

yours and for your protection." He bowed his head as he made this formal introduction. "The answer to your question is that we have received news of an elven war-band coming from the north. Ar-Vang has taken the men to intercept it."

"I see." For a moment Ansylike was thoughtful and said nothing. She sipped at her ale and wondered how much she should say to this soldier. "Did you notice the silver chains around the necks of those bears?" she asked.

"I could hardly miss them! It proves that they're not ordinary creatures. They are the servants of Gromixillion, the elven war-lord. They were probably sent for you! He will try again. He must know where that sword of yours is. That's why you must have an armed guard round you at all times."

"What does this elf want? Does he want the sword?"

"He wants to kill you! I suppose he wants the sword too, but you are far more important to him. I'm surprised that he could trace you in these woods, though. They're enchanted. His magic is not the sort that can break through spells that the wizards have cast."

"How do you mean?" Ansylike was puzzled. "Are there different sorts of magic?"

"Indeed there are! Gromixillion has the ability to enchant creatures and people. Creatures are easier, of course. The magic is in the silver chains. They bring the animals under his control. He can only work that sort of magic on people if they agree to it or if he can deceive them. He cannot trace people who are hiding from him, except by using his animals as spies and they can't operate in an enchanted wood! He must be getting help from someone."

"Maybe he was just lucky?" offered Ansylike.

"No chance!" Gunsel laughed. "The sooner we have his head on a pole, the better. Anyway, I have work to do. If there's anything that you need, just let me know. You'll be safe here now." He bowed his head again and strode off to check that the guards were alert.

"What did you make of that?" came a voice from below. Ansylike jumped and looked down to see Glade, standing at her side.

"You startled me! Do you always creep up on people like that?" she asked crossly. "It's very rude!"

"Sorry. I didn't mean to upset you. I've spent so long practising at keeping quiet that I sometimes . . . well, forget my manners."

"Well, so you should be! Sorry, I mean."

"I am!"

"Good!"

"Are you going to forgive me, then?"

"Oh, all right. What do you want?" Ansylike did not sound as if she had forgiven him. She was annoyed and worried and Glade was the only person who happened to be around for her to take her anger out on.

"Don't snap at me. I have feelings too!" he insisted. "I don't have to help you. You can ride at the head of the army if you want. That's what they have planned for you!"

"I'm sorry. It must be the ale that's making me bad-tempered," apologised Ansylike, with as much grace as she could manage. Her nerves were on edge and she was quite ready to snap again!

"If we're going to get out of here, it'll have to be tonight. When Ar-Vang returns there'll be no chance of sneaking off. You'll need my help to get through the woods. I know a way that will make it difficult for them to track us. I'm going on one of my herb-collecting trips. I'll have a word with Andric and tell him where to meet us. Have a rest and don't drink any more of that ale. It puts you in the mood for fighting!"

Ansylike looked at the tankard she was holding. It was nearly empty. She had sipped her way through a quart of the stuff. No wonder she was feeling grim! She put the pot down and made her way unsteadily to the stairs. If she could get her head down for a couple of hours, she might feel better.

It was well after midnight before they assembled in the forest. It had not been easy to leave without attracting any attention, but they'd managed it. Glade led them, by the light of the moon, to a rocky slope.

"We'll lose them here," he explained. "They can follow our tracks to this point, but no further. We'll keep to the stones and make our way to the cliffs. Not far from there is an elven village. It's one of the neutral places where we can take refuge. By tomorrow night we'll be in safe hands!"

Through the darkness they made their way, climbing ever upwards until they reached the long shadow of the cliffs. From a distance they had seemed to be nothing more than an escarpment, a thin line of rock on the horizon. Lit by the moon they seemed ominous and threatening. Above them, the jagged peaks of twisted stone reared like claws, poised to strike down at the land and tear it to shreds.

"Do we have to go up there?" Ansylike stared at the wall of rock that faced them. "It'll take days!"

"You're right," agreed Haldriel. "We can't climb that in a single day and I can see no caves that we can hide in. The soldiers of Ar-Vang can hardly fail to notice us up there. We'll have to go around it." He looked at Glade who merely shook his head.

"There is no way around. The only way is over the top, unless the elves have invited you. There are tunnels, but there's no way of getting through the traps that line them. I hope you can all climb well."

"There's no way we can get over that. We'll have to try something else," commented Andric gloomily.

"I've got an idea!" said Ansylike. "Yes! I know what we can do."

The others watched curiously as she got on her knees and put her mouth close to the rock. "Granite!" she called. "I need your help. It's Ansylike. I need a lift."

The stone before them gradually transformed itself until a face appeared. The eyes opened. Even though they all knew what to expect, they stood back in fear. All, except Glade. He didn't know what to expect. He fell to his knees in absolute terror and scurried backwards as fast as he could. Groblic stopped him by putting a foot on his bottom. His hands still scrabbled at the stone while his eyes were fixed open at the giant in the wall.

"I'm here!" said Granite. "Going up?"

"Please," answered Ansylike. "We're in a spot of bother."

"Step in," he replied and opened a mouth that a wagon could have turned round in.

Groblic seized Glade by the collar and hauled him, still struggling, into the mouth of the giant. The rest followed into the grey cavern. Their ascent was rapid and it was only a matter of seconds before they found themselves safely on the grass again. Ansylike remembered how important it was to be polite, so she turned to thank the stone-giant for his assistance and for getting them out of trouble.

"Trouble!" he said. "You think you're in trouble. Zileika is in far more trouble than you are. Do you know that she's been captured? I suppose you don't. No matter. Just thought that you should know. We're even now. Don't bother me again for a while. I must sleep." Ignoring Ansylike's pleas for more information he sank into the ground and was seen no more.

"You know the sorceress?" asked Glade. He was still shaking and was on his knees in the grass.

"Yes," replied Ansylike, "we do." She considered the implications of this news. "We left some friends of ours at the tower, under her protection. I wonder what will happen to them now?"

"Look at this!" urged Haldriel, as he came running towards them. "I've been looking at the elven village. It's over this hill." He beckoned them to see for themselves. "Look! It's devastated!"

"Who could have done such a thing?" asked Andric as he made his way over the ridge and towards the little village that lay, nestled, in the valley below.

His heart felt like lead and thumped against his ribs as he got closer to the ruins that had once been a neutral zone. The smoke from the burning houses could scarcely mask the stench of death that hung over the place. The thin plumes of smoke and the swarms of carrion flies were the only things that were moving. All the buildings were burning. Nothing remained intact.

"That's the banner of Ar-Vang!" called Glade who was still on the ridge. "Take cover!"

"Too late for that!" commanded a voice. "Raise your hands and make no move for your weapons, or you die here!" The party cursed

themselves for being caught out again. It was just unbelievable. They
were surrounded by troops and many of them had crossbows ready to
fire. "March down!"

There was no alternative. They marched. In single file, with their
hands behind their heads, they trudged down the mountain towards the
village that played no part in the war, but had been destroyed anyway.
The smell of death grew stronger. With a shock, Ansylike realised that
the posts that surrounded the village had elven heads impaled on them.
Ar-Vang was not in the habit of taking prisoners.

The villagers had been slaughtered! Not a dog stirred on the streets.
The long shadows of early morning revealed fresh horrors and Ansylike
had to turn her eyes away to avoid looking at the butchery that had
taken place.

Chapter Eleven

RESCUE

One stone building remained. Here it was that Ar-Vang was holding court. His scowl and pursed lips did not promise them any favours.

"So, you tried to escape! This time I'll make sure that you don't!" He toyed with a dagger and sat behind a large wooden desk. "I didn't trust you from the start. I don't like elven blood except on my sword!" He stood up suddenly and ordered his guards. "Take them out and put them in irons." He waited to see that the guards were obeying his orders before he spat on the floor and resumed his seat. In his anger he failed to notice the crow that perched on the open window. It wore a silver chain around its neck. No-one else marked its flight as it returned to its master, Gromixillion!

It was in the dead of night that the attack came. It was as ferocious as it was unexpected. The elves rose from the ground and their arrows cut down the soldiers of Ar-Vang before they even knew that they were in danger. They whistled death through the moonlight and cut through armour as if it were cloth.

Ar-Vang didn't know that they were under attack until his chin was raised by the point of an elven leaf-sword. It was the last thing he saw before his throat was slashed and he fell lifeless onto the floor.

"There are prisoners here! Shall I release them?" a distinctly elven voice shouted from outside the door where Ansylike and the dwarves were being held. They were all chained to the walls. Andric had been beaten brutally and the blood from his wounds matted his hair. One of his legs was bowed and he kept himself upright on the other one. His captors were unworried by the state of their victims. Ansylike was the only one of importance to them and they were sure that they could make her do what they wanted. Given enough persuasion.

"Let me see them first. Are any of them elves?"

"No, Lord."

"Idiots!" hissed the elven captain as he entered the cellar. "Get them free, now!" Springing into action his soldiers had the chains undone in moments. Their fingers nervously worked the keys in the locks.

Ansylike was particularly grateful at being released. It was no fun being chained up in a wine cellar. She made hasty excuses and dashed off to find a toilet. Groblic was indignant. He was not fond of being locked up and being released by an elf made matters worse. It was too humiliating for words. Haldriel had been thinking. He was sure that rescue would come, so he had waited patiently. He thought over the situation and came to the conclusion that the soldiers of Ar-Vang must have used magic to keep themselves hidden. How else could they have appeared so suddenly on the ridge? If the tunnels were so heavily trapped, then they couldn't have passed through them. Someone had betrayed the elves. Who?

"Dwarves! Why the High Lord would want to speak with you I can't imagine. I've not seen many of your folk in these parts and I can tell you that you're not welcome. Still . . . enemies of Ar-Vang must be friends of ours." The elven captain chuckled. "Come with me. You can talk in one of the rooms upstairs." He led the way. For some reason he seemed to find the situation highly amusing.

"Where's Spud?" asked Groblic.

"Who?" The elven captain stopped on the stairs and looked back at the dwarves that were following him. "Does she allow you to call her 'Spud'? A humble root vegetable!" His surprise was plain. His arched eyebrows drew back until they formed a perfect vee. "The maiden-warrior of the prophecy is called Spud?" He roared with laughter. "This can't be real!"

Groblic and Haldriel exchanged glances. Groblic shrugged. He had no answers. Haldriel gave the elf a push.

"Get a move on. We've spent enough time down here and we're worried about our friends. I don't see what there is to laugh about. Gee up!" He obeyed and soon they were in a room that was considerably more comfortable than the chambers where they'd been chained. Groblic rubbed his wrists and muttered a curse at the guards who had bound him so tightly to the wall. Andric seemed to have suffered the most, but he was conscious. Two elves carried him to a bench and laid him out to rest.

"The leg is broken, but it will mend. The wounds on his head are deep, but there is no sign of infection. I can treat him here if you wish?"

The elven medic talked as he inspected Andric's injuries. He addressed his comments to the Commander who sat behind a heavy oak desk. "Shall I take him outside?"

"Do what you have to. Treat him here." The elf behind the desk was an imposing figure. He stood and it was immediately obvious that he was taller than any of the others. He wore black leather armour. Around his wrists hung an assortment of silver chains.

"My name if Gromixillion. I lead the elves in their battle for land." He snapped a finger and a guard entered the room. "Bring her in!" he commanded. Ansylike was escorted into the room and a chair was brought for her. The dwarves said nothing. This was the commander of the elven armies. The dreaded High-Elf, who fought a war against all humans, laughed and took a seat.

"Spud!" his laughter was mocking. "Did you really think that you were going to kill me?"

Ansylike sat and stared at this cruel elf. She wished that she had her sword to finish him off on the spot, then wondered whether he could read her thoughts.

"Bring me the blade!" he ordered and an elf in full chain armour went off to obey his command. He clattered out of the room. "We'll see if you are up to it!" he shouted. His cheeks were aflame with rage. "Did you see the heads of my people on stakes out there? Did you see them? These folk have never done any harm to anyone!"

"What's that got to do with us?" asked Haldriel.

"Everything!" came the terse reply. "Without me the elves will be defeated. Have you seen how they butcher us? Have you counted the number of elven heads that are dangling on wooden stakes out there? This village decided to be on no-one's side. The people were unwilling to get involved. Now they're all dead. Every man, woman and child . . . all dead. No-one is neutral. All must decide which side they are on."

"That means us, I suppose?" asked Haldriel. "You want us to pick which side we're on?"

"Your sword, I believe." Gromixillion held the leaf-blade that was given to him by one of his servants. He cradled it in his arms. Suddenly he pulled it free of its scabbard. "Take your weapon, Spud!" he insisted. "Defeat me in combat!" He offered her the sword. Take it! Are you afraid?"

Ansylike had no idea what she was supposed to do. She didn't like being called 'Spud' by this elf, but that was no reason to kill him. She'd put up with worse insults than that! She said nothing and didn't take the sword. "Let me make it easier for you," urged the elven commander. He held the point of the sword towards his heart.

The hilt was only a finger-length from Ansylike's face. "If you are the one to kill me, then do it now. Just push the blade and kill me! Go on!" He paused with the point of the sword at the base of his ribs, then spun the blade into the air. "This is what I think of your prophecy and the fools that believe in it!" He cracked the sword down, over his knee, and broke it in two. "Now you can have it back!" He dropped the pieces into Ansylike's scabbard and gave it back to her. "Wear your broken sword!" She had no alternative so she strapped it round her waist and waited for him to continue. Perhaps she should have killed him when she had the chance, but it was not easy to kill in cold blood. Strell had been right. "Take them to the castle!" ordered Gromixillion. "Our work here is done. Finish burying the dead and follow me when you can."

"All of them? The humans too?"

"All of them. There are no enemies after death. I don't want Ar-Vang's head on a pole. Give him the honour of a warrior who died in battle. Let all see that we have respect for our foes. Now take this lot away."

"I don't want to move this one yet," complained the medic who was tending Andric. "I must finish setting the bones."

"Take the rest and leave him here. I can show mercy to my enemies. Even the ones who are trying to kill me."

Ansylike was going to protest, but Groblic nudged her and she thought better of it. At least they were not going to be killed. They had found the elves at last, or been found by them, and the dwarves would be able to make their offer. She wondered why Haldriel had not explained the real purpose of their mission. As she was led out, she cast an eye at Andric, who was having his leg set. By the look of pain on his face she could see that it was really hurting. Ar-Vang's men had not been at all gentle. They all owed their lives to the elves! Being caught up in a war was certainly complicated if you didn't know which side to fight on and it all seemed so senseless.

The ride was uneventful. Ansylike was fairly good with horses, but the dwarves were not, so they'd been loaded onto a wagon. She chose to join them as it would give her the chance to talk and plan what they were going to do next. Haldriel seemed to think that all was going very well. Groblic was not so sure. Glade made few comments. He was not a good traveller and longed for his feet to be on firm ground again.

The cart bounced and joggled them about and they were all glad when they came in sight of the elven castle. It was small, as castles go, but its defence were impressive. A wide moat surrounded it and the guards on the battlements stood in alert ranks, their bows at the ready. Banners flew from the higher towers and smoke rose from a score of chimneys. Evidently it was a busy place. Over the drawbridge they went and under arches, until the squadron drew up in a courtyard. Glade slid off the wagon and fell to his knees in the dust. He clutched his stomach and closed his eyes. Ansylike had suffered less on the journey and was only feeling tired. The dwarves were in good spirits and chattered to each other as they admired the construction of the castle. Stone buildings were a fascination to them. This one was spectacular!

Flying buttresses, high turrets from which guards peered down at them curiously and arched doorways were the subjects of their attention. Ansylike was more taken with the gibbet that stood in one shadowy corner. It was a type of gallows from which criminals were hung. She had seen such a thing, many moons ago, in a town she had passed through. Thieves were hanging from the ropes while the onlookers cheered at their deaths. It was not a happy memory! She sincerely hoped that such a fate would not befall her and the companions that had come so far into The Desolation.

"Admiring the gibbet?" asked one of the elven guards, who took up a place beside her. "Don't worry. It's a trophy of war. We captured it. Only elves have hung from that thing. We don't torture our prisoners. If Gromixillion decides that you're to die then you are sure of a swift, clean death. We favour the axe, but a sword will do the job just as well, if you prefer it!" He ran the nail of his index finger across the back of Ansylike's neck and she shuddered. He laughed. "That fate is not for you. Don't shiver! You may become the queen of these lands before long!"

"Queen?" she asked. "Are you serious?" By the expression on his face she couldn't tell. It was a dreadful prospect. Even the gibbet seemed inviting by comparison!

She looked around for Groblic, but he and Haldriel were still admiring the architecture. The elf walked off and left her to her thoughts.

"Not what you had in mind?" came a voice from beside her. She jumped.

"I thought I told you not to sneak up on me!" she hissed at Glade. "You really are a pest!"

"All that about not believing in the prophecy is lies," he continued, without taking offence. "He believes all right! he thinks that he's found a way around it."

"What do you mean?" Ansylike took a sudden interest in what Glade was saying. "Do you know exactly what the prophecy foretold?" She seized his shoulder and shook him in her impatience. He went suddenly pale and his eyelids fluttered. "Sorry. That was unkind of me." Her hand was wet and she was just going to wipe it on her tunic when she realised that it was covered in blood. "You've been injured!" she exclaimed. "Why didn't you say?" Glade breathed heavily.

"It's nothing much. Just a scratch. I'll be all right."

"Rubbish! Groblic!" she called at the top of her voice. "Here, now!" As Groblic and Haldriel ran over to see what the emergency was, she held Glade to her side. How could she have failed to notice the blood that soaked his jacket?

"This is a serious wound," said Groblic as he examined the gash on Glade's back. "He must have lost a lot of blood. He'll need more help than I can give him."

An elven warrior came over and peered over Groblic's shoulder. He took one look and waved to some passing soldiers for assistance. Before long a small crowd had gathered and a stretcher was carried out to bear Glade away.

"I wonder when they're going to feed us," said Haldriel. "I'm famished."

"He was just going to tell me about the prophecy," returned Ansylike. "I don't think that we've heard the full story yet."

"I can tell you," offered an elf who was standing close by. "You'll know soon anyway."

They all turned to look at him. He was short by elven standards and wore his hair in braids. His clothes were a mixture of colours as if he had selected them from his wardrobe in the dark. Even his socks didn't match and one leg of his trousers was longer than the other. His boots curled up at the ends. "I know all of the prophecies. I've spent much time reading. Do you want to know?"

"We do," replied Ansylike. "Tell us all you know!"

"That may take some time. Will you join me?"

Chapter Twelve

GARRET

"Where do you want us to go?" asked Haldriel with more than a trace of suspicion in his voice. He was trusting by nature, but that didn't extend to elves. They were a shifty lot and he knew that their sweetest words were often laced with poison.

"To my quarters. I have a comfortable room for myself and there are plenty of spare rooms that you are welcome to use. Weary travellers can always find lodging at my humble abode." He flashed a smile at them and grinned as if he had said something tremendously amusing. "You can call me Garret. Most people do."

"Do what?" asked Ansylike.

"Call me Garret."

"You just said that. What do most people do?"

"Listen!" insisted Groblic as he jostled her arm, "and follow me."

"The staircase is a bit of a nuisance!" commented Garret as he wound his way up the stone stairs. "These towers look very nice from the outside, but no-one thinks of the folk who have to live in them."

"Going round in circles is something that one gets used to," replied Groblic and he looked back at Ansylike who was following him.

"Where has Glade been taken?" she called. "Will he be looked after properly?" She felt more than a little guilty. She should have known that he was not well. If the journey had been much longer, he might have lost too much blood and died in the cart.

"He'll be in good hands," replied Garret. "Now here we are at last." He turned an iron key in the lock of a stout door and beckoned them to follow him. "My quarters, such as they are," he declared. "My hospitality is legendary."

"Some room!" exclaimed Groblic who had shuffled his way past the others and was the first to follow Garret. "I've never seen so many books in my life. There must be a whole library in here! Are any of them magic?"

He stared in wonder at the walls that were lined with volumes of leather-bound tomes.

"Each has little magic, but they're not lists of spells," came the reply. "I have magic of my own and I don't need the use of the ancient knowledge. Make yourselves at home." He indicated a soft, furry bench and a couple of deep chairs. "I'll get us some food and a little ale. I never think well on an empty stomach. I'm sure that you could all do with a meal inside you." He left for what was obviously the kitchen and left the dwarves and Ansylike to keep themselves amused.

"I hope it's more than a little bread roll!" hissed Groblic confidentially.

"All our rolls are very well bred!" came a reply from beneath him. He froze and his eyes widened. "Just make sure you don't drop any crumbs! They make me itchy and I can't scratch."

That was enough! Groblic leapt to his feet and faced the chair.

"The furniture is alive!" he exclaimed.

"As long as you don't give it any offence I'm sure it won't harm you," advised Ansylike, who had seen this sort of thing at Zileika's. "If there are any beans on the menu I thinks we should all give them a miss!" She broke into a fit of giggles and curled up on the couch.

"I don't see what's so funny about that!" came the voice of the couch beneath her. "Heed her advice!" The fur beneath her stiffened indignantly and tickled her, so that her giggling only became worse.

Haldriel didn't know whether to be amused or frightened. He was bewildered and hoped that they would not have to sleep on talking beds! If he talked in his sleep he didn't want to be answered back!

"Food is ready," said Garret, entering the room. "I heard you speaking to the furniture. It gets a little grumpy at times, but take no notice of it."

"I'll sit on the carpet," replied Groblic warily.

"Typical!" retorted the carpet. "It's not enough that people walk all over me! Now they want to sit on me too!"

Groblic jumped into the air. Ansylike hugged her arms around her chest, curled into a ball and burst into laughter. She was delighted at the reactions of the dwarves and fully enjoyed the entertainment that Garret had provided at the expense of his guests. No wonder his hospitality was legendary. He'd said that people never forgot it. Now she knew why! He was an Animator! One of the rarest sorts of magicians, so they said, as few people saw it as a very profitable line of business.

When they were all seated around the table and had filled themselves with a variety of food that didn't, thankfully, include beans, Ansylike asked Garret what he knew of the prophecy. She'd noticed that the table had not said a word. Perhaps it was shy.

"It's a tricky one, that," he began, "but most interesting. I'll tell you what you need to know and spare you the details. Ansylike, here, will have a permanent bond with the ruler of the elves, until one of them dies."

"A 'bond' means marriage, doesn't it?" asked Groblic. The concern he felt was clearly visible in the lines on his face.

"Maybe. That's how Gromixillion sees it anyway." Garret's words were slow and thoughtful. "There's more. Ansylike is also destined to kill the elven ruler. She can't, however, kill anyone that she's bonded with. I told you it was tricky." He looked at their blank faces. "For Gromixillion it is simple. He resigns as the elven commander. In his place he puts another, whom Ansylike kills. He marries her, takes over command and executes her." He paused for his words to have their effect. "There's something about a 'dancer behind the throne', but that bit is a mystery to me."

"Then we're safe until Gromixillion gives up his command. While he's still in charge we have no worries," was Haldriel's cheerful comment.

"Exactly when do you think that he'll appoint another leader?" inquired Groblic.

"Tonight, I expect," replied Garret. "You'll have to think of something soon."

"Do you mean that you haven't thought of something that can help us? Why tell us all this if you haven't got an idea as to what we should do?"

Ansylike was more than a little impatient. She was prepared to face death in battle, but she had no intention of being married! No chance!!

"I do have one other piece of information. I think that you should find out who is being held prisoner in the east tower. When Ansylike is dead, she is to become the new bride of Gromixillion! Kill her and you will have some extra time. She is well guarded, so you must take care."

"We have no weapons, so we must use stealth," advised Haldriel. "Let's get going now!"

"We'll need Glade," suggested Ansylike. "Find him first and he can do the sneaking and creeping bit. He's certainly good at that. It's a pity that Andric can't join us. I wonder what they've done with him."

"I'd offer you weapons if I had any," added Garret, "but I have none. Instead I'll give an animation spell to one of you. Who shall it be?"

"Me," said Groblic. "I hate magic and I don't want to use it, but if it will keep Spud safe, I'll accept it willingly!"

He stood and dared anyone to question his rash decision. They didn't.

"Then take this paper." Garret handed over a small piece of parchment. "Hold it in your hand and concentrate on the object that you want to become alive. The spell will not last long so use it wisely. I wish I could be of more help to you. There will be no end to the fighting while Gromixillion lives. I hope you are successful."

"Excuse me," said Ansylike and started to take off her clothes. "I've just remembered something." She stripped to the catsuit that she was wearing under her ordinary clothes and stood against the wall. "Well, what do you think?"

"Amazing!" whispered Groblic, as she changed colour, before his eyes, to match the stone. "I can hardly see you!" Ansylike walked towards him and shimmered back to her usual self.

"I'll try it again, wearing my sword and see if the magic still works."

She buckled on her weapon belt that held her broken sword and stood against the wall again. The effect was the same.

"I'm not sure I like the idea of you going out with so little on. It's not decent," complained Groblic, "but I suppose no-one will see you."

"I hope not!" replied Ansylike. "I hope not, or we're all in trouble. Now let's get going. I'll find Glade and you can see how many guards there are on the tower."

It was not a wonderful plan, but it would have to do. They were all glad to be back in action. They had a chance and if they failed, well, it would only mean their deaths. It was better to die fighting than to wait for the axe to fall! Ansylike led the way down the winding stairs and to the arch that opened to the courtyard. She crouched and slid along slowly with one hand on the wall. Groblic and Haldriel strolled out and made their way to the east tower. Every so often they paused and looked around as if they were still admiring the buildings. None of the elves seemed to take much notice. They were far too busy. There were no guards outside the tower and the door was unlocked so Groblic and Haldriel slipped inside. A surprise awaited them!

It was easy for Ansylike to find Glade. The medical centre was clearly signposted and she crept in, unobserved.

There were few patients and no staff to be seen. Glade was sitting in front of an open window, snoozing in the last rays of the sunshine. She put a hand over his mouth so that he wouldn't cry out if she startled him, and whispered in his ear. He squirmed in panic for a second, then relaxed when he recognised her voice.

"Are you well enough to leave? We must act now and we need your help."

"I'm fine," he replied, sliding out of his chair. "You go out and I'll say I'm going for a walk to stretch my legs." He grinned.

They met up outside and cautiously made their way to the tower. Glade didn't attract any attention, as he intended. He had an uncommon knack of being overlooked. He wondered what was going on, but had the sense not to ask for explanations. It must be some sort of emergency so he just did as he was told. The reasons could come later.

"Well, Haldriel, I think we have some business to finish!"

"You! How did you get here? The last time I saw you . . ." Haldriel left the sentence unfinished and stared at Tharl. Obolin and Cledrin stood on either side of him. They were no longer toads. Fully restored, they confronted Groblic and Haldriel and they were armed and ready for battle. It was obvious whom they were eager to kill!

"I've been waiting for you. I knew that you'd come here. I've even got some weapons ready. Choose and prepare for death!" Tharl spat the words out. His voice was dripping with poison. "You too, Groblic." He indicated a table where a range of weapons was spread out. "There are three of us and only two of you, so we will have to wait until Spud gets here. I'm sure it won't be long. We'll be evenly matched then."

This was not entirely true! Haldriel was skilled with a crossbow, but he was not an ace with any other weapon. Ansylike's magic sword had been broken. Without it, she was no more than average. Groblic was a match for any of his opponents. It looked as if the contest had only one possible outcome. Defeat!

Haldriel and Groblic looked carefully at the array of weapons before them and took their time choosing. There was no rush. A war-hammer with a cruelly spiked head was Groblic's choice and he balanced it in both hands to measure its weight before he picked up a small, sturdy shield. Haldriel's decision was more difficult to make. He knew that he would have to face Tharl. With a sword or an axe he would stand no chance. He had to use his head and outwit the superior warrior by cunning. He chose a whip and a stiletto blade. It was risky.

"And here is our third opponent!" gloated Tharl, as the door swung softly open. Then he scowled. "Who are you?" he demanded as Glade walked past him to choose a weapon. He'd expected Ansylike. He had orders not to kill her, but Cledrin had volunteered to defeat her in battle. He wanted to humiliate her for rejecting him in favour of Groblic. He burned with a jealous rage. He wanted to make her crawl and beg for mercy! Unseen, Ansylike slipped past into the shadows and hid under the table, keeping one hand on the wall.

"There are three of them now. Let's begin!" urged Obolin as he squared up to Groblic. "One of us must die here, old friend." Although there was sadness in his voice, it was obvious that he was prepared to fight to the death. "I must kill you," he continued. "I've sworn to help the elves regain this land. They will be happy here and will never return to trouble us." He hefted his shield up and raised his hand-axe.

Tharl held a mighty battle-axe. One well-aimed swing could send a man's head flying from his shoulders. Haldriel had seen it in action and knew that he would have to stay out of reach.

Cledrin was disappointed that he was not to fight Ansylike and vowed silently to pound the little pipsqueak, who was still selecting a weapon, into a bloody pulp! It would satisfy some of his anger. He held a mace, an armoured club, in his right hand and wore a spiked metal glove on his left, behind his shield. "If you're ready?" he thundered. Glade cast a glance over his shoulder and saw what he was up against. He picked up two short swords and turned to engage Cledrin who bore down on him, keen to make a swift end to their combat. Glade side-stepped, but Cledrin anticipated his move and his mace passed within a coin's width of Glade's ear. Cledrin raised the mace again and aimed a blow at Glade's unprotected back. To keep his balance, he raised his left arm and held the shield behind him. Over-confidence and anger proved his undoing.

Glade sprang up, parried Cledrin's mace and struck into his chest with the sword in his right hand. At the same time he hooked a foot around Cledrin's ankle so that the dwarf fell on to him and the point of the sword sliced through his armour and appeared through his back. Glade was flattened under the weight of his foe and, weakened by the blood that he'd already lost, passed out.

Obolin and Groblic traded blows and soon their shields were battered and discarded. This gave Groblic an advantage as his fists were as good as clubs and could split a skull, even a dwarven one. Ansylike watched them, deciding whether to intervene. They all seemed to be managing very well, so she headed for the stairs.

They were much like the stairs that Garret had led them up so she knew what to expect. On and on they wound, until she reached a landing with only one door. She'd thought that a guard would be standing here and was surprised to find it deserted. As she reached for the handle a voice came from the lock.

"Gently," it whispered. "I'm feeling fragile. I'm not meant for travelling. Lying on my back on that cart . . . ooh! Do you know that some men actually sat on me?"

"Do I know you?" asked Ansylike, bending down. "Are you the same . . .?" She broke off as the door was opened inwards.

"My pretty one!" exclaimed Zileika. "Come to visit so soon. Do come in." She gestured with an open hand, but Ansylike hesitated. A bolt of blue flame lashed from the palm of the sorceress and burned a groove in the stone floor. Ansylike decided to accept the invitation and entered the room.

"You could have warned me!" she hissed over her shoulder to the door."

"Chip off!" it replied.

"Sit there!" commanded Zileika. Ansylike obeyed. "It really is a pity that you have to die soon. We could have been such good friends. Perhaps I could persuade that elf to leave you with me for a while. Perhaps not. He's so impatient. You know what men are like."

"Yes, I do. Tell me what you're doing here. Your magic seems to be as effective as ever. I thought you would have lost it all if you left the tower . . . This is the same tower, isn't it?"

Ansylike looked at the bead curtains, the pictures on the walls, the couch and it was all the same as the room that she'd visited before. "How did you manage it?"

"I had a little help," she laughed. "Gromixillion has already captured three of the magicians who imprisoned me. We haven't got them all on our side, yet. We will, though. The spell was loose enough for me to move the tower to here. I can't leave it, but I can move it with me. That's close to freedom, isn't it? Actually, I only moved the stones. The furniture and stuff were brought by cart." She stopped and sat on the bed. "I'm bad," she sighed. "Always have been. Reducing the examining board to dribbling babies was my greatest trick. With more power I could have destroyed them completely. They were going to say that I wasn't mature enough to practise magic. Stupid old slugs. They just crawled around and did nothing. 'We can't upset the natural balance,' they used to say."

"They did have a point," suggested Ansylike gently. "You are a little reckless."

"I'm the sorceress. What do you expect?"

"How many sorceresses are there in The Desolation?"

"Only me. I'm the only one." Zileika tilted her head back and shook her hair proudly, but there was sorrow in her voice. It was not easy to be one of a kind.

Ansylike sat down and leaned forward. She rested her elbows on her knees and cupped her chin in her hands. She knew what it was to be lonely. Fear led people to do strange things. Loneliness was the father of fear. She didn't know what to say, but she knew that she couldn't kill Zileika. She was tragic and pathetic, but not evil. Still dressed in blue, she sat in front of a mirror and brushed her hair.

"My, you are a pretty one!" she said to her reflection.

"Only as pretty as you," came the reply. Evidently the mirror was enchanted too.

Ansylike realised for the first time why the sorceress used these spells. She had become so lonely that she'd started to talk to the furniture. In her case it answered back! She shook her head and decided to seek advice from Groblic. There was nothing she could do here.

Haldriel had chosen his weapons wisely and he managed to keep out of the range of Tharl's battle-axe until the moment came when he caught its handle and both of Tharl's wrists with his whip. His stiletto blade was gripped firmly in his left hand and he thrust it up, through Tharl's jaw and into his skull. Death was swift and painless. His friend and companion dropped lifeless to the floor. At that moment he felt a searing pain in his chest and he looked in disbelief at the arrow-head that stuck out from his tunic. The whip slid from his hand, the dagger clattered to the ground and he staggered forward. Obolin and Groblic ceased their contest and shouldered their weapons as the troop of elves entered the tower. Arrows were aimed at both of them.

"Hands up or you're meat for the gibbet!" The elven captain looked at Haldriel who was on his knees, clutching at the arrow in his chest. "Don't kill him!" he commanded. "String him up!" He turned his attention back to the dwarves. His eyes were slits of green ice. He wore black leather armour and boots. Around his waist was a single silver chain. "Them too. Onto the gibbet with them. We'll let them hang for a while, then whip them to death!"

"No imagination!" laughed Groblic. "I thought that elves were inventive. Whipped indeed!"

"And dangled," added Obolin. "They really have no idea how to kill. I suppose that's why we were able to boot them out of our lands."

"I am Spiron, Commander of the elves. My word is law. Gromixillion has resigned. I am in charge. The old ways are past. I will deal with you in the way that you treated us in the days of old. I will raise a mighty army and lead it back to the land that you call your own. Every dwarf will die and their bodies will hang for the crows to feed on!"

"You trusted these people?" asked Groblic.

"I must admit to the odd error of judgement," admitted Obolin impassively. "It looks as though they are going to kill us. It only happens once so I hope they make it entertaining." He turned and spat on the boots of an elf who had taken up a position behind him.

"You can cut his tongue out for that!" rasped Spiron to the elven guard. "But not yet. We'll get a bit more amusement out of them."

"Don't worry. He talks from the other end most of the time!" retorted Groblic. He laughed. Neither of the dwarves were going to show any fear in front of the elves. They knew that they were going to die. Their lives were lost, but their honour was intact!

Glade had slithered out from beneath the body of Cledrin and was hiding under the table when the sentence of death was pronounced on his friends. Now was not the time to appear! He waited and hoped that Ansylike was not going to come down the stairs and walk into the clutches of this blood-thirsty mob.

She didn't. She heard every word from where she was, crouched on the steps, but she was unarmed and knew that she would have to tread warily. The elves were careful to guard the table where the weapons were displayed. There was no opportunity to grab one. She'd have to sneak past when they weren't looking and find something to fight with outside. As she watched, she saw Glade creep through the door on his hands and knees. "At least he's safe," she thought. Suddenly a voice rang out from above.

"There's one escaping! Guards, get him!"

With dismay, Ansylike watched as Glade was seized by the scruff of his neck and hauled back. She braced herself against the wall and edged her way out. It was obvious that Zileika was betraying them. She was on her own now. All her friends had been captured and would die if she didn't think of a rescue plan.

By the time Ansylike had reached the gibbet, the dwarves and Glade were hanging on it. An elven medic was tending to Haldriel.

"I don't know what we are coming to," he complained. "I thought Gromixillion was bad, but Spiron is even worse. I've never seen prisoners treated so cruelly. Given half the chance I'd desert. So would most of the troops!"

"Really?" asked Ansylike.

"Trees aflame! You startled me!" exclaimed the elf, then lowered his voice. "They'll catch you if you stay here, then it will be all over. Go to Garret's tower. You'll be safe there. I'll see that your friends don't die. Hurry!"

"Will you help me?" hissed Ansylike.

"Yes. I am called Skink. Tell Garret I sent you and tell him that Spiron is in command. He will know what to do, I hope."

There was no way to tell if the elf was to be trusted, but Ansylike had little choice. She needed a friend and there was no-one else. She made her way, cautiously back to Garret's tower and soon was sprinting up the stairs. He was glad to see her, but his smile soon faded when she told him the bad news.

"All captured, you say. That's serious. There are any number of elves who would like to see the back of Gromixillion and Spiron. The trouble is that they are unwilling to do anything about it. Too used to obeying orders, I suppose. We can't count on any of them. There's no chance of a rebellion, if that's what you were thinking."

"Then what can we do? Have you any ideas?" Ansylike was getting a bit desperate.

"No ideas at all. I knew something like this would happen. I just hoped that it would all turn out well. I was not expecting to play any part in it!"

"Typical!" Ansylike was more than a little vexed. She would have to sort it out herself. All these adults, grown men, and they didn't seem to have an iota of common sense! She curled up on the bench, then stretched out, her hands linked under her head and closed her eyes. She pursed her lips and blew out a sigh of frustration. Pondering over the problem she came up with a solution. "If I kill Spiron, as expected, who will be the elven commander? Does Gromixillion automatically take over?"

"No, of course not. There will have to be an election. He'll win, of course. No elf would dare to stand against him." Garret did not know why Ansylike had asked the question and he just hoped that she was going to come up with something positive. Lying on the bench in her catsuit she looked more like a child than ever. He couldn't believe that a mere slip a girl would hold the key to their future.

"Then we can win!" she declared. "Will you fetch me the rest of my clothes, please? I'll need somewhere to hide a blade and I can't hide anything in this. It's as tight as my skin!" Ansylike stood up and resumed her normal colour.

Garret returned with her clothes and she put them on. Then she drew her broken sword and tipped the scabbard up until the piece that Gromixillion had snapped off fell onto the table. She held it before her eyes. It gleamed with a silvery-blue light. Then she tucked it up her sleeve.

There was a gentle knock on the door. Garret opened it to find Skink waiting on the landing.

"You can't hide her here for long. They're searching the castle!"

"They can find me. I'm ready!" interrupted Ansylike. "I'll go down first. Make sure that Andric is all right and bring him along. It's vital that I have him with me."

"I'll get him," replied Skink. "Garret, will you come with me?"

Ansylike skipped down the steps and into the arms of the band of elves that were searching for her.

"No-one is in," she commented lightly. "I'm just exploring. Wonderful castle you have here."

"Just come with me and there won't be any trouble!" insisted the leader of the squad.

"Delighted!" laughed Ansylike. She linked arms with him and followed as he led the way. The elf was mystified, but happy that he'd found her. Captives were not usually so co-operative.

The assembly room was a huge hall with an arched ceiling and an intricate mosaic floor. It was designed with special occasions in mind. Light entered from scores of windows through stained glass. It was every colour that she had ever seen and a few that she hadn't! Ansylike stood in the doorway and gazed up. She had never seen anything so beautiful.

Her eyes lowered to the armed guards in mailed shirts that lined the walls. Each carried a tall spear. At the end of the hall there was a stage made from a single block of stone. Two thrones were set in the centre. They glittered with the precious metals that inlaid the wood, and sparkled with jewels that caught the light. Each would've been worth a fortune and Ansylike considered whether she could get close enough to tweak one of the diamonds out.

While she was intent on the thought of riches, Spiron walked onto the stage and gazed at her.

"Take her sword!" he commanded. Two guards rushed to obey. Ansylike didn't want them to seize her arms, so she unbuckled her belt and let it fall to the floor. "Bring it to me." The guards hesitated, their fear was obvious.

"Let me help," urged Ansylike gently and she bent slowly at the knees, keeping a wary eye on the guards until she could reach the belt.

She straightened up and held the scabbard of her sword in both hands and offered them the weapon. One of the elves accepted it. His face showed that it had taken great courage for him to perform this task. Obviously he expected a burst of magic to end his life as soon as he touched it. He let out a sigh of relief. "Your master is waiting. I don't want you to get into trouble. I have no quarrel with you. Take the sword to him."

"Thank you, Lady," the warrior replied. He dared not let Spiron see him bow his head so he just lowered his eyes, turned, and carried the sword up the long hall, cradling it in his arms.

"Your blade will rest here tonight. You will be brought here again tomorrow with all your friends. Then we shall test the truth of the prophecy. Sleep well. Rooms have been prepared for you. Enjoy our hospitality." Spiron's voice was almost friendly. "Without the sword you are no threat, so both of us may sleep soundly! Farewell." he walked from the stage and a troop of guards moved to encircle it. The sword would be well protected and there would be no chance of sneaking it back! Not that Ansylike had any intention of trying anything like that. She had a better plan!

Chapter Thirteen

SPIRON

Ansylike was relieved to see that her friends were safely gathered around a long table and were eating happily when she arrived with her armed escort. She'd tried chatting to them on the way, but they had not responded. They merely told her which way to go and kept their hands on the hilts of their swords. They were not very good company! One of them opened the door of a windowless, stone building and gestured for her to go inside. For an awful moment she thought that Spiron was lying and that she was to spend the night in a cell. She was much relieved. There was no sign of Glade nor Andric, but all the dwarves were well. Even Haldriel was enjoying his dinner. He moved a little stiffly and his face was bruised, but he managed to laugh at Obolin's jokes. Some of the coarser ones caused Ansylike to blush. They had not only saved her a place at the head of the table, but also kept the best cuts of meat and the tenderest vegetables for her to eat. She ate well, but drank only one glass of wine. She knew that she would need a clear head if her plan was to stand any chance of success.

Obolin made grunting noises as he stuffed more and more food into his mouth. It seemed as if he'd never stop. He drank wine, ale and mead, between huge mouthfuls of roasted meat, toasted bread rolls and the delicious mushrooms that they'd all come to enjoy. After the second course he had to loosen his belt. By the time that he was full, he had undone his belt and dropped it to the floor, where it lay, curled in a pool of ale and gravy. His table manners had not improved one bit. As he collapsed back in his chair, he looked fat enough to give birth to a calf! He snored deeply into his beard and passed into the sleep of the truly greedy who have finally had enough.

Groblic wanted to leave the table early and made his excuses. Through an arched doorway, he went and was surprised to find himself in a maze of passages. The building had not looked that big from the outside. There were many rooms to explore, most of them empty: bedchambers, designed to accommodate varying numbers; storerooms loaded with supplies; libraries of dusty books; and an armoury! A strange sort of armoury. The weapons were in glass cases, not hanging from the walls. There were cases of shields, magnificent ones, some made with dragon hide, some metal, some wood. All were of the very best craftsmanship.

The same was true of every type of weapon. There were fine elven blades, cutlasses, scimitars, broadswords, short-swords, maces, war-hammers, daggers. The list was endless.

In a daze, Groblic went from case to case, until he came to the battle-axe. He looked at it in shock. It was "Gwarl-Drimbre". This was a weapon from the dark days. Supposedly it was buried with a dwarf lord, but here it was for him to take. So much for legend! Unable to resist, he opened the case.

He gripped the handle of the mighty axe and held it above his head. It was well balanced and remarkably light. With this, he could cut down the elves three at a time. There would be no stopping him.

"I think we should put Obolin to bed," suggested Ansylike. "He'll not sleep well in that chair."

"It serves him right!" replied Haldriel. "You lift his feet on to a stool and I'll fetch a blanket to keep him warm. It's time we all had some rest." He rose from his chair and left to find the bedroom.

Haldriel wandered down a corridor and found himself in the armoury. He peered, without much interest, at the array of weapons, but his eyes were soon widening when he found the silver crossbow!

It was enough to bring tears of happiness trickling down his face. As a boy he had been told stories of Therrol, the mighty, wise warrior and his silver bow. He had always pictured the weapon in his mind to look exactly like this. Therrol was a great dwarven leader. Others always followed where he led and his decisions were respected. His aim was deadly and his silver bow never missed. He had fallen in battle long ago, finally slain by the elves, but they had buried him with full honours and sealed his tomb with magic spells. His crossbow was supposed to have been buried with him, but here it was! Haldriel was sorely tempted to pick it up. Such a weapon would be needed to defend the land if the elves attacked again.

"So there you are!" exclaimed Ansylike. "I thought you must have been weaving that blanket yourself! Bring it here and wrap it round Obolin."

Haldriel smiled and did as he was told. It was nice, in a way, to be scolded. Just like being at home! He chuckled as he made Obolin comfortable, then turned to face Ansylike.

"Groblic has gone to bed," he informed her. He decided to say nothing of the silver bow. That could wait. It might be a little insensitive to talk of how he'd been dreaming of killing elves and leading dwarven armies into battle against them. "Now shall we go?"

Ansylike's room was simply furnished, but she was only interested in the bed. It had been a long, hard day. She rubbed her eyes with the backs of her hands. A good wash and a sleep. That was what she needed! Then she noticed the nightdress that was lying, neatly folded on the pillow. She held it up and found that it was made of a light, silky-smooth fabric. Rubbing it gently against her face, she wondered whether it was made from spider-threads. Then she stuffed it back under the pillow and stripped off to wash. Soon she was tucked up under the sheets and fast asleep.

Morning came, as morning always does and Ansylike woke when she heard a light tapping at the door.

"Spud! Can you hear me? Can I come in?" It was Haldriel.

"Wait a moment," she replied, and pulled the nightdress out from under the pillow and slipped it over her head. Then she went to the door and opened it to find Haldriel standing alone.

"I'm worried!" he explained. "Obolin and Groblic are awake, but they don't seem to be acting normally. It's as if they're in a trance. They answer questions, but their faces have no expression. I think you'd better come and see for yourself."

Without pausing to put on her boots or any other clothes, Ansylike followed as Haldriel scurried back to his room. Groblic and Obolin were sitting on their beds. They were dressed, but their eyes gazed into space. Neither made any move when their friends stood in front of them.

"This is some sort of magic, I'm afraid!" said Ansylike. "How could it have happened? They seem to be dazed." She patted Groblic's cheeks, but he didn't even blink his eyes.

"I think I know!" hissed Haldriel through clenched teeth. Quickly he explained about the silver bow and how he was almost tempted to pick it up. "Perhaps the others fell victim to a similar greed!"

"Let's see the bow and we'll check if anything else is missing," suggested Ansylike. She followed Haldriel and they soon discovered that there was no armoury in the building. It had all been an illusion! It was a trap and Groblic had fallen into it. Obolin's temptation, they decided, must have been the food and wine. He was unable to resist the chance to stuff himself like a pig at a trough! Haldriel had passed the test when he'd left the bow in its glass case. But what of Ansylike? If anyone was to be enchanted, it should be her!

"We were offered what we most wanted. Something that we couldn't resist," explained Haldriel slowly. "What did you most want? Think carefully. The danger may still be waiting for you."

"All I wanted was to sleep," sighed Ansylike. "There was nothing I wanted more than a soft pillow and clean sheets."

"That can't be it. You did sleep in the bed, didn't you?"

"Under the nice, clean sheets with my head on the pillow."

"The bath, then? Did you resist the temptation to have a bath?"

"There wasn't one. There were basins of water and I had a wash. Then I went to bed."

"Wearing that?" asked Haldriel. "I suppose . . ."

"No, wait!" interrupted Ansylike. "I found this nightdress on the pillow. It was obviously meant for me, but . . . Well, it's lovely, but . . ."

Haldriel was silent for a moment. He thought over the possibilities. The guards would come for them and expect them all to be in the same state as Obolin and Groblic. It was best if they were not disappointed. A plan took shape in his mind. The elves were crafty. Spiron was taking no chances. He probably intended them to die very soon.

"Keep the nightdress on and go back to bed. Don't fall asleep! When the guards come for us you must pretend to have fallen under the spell. Just behave like old Groblic over there. I'll do the same and we'll see if they spot the difference. It should give us an advantage."

"It's certainly worth a try," agreed Ansylike. She paused, uncertain of her words. "If this doesn't work and we fail, I won't have another chance to thank you for all you've done for me. I just want you to know how much I've enjoyed this little adventure and your company. I suppose you know that I was a bit suspicious of dwarves to start with. I thought that you were all, somehow, different. Now I know that you are!"

Haldriel laughed! "We are, indeed! I think I've learned a lot too. There is no reason why our differences should put us into conflict. We have our ways and you have yours. We can live side by side in peace if we make the effort to understand one another."

He held out a hand for Ansylike to clasp and she accepted it.

"We make a good team!"

"The best!" agreed Haldriel. "Now get back to bed and I'll practise acting like a zombie."

It was nearly noon before the guards came for their prisoners. They didn't bother to knock at the door. Ansylike was shaken by a hand on her shoulder. She pretended to wake and gazed blankly.

"Dress and be quick about it!" commanded the elven guard. "We are expected soon and you will have little time to eat. I'll wait outside."

She had been careful to leave an arm above the bed covers so that the elf could see her nightdress. She wanted to convince them that she had slept in it all night and was already under their spell. Keeping an eye on the door, she dressed and had a swift wash. The water in the basins hadn't been changed, but she could hardly complain to the management about the poor room service!

When she was ready she opened the door and stepped meekly outside. The dwarves were lined up with Haldriel at the back so she took her place behind him and they filed out into the sunshine.

The first stop was a dining room and they were all given enough food to keep them going. It was nothing special, like the meal of the previous evening. There was no wine, nor ale, but jugs of fruit juice and water stood in their stead. They all ate quickly. Groblic and Obolin ate methodically and showed no signs of enjoyment. Ansylike and Haldriel copied them. Guards stood around the table, intent on every move that they made.

The next stop was the large hall that Ansylike had paid a brief visit to, but this time it was packed. They were led up towards the stage where chairs had been set out for them. The walk up the aisle was tricky. Ansylike wanted to look at the marvellous glass windows and their coloured light, but she kept her eyes fixed ahead of her. She was determined to show no trace of curiosity. Despite her efforts, she almost gasped when she saw that Andric was seated on the stage. It was a momentary lapse, but it was enough for Spiron to notice. He stood on the stage, in the centre, watching them keenly. Seeing that Ansylike was not under the spell, he turned his head slightly and rasped an order, knowing that his men would rush to obey. For many, long years he'd dreamed of power and now he had it and was determined to use it to the full.

"Bring the sorceress to me!" He stood, motionless, as Zileika was dragged before him. "It appears that your magic has failed! I told you what I would do to you if you let me down!"

Forced down onto her knees, with an elven guard holding each of her arms, Zileika burst into a flood of tears and begged for mercy.

"I did the best that I could!" she pleaded. "The dwarves are all enchanted."

"One of them isn't! I can tell," replied Spiron coldly. "Nor your friend. I wonder whether this is deliberate. With your magic you could have served me well. You know that I have total power over it. Now we will see how you manage without it! You know what this is?" He produced a glass bottle that he'd been concealing in his sleeve and smiled cruelly.

"No!" screamed Zileika, but it was in vain. Spiron had no mercy. He smashed the bottle against the nearest throne, spraying a blue liquid across the floor of the stage. The sorceress sank forwards and buried her face in her hands. Sobs of rage and sorrow convulsed her body.

Everyone else in the hall was silent and motionless as if no-one dared to breathe. The assembly was stunned and remained as solemn as statues. Ansylike and Haldriel gazed in horror at the fate that had befallen the sorceress. Stripped of her magic, she was lost. As they drew closer, she called out to Ansylike, raising her head and shaking her hair back defiantly.

"I did my best. I knew that you wouldn't wear the nightdress. He wanted me to put the spell on the bed, but I had to give you a chance to beat this evil dung beetle. The plans that he has for us are wicked!" Her words were cut off as Spiron lashed out with a booted foot and caught her squarely across the jaw. She fell heavily backwards and lay sprawled on the floor. The assembled elves gasped and some stood as if to voice their protests, but Spiron turned to face them and they were instantly subdued. In his suit of black leather and chain-mail, he was an awesome figure. His cold green eyes glittered. At his feet, in a pool of blue light, the sorceress squirmed and writhed in agony and despair. Blood trickled from her mouth and she spat some out as her magic powers continued to drain away. Evidently, the bargain she'd struck with Gromixillion had a few drawbacks!

The dwarves and Ansylike walked slowly onto the stage. The thrones were set far back and a long wooden table had been put in their place. In the centre of it was Ansylike's sword, still in its scabbard. Spiron took up a position at the far end and turned to address the crowd.

"Here is the one whom prophecy spoke of. She is destined to kill the elven war-lord. Now watch her try! She has one helper." He waved a hand at Haldriel. "I will have one too." He gestured for Groblic to

come forward. "Stand at my side and we will cut these trash to shreds."
Suddenly a gleaming war-axe appeared in Groblic's hands. Things
looked a bit difficult and Ansylike began to have her doubts about her
plan. "Take your weapon!" ordered Spiron, as he flung a dagger across
the table. "One of you has the sword and the other uses the knife."

Ansylike picked up the dagger. The hall was silent. Haldriel drew the
broken sword from its scabbard. Spiron's eyes widened.

"That can't be the same sword! That can't be the one! No dwarf can
hold the sword in The Desolation. It would strike him down and . . ."

"You don't read many books," sneered Haldriel, "or you would
know that the sword can be used by anyone who has held it outside The
Desolation. I examined it after Spud first used it! Will you face me in
battle or surrender now?"

"Impudent louse!" screamed Spiron. "I'll crush you under my foot."
He was confident. The sword was broken and the dwarf could only
slash with it. His moves were easy to predict and Spiron knew that
Haldriel was no great swordsman. He was only in any danger if
Ansylike held the sword and he was certain that he could deal with her.
Groblic waited for the command to move forward and attack, but
Spiron had not said anything to him other than to stand at his side.
Sword clashed against sword and sparks glittered as the elven war-lord
and the leader of the dwarven expedition met in combat. Around the
table they fought, with neither able to get the advantage. Ansylike bided
her time as there was nothing she could do until she had a clear target.
Then Haldriel stumbled and fell backwards. She put the dagger on the
table and slipped the broken end of her sword into her palm. Spiron
raised his sword, point down, ready to skewer Haldriel. Ansylike knew
that it was time to strike and hurled the sword-tip at Spiron.

It sped through the air faster than an arrow and found its mark.
Deep into the neck of the elven war-lord it pierced, draining the life out
of him. His own sword fell from his grip and he clutched at his neck as
if he could pull the blade free and save his life. Blood oozed through
his fingers and down his black armour. There was no way he could stop
it! He fell backwards, lifeless, on to the planks of the stage and started

to fade before their eyes.

His body dissolved into a haze of grey smoke, then disappeared into the wind. Only his armour and sword remained. And the silver chain that he had worn so proudly around his waist. He was no more than a puppet of Gromixillion, although he never knew it.

A cheer rose from some of the assembled elves, but Ansylike had no reason to celebrate yet. She went to the huddled form of Zileika. The sorceress shed bitter tears, but she almost managed to smile as Ansylike raised her to her feet.

"We'd better get out of here. The battle isn't over. They'll be fighting amongst themselves before long." Hardly had Ansylike finished speaking, when the first skirmishes broke out.

Most of the elves carried weapons and soon their swords and daggers were drawn. One of them leapt onto the stage.

"This way!" he insisted, pulling back a curtain to reveal a door. Ansylike was relieved to see that it was Garret and followed his advice. Zileika collapsed back onto the floor and waved for the others to leave her and they had little choice.

The spell on Groblic and Obolin was broken and they came to their senses and hurried after their friends. Without weapons they could do little, but Obolin hesitated, then stopped and looked over his shoulder. They were not being followed yet, so he went back and retrieved the sword tip that Ansylike had killed Spiron with. Then he scurried after the others.

Andric was waiting and urged him to catch up. It would not be long before they were missed and they would stand no chance if a squad of guards reached them. So far they'd been lucky, but now they needed to find a safe spot while the elves fought each other.

There was no way of telling who would win, but Andric suspected that the followers of Spiron, who were better armed, would come out on top. They fled as the sounds of battle behind them grew louder and more fierce.

"This is a back door where servants enter," explained Garret. "It leads to a courtyard. On the other side is the stable. There are horses.

Take them and leave while you have the chance."

"We're not leaving!" insisted Ansylike. "We still have things to do."

"Gromixillion will return. You have fulfilled your part of the prophecy. Now you must go, or he will take you as his bride. Your friends will be held hostage. Unless you do as he wishes, they will suffer in the dungeons. Could you bear that?"

Garret's words were rushed, but Ansylike got the message. Gromixillion would resume command. Then he would marry her. She would not be able to harm anyone with whom she was bonded, so he would be safe. With her friends at his mercy, she could not refuse.

Chapter Fourteen

GROMIXILLION

Glade finished saddling the horses and checked that the leather straps were secure before he decided to have a look outside. He was worried about his friends, but he knew that there was little he could do to help. It was up to Ansylike and he hoped that she had a good idea for defeating Spiron. As he stood in the shade of the stable's gable-end, he saw the shadow of a bird. Looking up, he saw the crow come to rest on a high window of the assembly hall. It was clear that Gromixillion was keeping an eye on what was happening. Glade put a stop to that with an arrow from his short-bow. The bird was dead before it had time to utter a squawk!

"Excellent shot!" complimented Skink. "I didn't think that your bow would have the range. I clearly underestimated you."

"You snuck up on me! How did you do that?" Glade was not used to being surprised. He prided himself on the way that he could move without making a sound. His hearing was sharp. He could hear a rabbit break wind from a hundred paces.

"Magic. I cheated. I have a few decent healing spells, but I've some others that help me to move around quietly. Would you like me to demonstrate?" Skink peered intently at Glade, as if eager to show off his powers. His clothes were no different to those of the other elves, so there was nothing to mark him out as a medic. In fact he looked more menacing than average. His hooked nose and blue, beady eyes made him look a little like a bird of prey. His fingers twitched nervously. Glade trusted him, despite his shifty manner, but he couldn't see how either of them could do much. Garret had told him to make sure that the horses were ready, in case they all needed to make a quick exit, and that he'd already done.

"Is there another way out of the assembly hall? A back entrance, or something like that?" he asked. An idea was taking shape in his mind.

"Over there." Skink pointed a bony arm and, at that moment, the door opened and they saw Garret appear and dash towards them. He was closely followed by Ansylike. Behind them ran Groblic, then Haldriel, Obolin and Andric, who cast anxious glances over his shoulder. It didn't take long for them to reach the barn. Soon the doors were closed behind them.

"You'll need to act fast!" advised Garret. "Get out before the guards on the gate are ordered to stop you. All will be in confusion for a while, but it will not be long before you're missed."

"I'm not going without the sorceress! I can't just leave her here. I think her magic is lost and she needs a friend more than ever, now." Ansylike was determined. "You go and I'll try to follow. You'll be safer without me. The danger may have passed now."

"It hasn't!" insisted Garret. "It will not be long before Gromixillion returns. Then we'll all be in the soup. You can't threaten him now. You have killed the war-lord and that was the only part of the prophecy that bothered him. You'll be at his mercy!"

"I think he's right," agreed Andric, looking at the elf. "We can't stay here and wait for him. Unless you have a plan?" He looked at his sister hopefully, but it was obvious from the way that she sighed and wrinkled her nose that she was also lost for ideas. There was a moment of silence while each of them considered what was their best course of action.

"I can't leave her. I'm going back. Leave us a horse and we'll follow." Ansylike took her sword and strapped it securely round her waist.

"Wait! I'll go!" insisted Glade. "If anyone can get Zileika out of there, it's me. I'm the best at sneaking and creeping, as you've pointed out. It doesn't make sense for you to go. You'll be noticed as soon as you leave the barn!"

"I may be able to help," offered Skink. "No-one will pay attention to me. I'll come with you."

"All right," agreed Ansylike. "I'll wait for you here. We'll get some more weapons and make a stand if the worst happens. They'll not take me alive!"

"That's more like it!" proclaimed Haldriel. "They'll perish on our iron! Let's see what we can find to defend ourselves with. Those elves won't be a match for us. I reckon they're all soft!"

Garret laughed and Haldriel quickly apologised, explaining that he hadn't meant that all elves were soft. Garret was not offended and Skink found Haldriel's embarrassment highly amusing!

Time, however, was passing and the need for action was urgent. Andric went stealthily to check the main gates and to count the guards. It did not take him long to discover that the gates were securely locked and the guards had been doubled in number. They would not be able to fight their way out! He counted fifty armed troops on the walls and there were probably more in the stone guard-house. They looked as if they were expecting trouble. He went back to the barn to tell the others the bad news.

Ansylike and the dwarves were having better luck. An assortment of weapons was soon gathered together. There was more than they could possibly use. Unfortunately there were no crossbows and Haldriel wished he knew where his had been taken. He would just have to make do with an axe. There were plenty of throwing knives for Ansylike to choose from and she weighed each one in her hand to check its balance. Groblic found a blacksmith's hammer that suited him perfectly. When Andric appeared at the door and sidled in, they looked ready for battle.

Glade and Skink were unobserved and got to the back door of the hall. They could hear shouting from inside and the clash of sword on sword. Evidently the battle was still raging as elf fought elf. They went quickly in and through the corridors. The stage was empty, except for the furniture and the sorceress, who was propped up against one of the thrones. She surveyed the scene calmly. Without her magic she had no reason for living, so she waited for death and hoped that it would come quickly. "Can you walk or shall we carry you?" came an unexpected whisper. Zileika was used to talking furniture and believed for a moment that the voice was that of the throne. She paused for thought and regarded it carefully. "It's Glade. Ansylike sent me back for you. We must hurry. She's in great danger!"

The sorceress looked down at the face under the throne and smiled. Perhaps there was a reason for living, after all. Her magic had never got her what she really wanted. She'd tried to be popular, but no-one liked her for long. Now she had a friend who was risking her life for her, although she owed her no favours. She nodded to Glade and began to crawl towards the back of the stage. Once in the corridor she stood up, a little unsteadily. Skink supported her and they made their way, once again, to the back door. Behind them the fighting continued.

Ansylike was glad to see the sorceress, but horrified by her injuries. The side of her face was badly swollen and she had to speak through clenched teeth. One of her eyes was almost closed and the pupil was blank.

"So you didn't abandon me," she hissed. "I'd given up hope." She managed a flicker of a smile.

"Can't you do anything for her?" asked Glade, pulling insistently at Skink's sleeve.

"I'll do my best," he replied. "Sit her down over there. It'll take time though. I think the cheek bone is broken and her eye is damaged. She won't be able to travel today!" He looked at Ansylike to see what effect his words would have.

"Do your best," said Haldriel. "Our plan of escaping is no good anyway. There are too many guards for us. We can get over the wall, but there's no way that we can get the horses out. They'll find us in no time if we leave on foot! We'll have to come up with another idea."

"Then let's go back to Garret's tower," sighed Ansylike. "There's no point in hiding here and I need to think. If we have to fight, I'd rather be in a stone building than a barn!"

There was sense in this, so they headed for Garret's quarters. Skink went first to fetch some healing herbs and promised that he wouldn't be long. It was with heavy hearts that they made their way up the stone steps. None of them could see a way out of their current dilemma and death seemed to be waiting for them all!

When they were seated comfortably, Ansylike told them of her plan. Before she began, she warned them that it was a bit desperate. They all agreed when she was halfway through!

"Let me get this straight," said Groblic. "You propose to talk to the elves before Gromixillion gets back and offer them the chance to return to our hills?" He shook his head. "Why would they want to accept your offer when they can march back with an army and get their revenge on us? They can take the land back and drive us out!"

"A lot would die in the process. Not all of the elves enjoy fighting and I'm sure that none of them want to perish in another war with the dwarves. They lost last time!" Ansylike reminded him.

"True," added Obolin, thoughtfully. "It would certainly mean a major battle if they came at us with an army. They have no way of knowing whether they would win or lose."

"I propose something else," said Ansylike carefully. "Before Gromixillion can take command, I want the elves to appoint a new leader. I'm thinking of someone who can unite them and also put an end to the war with the humans."

"Nice, if you can manage it!" snorted Skink, who had finished dealing with Zileika's wounds. "I suppose you mean a half-elf? You for instance?" His tone was gently mocking. "You're too young!"

"Andric isn't!" she retorted swiftly. "He's also a half-elf! Besides, he'd make a better ruler than I could. I'd find the paperwork a little boring!" She laughed at the expressions of amazement on the faces of her friends.

"No!" exclaimed Groblic. "It'll never work!"

"I told you it was a rather desperate idea. One of the things that Strell told me was that I would never be the leader. The man that I loved would rule in my place. There is no-one that I love more than my brother." The faces of her companions were lined with disbelief.

Groblic's mouth moved, but no sounds came out. Skink was silent as he thought over the possibilities. His eyes fixed on the window and he gazed out at the sky.

"One of those birds!" he exclaimed. "One of the spying birds that Gromixillion uses. He can't be far away. We'll have to act fast." He looked at the sorceress. She was sleeping soundly in a chair and appeared not to have heard any of their conversation. "We'd best leave her here."

His words caused them all to spring up. None had thought that there would be so little time. They got moving fast and hurtled down the stairs as if their lives depended on it. Across the courtyard they ran and up to the main doors of the assembly hall. The sounds of fighting had died down, but they could hear voices shouting in anger. It was not the best moment to make an entrance, but there was no choice.

The dwarves went in first and gradually the elves fell silent. Many were dead and more were injured. All turned to look at the dwarves as if they were to blame for the slaughter. It was time for Ansylike to take charge of the situation, so she made her way forward. She held her head high and hoped that she looked confident. She didn't feel it! She cleared her throat, but Garret spoke first.

"I summon the Council! It is my right. The leader is dead and I call the Council to appoint a new one."

"This is hardly the time! We must bury the dead and tend to the injured!" protested a tall Elder. "Take back your summons!"

"I will not!" called Garret. His voice rose above the heads of them all. "I insist!"

"Very well," agreed the Elder. "It is your right. No-one here can question that. Let it be so."

Ansylike had never seen an old elf. Now a score of them detached themselves from the crowds and made their way up to the stage where they stood in a semi-circle, facing out. They looked quite impressive.

"Now's your chance, Spud. Go to the front," urged Groblic. As she seemed uncertain how to proceed, he took her by the hand and led her forward. Their friends followed, still armed with their newly scavenged weapons.

One of the Elders moved to the front and addressed the audience. There was a general shifting about as the elves sat down. The wounded tried not to groan too loud!

"We are called to find whether there is one among us who is willing to stand for leadership. All who wish to be considered will make their way to the front. I must remind you all that this is a grave duty and not to be considered lightly. Are any of you willing and able to be our leader?" He scanned the faces before him, but not a head nodded and none came forward. All knew that Gromixillion would soon return and leadership was his by right. Who would dare to stand in his way?

"I wish to be considered!" called Andric, as he made his way forward, ignoring the gasps of surprise. "I have much to offer you. I want to tell you first of the reason why we came here. Then you can decide. Can we all come onto the stage? My words are for everyone to hear and I want you to listen to what my friends have to say."

There was no reason to refuse. Anyone could ask to be considered as leader. The Council of Elders would have the final say, of course, but there was no denying the right of anyone to address the assembly. That was the way it had always been. Ever since the elves had left the forest of the north and moved into The Desolation, they had done things this way. Few, if any, expected the dwarves would be wanting to talk to them!

Andric kept his speech brief, then invited Haldriel to talk. The elves listened in awe. They couldn't believe their ears. This was an invitation to return to the hills of their ancestors! There was work to be done and many were keen to be on their way before Haldriel had finished talking. Groblic spoke touchingly of the friendship that had grown between him and Ansylike. It was a sign, he explained, that dwarves and elves could co-operate and live in harmony.

Finally, it was Ansylike's turn. She reminded them of the prophecy and how she had seen it coming true. If Andric was elected, then another piece would be complete. As his sister, she was bonded to him from birth, exactly as foretold.

As she spoke, the Elders began to nod. They were convinced. They only needed a moment to confer before they reached their decision. It was unanimous. All of them agreed that Andric would be their leader and a huge cheer burst from the crowd of elves. There was much laughing, shaking of hands and slapping of backs as the fighting was forgotten and friendships were made anew.

Skink took the chance to have a look at the wounded and Glade followed after him, doing what he could to help. Garret walked among the elves, shaking hands and smiling, joining in the general air of happiness. All thoughts of Gromixillion seemed to have been forgotten. The dwarves laughed happily and cursed themselves for ever doubting that Spud's plan would succeed.

So it was that they paid little attention when one of the Elders presented Andric with the silver chain that Spiron had worn around his waist. Andric accepted it gratefully and allowed the Elder to fasten the buckle to him. He wanted to cry out as the mind of Gromixillion invaded his head, but he couldn't manage a squeak! Smiling as if nothing was wrong he went over to one of the thrones. He sat down and said nothing, merely waiting for his master whom he knew to be close by. Very close by!

Zileika woke and found that she was alone. She raised a hand to her jaw and, surprisingly, felt no pain. The swelling around her eyes seemed to have gone down a little and she could see out of it, although her vision was blurred.

"I wonder where everyone has gone?" she said aloud.

"Down to the assembly hall," replied the chair. "They left you to recover."

"Do you know what they're going to do?" Zileika thought nothing of having a conversation with a chair. For her it was not out of the ordinary.

The chair retold what it had heard and the sorceress thanked it before heading for the stairs. She was worried. Ansylike was sweet and innocent. Awfully innocent! She dreaded what fate might have already befallen her. She cursed the fact that she'd lost her magic powers. Halfway down the flight of stone steps she paused to get her breath and wiggled a finger at a beetle that was climbing the wall. With all her powers of concentration, she could not affect it in the least.

The elves had meant what they said. Their threat hadn't been empty. Gromixillion had explained his offer most carefully. She could travel where she pleased and her powers would be intact, as long as the flask of blue liquid remained unopened. The bottle that Spiron had smashed! Now she was totally without magic. She could not use it and could not be helped by it. It was like being an ordinary mortal! How degrading! Briefly she wondered how people managed without magic. They seemed to get by, but it must make their lives very tedious.

When she got to the bottom of the stairs, she stopped for another breath and leant heavily against a stone column. The rock was cool against her bruised skin. Suddenly she heard the sound of the front gates being opened. Breathless, she waited, hoping that it was her friends getting ready to escape. In her heart she knew that it couldn't be so. She sidled back into the shadows and waited. Sure enough the sound of horses reached her. She didn't need magical powers to know that Gromixillion was back! His armed escort took a while to pass. Fearfully, she counted them as they passed. At least a hundred on horseback and more than twice that number on foot. They marched confidently. They were not expecting any resistance. It looked grim!

She scurried towards the assembly hall, but there were already guards outside. She hastened to the back entrance and got in, as a squad of troops marched round the corner.

The sorceress was not in time to prevent Andric from accepting the silver chain of Gromixillion, but she saw it fastened around his waist and knew at once what it would do. She tried to catch the eye of one of the dwarves without making it plain to everyone that she was there. Skink noticed her and gave Glade a nudge. Neither of them guessed what the trouble was. In the general mood of celebration they couldn't imagine what could be going wrong. Despite that, they knew enough to

be cautious and made their way slowly towards Zileika. While she was
still explaining to them, the main door burst open and the first of the
guards pushed his way inside. At once the air changed and smiles
disappeared from the elven faces to be replaced by looks of fear.

A heavily-armed guard formed a corridor from the door to the stage
and Gromixillion strode through it, well-protected. His black leather
gleamed and the silver chains clinked and jingled as he walked towards
the stage, looking neither to the right nor the left.

None of the elves made a move against him. Some unbuckled their
weapon-belts and let their swords and knives slip to the floor. He had
been their leader for a long time and they had learned to obey him
without asking questions. Now he was back and the throne was his to
demand. He had only to defeat Andric in combat and win the approval
of the Elders. What could stand in his way?

Ansylike tried to hide in the crowd, but she was grabbed by two elven
guards and dragged backwards onto the stage. They took her sword and
her daggers and placed them on the table. Then they sat her on one of
the thrones and told her to keep still. There was little choice. She
wondered why Andric had stood, but offered her no help.

The dwarves were soon rounded up and disarmed. Against such a
force they could have done very little. Groblic, however, had the
presence of mind to clutch a small piece of paper between his fingers. It
was his gift from Garret and he waited for the right moment to use it.
He had not given up hope. It was the animation spell. Not a powerful
weapon, but it was an edge and any advantage was not to be ignored.

Gromixillion turned his attention to the elves and called for the
Elders to come forward.

"You have elected this person as your leader." He waved scornfully at
Andric. "That is your decision and I cannot disagree with it. I respect
our traditions. Now, however, I will ask him to give me command. He
will not refuse. Does anyone challenge my right?" He waited and
tapped a booted foot on the planks. "No?"

"I challenge you!" called Ansylike. She didn't dare to stand up as
there were two elves with long bows ready to kill her. Whichever way

she moved, one of them would get her. "I challenge you to combat. A fair fight. My sword against yours. You're not afraid of me, are you?" She taunted him, but he was cool and not stirred to anger.

"I accept," he snapped and drew his blade. It was no ordinary sword! It caught the light and held it. It was a dull black from hilt to tip, forged from a single piece of the rarest metal. A blade from the Dark Days. A slayer! Once it was drawn from its scabbard it would not rest until it had tasted blood.

"Dwarf-killer!" hissed Haldriel.

Gromixillion appeared to ignore him. The dwarves could be easily disposed of later. "I am a man of honour," he continued. There was no sincerity in his voice. "I accept your challenge, but I nominate a champion to fight for me. Andric will fight in my place. You may also ask one of your friends to fight for you."

Ansylike had not anticipated this! In horror, she watched as Andric accepted the Slayer. Her own broken sword was no match for it. Andric was a very good swordsman and she could not see how she could beat him. Gromixillion had, it seemed, thought of everything!

But not quite. Zileika decided that it was time to make a move. She had no intention of letting her friend be killed. For a moment she hesitated, then approached Andric.

"Let me take this off for you," she offered, pointing a slender finger at the silver chain around his waist. "It will only get in your way."

"Touch that and you're dead!" screamed Gromixillion. "The chains are enchanted and you will be burned to a crisp!" He had plans for the sorceress and he didn't want to see her die.

"You forget what you've done to me!" snarled Zileika as she unclipped the chain from around Andric's waist. "I have no magic and I cannot be harmed by it. So much for that spell. Now let's see you fight your own battle for a change!" The silver chain fell to the floor and Andric was released from the control that Gromixillion had over him. The black sword clattered to the ground and pulsed, as if it had a life of its own. Andric awoke as if he had been in a deep sleep and allowed Zileika to lead him back to the throne. There he rested in a daze.

"It's up to you, now!" called Groblic. "Get him, Spud!" With as much confidence as he could muster, he cheered her on. He was very much aware of the sword that was pointed at his back and knew that he would be dead if he attempted to intervene. The rune-paper was still clutched tightly in his hand. He still had one surprise left! The other dwarves were silent. They feared the worst. Even Haldriel resigned himself to defeat. He was renowned for his optimism, but at this moment he prepared himself for death. He looked at the guard who stood before him and weighed up the chances of seizing his dagger before he got an arrow in the back. Slim, indeed. Their only hope was with Spud. She stood no chance!

Gromixillion picked up the sword that Andric had dropped. He whirled it around and struck the table. It collapsed, cut cleanly in half. It was a show of strength, nothing more, but the elves were clearly impressed. They murmured, whispered and groaned, depending on who they hoped would win. Ansylike drew her sword and held it up for all to see. She knew that she would lose in a straight fight and looked for an advantage. Her blade caught the last rays of sunlight and glittered as she held it out.

"Look out! Behind you!" called a voice above Gromixillion's shoulder. He turned for only a second and then Ansylike's sword cut through his armour and bit deep into his heart. It sliced through the black leather, cut the silver chains and pierced his ribs. He fell back, dragging the blade from Ansylike's hands. Groblic's spell had worked! It had distracted Gromixillion just long enough for Ansylike to strike under his guard. His own sword fell from his hands as he sank to his knees. The sorceress ran forward and seized it in both hands, pushing Ansylike out of the way.

"Get back!" she insisted. "This will drink blood and I can think of no better victim for it than this evil elf!"

She raised the blade and drove it down through Gromixillion's neck, feeling the surge of power as it drained the essence from him, then she pulled it free and replaced it in its scabbard. Not a single drop of blood came from the mortal wound.

The guards were free of the control that they'd been under and none attacked the girls. They lowered their weapons and began to leave the hall.

"I think this calls for a celebration!" shouted Andric and his words were greeted by a mighty cheer that echoed around the hall. He went to his sister and the sorceress and hugged them both.

The rest of the day was spent in preparation. There was much to do. The ovens were fuelled and lit and extra help was enlisted for the kitchens. Ansylike made sure that she kept well out of the way. She joined Zileika in her tower and spent the afternoon snoozing. They had all earned a rest, but the dwarves and Andric seemed incapable of slowing down. Wherever there was work to do, one of them could be found giving a hand.

Groblic split logs for firewood. He was tireless and amazed the elves with his stamina. Haldriel and Obolin assisted the master chef in the kitchens, scurrying about with pots, pans, bowls and dishes. Glade had not forgotten about the horses that he had made ready for their escape. He unloaded and unsaddled them, fed them and brushed them down. He was quite happy with horses, as long as he didn't have to sit on one!

Andric decided that the assembly hall was the scene of too much bloodshed to be used for the celebrations. He made enquiries about an alternative site and chose a hall that hadn't been in use for a long time. It meant a lot of extra work to get it ready, but all were enthusiastic and there were plenty of willing hands.

It was brushed, dusted, mopped and polished. Tables were brought in, chairs and the thrones which were set together at the head of the hall. The entire floor was covered in rolls of green carpet that looked amazingly like grass. As he was supervising the operations, Andric's attention was caught by the curious murals that decorated the end walls behind the thrones. They were paintings of a quaint village with rather strange buildings.

They were tall, with small turrets, like little castles, but made of wood. He could see trees, arranged in rows. They might be an orchard. He thought of asking one of the elves what it was meant to signify, but decided against it. There was too much to do and he didn't want to distract anyone from their work. With satisfaction he watched as the elves busied themselves about their tasks.

It was getting dark and Zileika had lit a few candles before there was a gentle knock on her door. She opened it to find Glade grinning at her from the height of her waist. He seemed to be in perfect health and he grinned widely at her before delivering his message.

"It's nearly time for the celebrations to begin," he explained. "You'd better start getting ready." He turned and made his way back down the stairs.

"Thanks!" called Zileika, after him. "We'll be there soon."

She closed the door and went to wake Ansylike.

For once, Ansylike decided to wear a dress. It was a formal occasion, after all. She chose a dark green that matched her eyes. After she'd bathed, dried herself and arranged her hair as neatly as she could, she tried it on. It fitted as if it had been made for her. A pair of green sandals were a perfect match. When she was ready she joined Zileika who was wearing blue, as always.

When they reached the bottom of the tower, there was a surprise waiting for them. Andric, the dwarves and Glade were ready to escort them to the hall. Groblic took Ansylike by the hand, as proud as if she was his own daughter. He led the way. Andric offered his arm to Zileika and she gladly accepted. The smell of roasted meat, freshly baked bread and steamed puddings welcome them as they drew nearer the hall.

The feast was better than anyone could have expected and the wine was the best that the elves had in their cellars. Long into the night they ate and drank, enjoying each other's company, telling tales and cheering as each fresh course was delivered to their tables.

As the first rays of dawn glittered through the high windows, Andric decided to play them a tune on his flute before he retired for some sleep. Many of the elves were already dozing, their heads on the tables. He decided to wake them up with a lively song that they could all join in with. None was more enthusiastic that Zileika, who slipped off her shoes and danced gleefully around the thrones.

Ansylike turned her head to watch her friend capering around to the music of Andric's flute and saw the mural for the first time. It was the scene from the 'magic carpet' that the sorceress had decorating her walls. She knew that she was no longer needed. Fresh adventures awaited her. It was time to leave!